Don't Blame the Devil

Also by Pat G'Orge-Walker

Somebody's Sinning in My Bed

Somewhat Saved

Cruisin' on Desperation

Mother Eternal Ann Everlastin's Dead

Sister Betty! God's Calling You, Again!

Don't Blame the Devil

Pat G'Orge-Walker

KENSINGTON PUBLISHING CORP.

www.kensingtonbooks.com

DAFINA BOOKS are published by

Kensington Publishing Corp.
119 West 40th Street
New York, NY 10018

All Kensington titles, imprints, and distributed lines are available at special quantity discounts for bulk purchases for sales promotion, premiums, fundraising, educational, or institutional use.

Special book excerpts or customized printings can also be created to fit specific needs. For details, write or phone the office of the Kensington Special Sales Manager: Kensington Publishing Corp., 119 West 40th Street, New York, NY 10018, Attn. Special Sales Department. Phone: 1-800-221-2647.

Dafina and the Dafina logo Reg. U.S. Pat. & TM Off.

ISBN-13: 978-0-7582-3542-8
ISBN-10: 0-7582-3542-9

First Printing: September 2010
10 9 8 7 6 5 4 3 2 1

Printed in the United States of America

I dedicate this story to my parents,
the late Reverends Margaret and Alonza,
Mount Vernon, New York's own
Delilah and Thurgood-light ☺

ACKNOWLEDGMENTS

And they shall be mine, saith the Lord of hosts,
in that day when I make up my jewels;
and I will spare them, as a man spareth
his own son that serveth him.
—Malachi 3:17

To all my supporters, your prayers and encouraging words
have sustained me, and it is with these words that I convey my
love:

Heart to heart I've shared my words with you
Heart to heart to my friends old and new
Please remember, after all that's been said and done
It's been heart to heart as one . . .

I thank God for His son, Jesus. Precious is the time God's
given me, and blessed am I to be counted among His own.
He's led me in a new direction for this story, and I thank
Him.

There is a bit of a personal story interwoven in *Don't
Blame the Devil.* I did not see my mother from the age of nine
until I reached eighteen. Therefore, though my mother and
the character Delilah had very different reasons for their ab-
sences, I share a lot of Jessie's pain and ultimate acceptance of
the outcome.

I also thank, with all my heart and my love, Robert;
you're my best friend and a husband whom God created especially for me.

Beautiful children—Gizel Dan-Yette, Ingrid, and Marisa,
along with my grandchildren and great-grandchildren—I thank
each of you for your contributions and gentle reminders that

at the end of the day, no matter what other hats I wear, I'm still just Mama, Grandma ATM, and Granny. My family—my sister Arlene Baylor and brother Anthony Acker, Sr., Uncle Elbert and Aunt Ovella in particular, as well as my other sisters and brothers along with numerous cousins, close friends who prodded, prayed, babysat, and sometimes fixed a meal or two—I thank each of you for your support and faith in what God has placed into my hands.

As always, I'd like to thank them for their prayers and support: Bishop John L. and Lady Laura L. Smith of the St. Paul Baptist City of Lights Ministry, and the congregation; Reverend Stella Mercado and the Blanche Memorial Baptist Church family; and the numerous churches and organizations who've supported my efforts for many years. I offer deep gratitude and appreciation to my editor, Selena James, along with the entire Dafina / Kensington Books family, and to my longtime friend and attorney, Christopher R. Whent, Esq., and publicist, Ella Curry (EDC Creations). Without a doubt my Facebook and MySpace family of readers, friends, numerous book clubs, and authors are the winds beneath my literary feet. Of course, there are several authors who are my sisters from other mothers: Jacquelin Thomas, Michele Andrea Bowen, Lutishia Lovely, Olivia Stith, Zane, Tracy Price-Thompson, ReShonda Tate Billingsley, Dr. Maxine Thompson, Dr. Rosie Milligan, and the woman who makes my phenomenal promotional items, Debra "Simply Said" Owsley.

A special thank-you to Doctors Manolis Tsatsas, Ruthee-Lu Bayer, and Yardley Pierre-Jerome-Shoulton; and to Ms. Diane Gissinger.

Finally, to my family members who left too soon in 2010: Aunt Connie, cousin Theresa, and niece Treva.

When diagnosed in April 2009 with cancer, my first reaction was to laugh. I thank so many of you who laughed along with me, prayed diligently for me, encouraged me daily, and then shouted hallelujah when the prognosis was *we got it all*. I always believed then, and continue to believe now, that when you know the Prince of Peace (Jesus), then you can have peace.

Chapter 1

The Beginning before there was a Delilah

Nine months ago she was the darling of the Apollo Theater. A gorgeous R & B chanteuse and often mistaken for a Dorothy Dandridge look-alike. Nine months ago, Claudine Dupree Jewel was someone on the verge of stardom because she'd made it into the downtown Manhattan nightclub scene. Downtown was where the white folks with money and connections migrated and played the queen-making game for some lucky Negress.

Nine months later, Claudine was an angry, fame-chasing, maternally lacking, pregnant, and unmarried nineteen-year-old.

It was 1947, and it came to a head during a snow blizzard in Westchester County, New York. She'd never completed high school and was barely existing on the little money she'd made and saved before she began to show. Nobody would hire a big-bellied singer, no matter how good the singer was.

In no time the money dwindled. Claudine didn't have money for the crowded, vermin-infested room she'd rented and barely enough to pay for a bus ride. But Claudine had what she called street smarts, so she made a plan. She couldn't afford prenatal care, so she just simply planned to wait until a few days from the date when Mother Luke, an elderly church mother who rented one of the other cockroach motel rooms, suggested she'd give birth, and then go to a nearby emergency room.

But Mother Luke's old custom of placing a hand on the belly and sizing up the dark line that ran from the navel to the pubic hairline wasn't quite scientific enough. If the pains that racked Claudine's back meant the baby was coming, then the old church mother was off by a couple of weeks.

So armed with just enough bus fare, and towels crammed into her underwear to catch the birth water, she stood on the bus, crushed between others who didn't care if she was pregnant or not. Twenty minutes later, a young and alone Claudine Dupree Jewel barely made it across the street after she'd stepped off the bus. Within fifteen minutes after arriving and some ignorant doctor yelling, "Don't push," while the blizzard howled louder than her screams, she gave birth in a small hospital labor room in Mount Vernon, New York. Shortly after, since she'd registered as a charity case and the bed was needed for paying patients, there'd been not too subtle hints tossed her way indicating that her stay would be short.

"We're sorry we can't allow you to stay past a day or so until you get your strength," the charity ward nurse began in her most uncharitable manner, "but the best we can do is give you a few diapers and a letter that will authorize a few bottles of formula from the hospital pharmacy. Once you leave, I suggest you try and eat healthy enough to give that baby some breast milk."

So that was all the kindness Claudine received. A couple of diapers, a letter for formula, and advice to eat healthy on money she didn't have so she could provide breast milk from her tiny yet swollen breasts. She got the news after she received a few hope-this-will-hold-ya stitches. Her five-pound-two-ounce pasty-colored baby girl, just hours ago, had almost ripped the petite Claudine apart.

To add further insult as she lay without the benefit of

even an aspirin for the bone-crushing cramps that followed, someone came over to the bed and urged her to hurry and name her baby. Paperwork needed filing before they kicked Claudine to the curb in another twenty-four hours.

Claudine didn't give it a second thought. "I'm naming her Delilah." Her chest heaved as the tears poured. "This little girl's gonna blind every man with her beauty and steal their very soul, just like that Delilah gal did in the Bible story."

The unsympathetic woman with the pen and paper remained disconnected as she added, "And don't forget to fill in the father's name and date of birth."

"He's dead." Claudine let out another groan, indicating that was all she would say about the matter.

The woman retrieved the pen and paper from Claudine's hand and left without any further information. It wasn't the first time a woman gave birth and didn't give the father's name.

The real truth was that Claudine didn't care what the woman thought. Despite her pain and the wails coming from her hungry newborn baby in the bassinet a few feet away, Claudine turned to face the wall and cussed damnation upon every Y chromosome that walked the earth. Of course, there was one man in particular whom she'd have shot if he were there. She was really angry at a silvery-tongued devil named Sampson, and despite telling the lie that he was dead, she was very sure he was still alive.

Sampson, the object of her hatred, was a few years older; a tall, butterscotch-complexioned bass player who'd gotten more than a phone number from her—he'd gotten her pregnant. As smart as she thought she was, she'd fallen for the old "We don't need no piece of paper to show how much we love one another" jive. The first few months were like magic. Then hocus-pocus—Sampson disappeared off the planet as soon as she mentioned she'd missed her period. She would never forgive herself for not learning more about him so she could've ruined his life like he'd done hers. The only way to get back at him was to never tell her daughter who her father was. Claudine never did; not even when Delilah grew up teased and called a bastard child and cried to know his name.

Like most of Claudine's decisions that weren't well thought-out, if thought-out at all, she also messed up when she named her baby with a less than noble motive. Claudine hadn't read the entire biblical story, because in the end that particular Delilah didn't make out too well, while in Sampson's case, he brought the house down . . . and not in a good way.

Only time would tell if Claudine's need for revenge would manifest in little Delilah's life, and to what degree. Whether it did or not, Claudine never waited to find out. As soon as Delilah, talented and gorgeous, turned eighteen, Claudine did to her daughter the same thing she'd always hated Sampson for. Claudine disappeared and left Delilah to fend for herself.

Chapter 2

The Storm in 2009

Delilah Dupree Jewel was dog tired of decades of life using her as its human Ping-Pong ball and toilet. She'd looked for love on her terms ever since Claudine abandoned her with nothing but youthful ignorance as a cover. It didn't matter that Delilah had beauty that either made one instantly love her or hate her. She'd lost count of how many times she'd heard *You may look like Lena Horne, but you ain't Lena Horne.*

How many times had she fallen for some man's game? All a pair of pants had to say was *Lena Horne better watch out, 'cause you about to snatch her shine. You look like her twin.*

Of course, Delilah wasn't totally blameless. If she found a diamond, Delilah would find a way to turn it into cubic zirconium. Self-sabotage, thy name be Delilah Dupree Jewel.

By the time she turned forty-something, she gave the idea of surrendering a try. *I don't have another tear left,* she told God for the umpteenth time. That time it was when the last of her sugar daddies turned out not to be so sweet. His wife, having thought more of the marriage than her husband, went after Delilah with a brick in one hand and a fistful of High John the Conqueror snuff. She'd planned to hit Delilah upside the head and then blind her.

"Don't you ever call my house again for my husband," the man's wife threatened.

Delilah was insulted that the woman thought so little of her. "As long as I've messed around with your husband, I've never called your house," Delilah barked. "I've got more class than that."

And that's when Delilah lost several teeth. The man's wife, apparently not happy with Delilah's apology, put a well-placed punch in Delilah's unrepentant mouth with the brick.

Getting her teeth fixed caused her to pawn a very expensive ring and laid her on the doorsteps of the poorhouse.

But eventually, as so many do as a last resort, Delilah wanted peace in her life; Jehovah-shalom. A lot of her decision also had to do with a failed singing and modeling career and a couple of other speed bumps along life's highway. And, of course, she expected God to do things on her terms and she set about to find Him. She wanted the great Jehovah-nissi, the God that would protect her from the demons of her past and most of all protect Delilah from her own self-destructive behavior. After all, she'd endured for almost half her life, to Delilah's way of thinking, God owed her big-time. Delilah decided she'd serve Jehovah-jireh. After all, she'd heard He was the great provider.

So with no family or close friends to hold on to and her Jehovah at her beck and call, Delilah headed back East from California. Once she returned to New York, she continued her search for the elusive peace, but bad luck kept dogging her as though it were an ugly birthmark on her forehead. Yet Delilah was still Delilah "the stubborn," and as time went on she became less of a worshipper and more of God's adviser.

Delilah had barely taken a bite out of the big New York apple when she'd upped the she-gotta-lotta-nerve ante and placed God on a schedule. But it all started to unravel one Sunday in Brooklyn, New York. The temperature was in the nineties and the weather wasn't the only thing hot.

Delilah Dupree Jewel put on her best and most modest yellow print dress, tucked her long, snow white hair under her big-curls blond Farrah Fawcett wig, and donned her oversized sunglasses. She'd done all that so she could sit in her car outside one of the various Brooklyn churches she favored. That was how she did her "churchy duty."

In her car she could avoid inner church politics such as, "My tithes paid for this pew," or "God knows our hearts and a little sinning is okay." If she was inside and had to hear that familiar mess, she would've killed someone before the choir sang their first hymn.

By the time Delilah made it to her car that Sunday, the temperature had soared to almost one hundred degrees. As she drove along she sweated profusely. Her dress was wet and clung to her legs. Of course, the air-conditioning in her car was on the fritz.

"Okay, Lord, I know I promised you I would give you another shot when I came back to New York," Delilah whispered angrily, "and I've kept up my end of the arrangement, but I need you to touch this air-conditioning or I'm gonna hafta go back home."

Satisfied that God would do such a small thing on her behalf, she relaxed a little and let out a sigh. One of her small hands clutched the steering wheel while the other fiddled with the knobs for the A/C. The A/C was as stubborn as Delilah. "If I had another way of getting around and wasn't already three months behind on this piece of crap, I'd leave it in the middle of the street."

As she pushed her neon red, leased 2003 Navigator through the busy streets of Brooklyn's East New York streets, she pleaded, "Come on, Jesus. I wanna get there before the choir goes up and the Rapture comes."

There wasn't much gas in the tank, but she believed God. Even if He wouldn't touch the air-conditioning, He would get her to church on time, even if it had to be on fumes. And then Delilah suddenly took up from an earlier prayer she'd had with God, and reminded Him, "I know I promised You, when You let me keep this latest car out of the clutches of the repo man, that I'd serve You more often, but I still need Your help. I need help in paying that three months' back note. . . ."

"Lord," Delilah continued, "there's that one thing I know I keep bothering You about. But if I don't bring it before You, who can I bring it before?" The sound of a blaring car horn shook Delilah. She realized that she was idling at a stop sign and not a red light. Since she was on her way to church, she decided not to flip the bird to the driver behind her.

Her attention was still on her driving, and she continued talking to God. "I know there're other problems in this cold, cruel world that occupy Your time. And just like I know folks say that You leave the past in the past, I want to thank You for being bothered with me and all my shame and hurt."

And then Delilah lowered her voice as though it were someone else in the car other than her and God. "I mean specifically the shame of having that breakdown, and me leaving my husband and putting my baby boy, Jessie, in foster care all those years ago. I'm sure they're doing quite well without me and my family curse. I remember throughout most of my teenage years, my mama taught me that it seems like the Jewels just don't shine that well here on earth. . . ."

"Y'all sing that chorus just one more time," Delilah murmured through her car window that particular Sunday as she pulled into the New Hope Assembly Church's huge parking lot. Happy she was able to park not too far from the sanctuary, she rolled down her window and braved the heat. The huge, air-conditioned church's windows were closed, but she could still hear them praising God. Delilah swung her tiny hands from side to side and tapped the steering wheel like a choir director. Oh, how she did enjoy directing a good song almost as much as she did singing one. "Awww, come on now. Give God the glory!"

★ ★ ★

Delilah's attempt at pleasing her God caused her to spread her worship among several churches in Harlem and Brooklyn. New Hope was surely becoming one of her favorites. It was the third time she'd visited and praised God from their parking lot. She'd come to choose her place of worship according to which she thought had the best music. So many times the music that poured through open stained-glass windows or oversized amplifiers tugged at her spirit and fed her soul.

And yet, true to her word, as soon as it became time for God's message to come forth with all the loud preaching that was brought with it, along with the begging for money part of the service, she'd always drive off before it began. Delilah always managed to feel good after giving God His worship, on her terms.

However, soon enough Delilah would receive a message of another sort. God, omniscient and the author of the final word for all mankind, had had just about enough of Delilah's customized worship service. God was about to checkmate the old gal and she'd never see it coming.

Chapter 3

Before she could put the car in gear, several people filed through the church's side exit door. She'd never seen that happen before a service ended. "Well, it's time for me to get out of here." She was just about to turn on her ignition when she heard a voice.

"Delilah?"

Delilah swung her head around and peeked out through the driver's side rolled-down window. She'd moved too fast; something she didn't normally do when she heard her name called, without checking to see if there was drama attached to it.

"Delilah?" There was no mistaking that male voice. It sounded closer and a bit more confident than it had a moment ago. But now it had more of an accusatory tone than a questioning one. "Woman, stop trying to act like it ain't you."

The tall, dark-skinned man lumbered toward the passenger side of Delilah's car. Only a few feet separated him from the Navigator.

"Delilah Dupree . . ." The man reached the car before he could complete her name for the third time. He had a dark jacket flung over his arm and wore a black-and-white polka-dot shirt and matching bow tie. His white pants didn't quite fit right, but the suspenders made certain they wouldn't fall off his lanky body. And the hair—a little sparser than the last time Delilah had laid eyes upon it—still appeared shiny and hard, as though it would crack if touched.

The sight of the man's hair pulled Delilah back to her senses. Anger replaced her fear and any other feeling she'd felt a second ago. *Dayum, is that fool still wearing a conk?*

Before she could put the car in drive, he was standing in front of it like he dared her to take off and risk running him over.

"Excuse me?" Delilah's mind went into warp speed but didn't take a single innovative thought with it. All she could say was, "I think you have me confused with someone else."

"Heffa, please." The man's dark eyes narrowed as he cautiously walked over to the driver's side and stared. His eyes looked like two brown pieces of steel as he placed his Bible on the roof of the Navigator. Without turning his cold eyes away, he pointed at the front of the car. "Now, unless you stole this monster, why does your license plate have *Delilah* on it?"

"So what if it does?" she shot back. She always knew that one day her oversized ego would land her in hot water with her vanity plate.

The man was about to say something more when several congregation members suddenly came along. Still wearing the smile of a Holy Ghost good time, one of the men greeted the deacon as he nodded toward Delilah. "Praise the Lord, Deacon Pillar. You sure gave God His due this morning."

"Well, God is good all the time. . . ." The deacon answered without removing his Bible off the car or his eyes off Delilah.

If the men felt slighted because Deacon Pillar didn't greet them with a handshake or even a glance—and never mind no introduction to the very attractive woman behind the wheel—they never showed it. The other man simply added before moving on, "And all the time God is good."

Before the men barely got out of earshot, Delilah started in on the man. "Deacon—so you're a deacon now?" Again, Delilah had spoken in haste. She'd forgotten that she'd not actually admitted to being *his* Delilah. What she'd meant to do was to just drive away, and if the Bible remained on the car's roof, then so be it. She didn't need a blast from the past to mess up her future. She certainly didn't want this particular one now.

Her tiny fingers buzzed across her steering wheel and her mind kept grappling with her situation. *So help me if I get back home to Garden City, Long Island, I will not be coming back this way again.*

Before her stood yet another reason why she didn't have friends or acquaintances; they usually brought the type of trouble she didn't want. She avoided friends the way she avoided fatty foods. Both would eventually lead to high blood pressure or a stroke.

But the man wasn't through. "If I hadn't been inside my church this morning and praising God in all His glory, I just might've wanted to cuss you out when I first saw you." He stopped and shook his head. "Lord knows, I should've just stayed inside until the church meeting started. . . ."

"You were up in *your* church? If you're so much into your church, then what kind of religion you got that makes you wanna cuss someone out when you first lay eyes on them?"

"I got the kind that's kept me for a lot of years since you took off for wherever your kind goes to."

"Well, good for you." Delilah's gray eyes didn't blink as they swept the deacon from his conk to his white loafers before she hissed, "Just let me get out of here before you lose what little religion you say you have, along with that precious, outdated conk and whatever else you got going on these days." It wasn't what she really wanted to say, but that's what came out.

"Lord help me to protect my blood pressure and ignore her nasty remark about my conk."

He'd worn a conk since he was seventeen. He'd worn one when he was twenty-six and met her. Back then she was a homeless, yet talented, eighteen-year-old Delilah. He'd even worn one when they eventually dated and set the world afire, and he'd wear one until he was a hundred and seventeen if he chose.

Deacon Pillar laid his arm across the sill of the car window and leaned in. He came close enough to Delilah to kiss her. "To my eternal shame, I always wondered, from time to time, just how I'd feel if I ever saw you again. And now God has delivered you right to the doorstep of New Hope Assembly and I'm not sure I like that. In fact, I know I don't."

Delilah moved over a few inches just in case she needed to swing. "Oh, so now you hate me? You just finished praising God and you want to cuss and hate me?"

"No, I don't hate you. I pity you."

"Pity me!" She became so angry her small frame seemed to almost levitate off the seat. "You pity me! Who the hell are you to pity me?"

"I'm the same one who pitied you forty years ago—"

"Save your damn pity!" Delilah's small chest heaved as though she were having an asthma attack. "Go on back inside your church. I don't need to keep coming around here. There're other churches. . . ."

"At least you've figured that much out." The deacon pointed his finger at Delilah and snapped, "Just so you know . . ."

"Just so I know what?" Delilah barked. "That finger don't scare me as much as that damn conk."

The deacon's face again stiffened at the insult, but he let it roll off and continued, "Just so you know, I truly have turned my life over to Jesus. I'm just telling you so you'll do the decent thing—in case you're lying as always—and truly stay the hell away from here—"

He was just getting started, but the deacon never had a chance to finish his rant.

Suddenly, from somewhere deep within her, Delilah gathered her wits and more strength than she'd felt in quite some time. "Well, at least you can't blame the devil for your still nasty attitude."

Delilah slammed her tiny foot down on the accelerator and took off. The Bible flew off the roof of the Navigator and landed at a stunned Deacon Pillar's feet, opened to the Book of Revelation.

Chapter 4

Deacon Pillar watched Delilah speed away almost in relief as he stood rooted to the hot cement. In one swoop, his long arms reached down and retrieved his Bible. "Give me strength, Heavenly Father."

The deacon tried to compose himself as he turned and headed back toward the side entry of New Hope. His habit of leaving the service early to prepare for the board meeting suddenly seemed like a bad idea. But his head felt like a piece of lead and he couldn't lift it, not even for appearance' sake, as passing congregants greeted him warily.

A few minutes later, the deacon's body relaxed, just a little, as he climbed the few steps to enter the deacons' board meeting room. It was a small room practically devoid of adornment and adjacent to the pastor's lavishly decorated study.

He opened the door and nearly collapsed onto one of two sofas in the room. He was so grateful it was empty. His brow furrowed and without thinking he'd begun to wring his leathery hands just before he leapt off the sofa and fell to his knees. "Father God, after all these years, why did you let me see that woman?"

And from somewhere deep within his spirit he imagined

God admonishing, *I allowed you to see her. I never told you to call out to her.* . . .

"Sorry to interrupt, Deacon Pillar." It was one of the church trustees. He'd whispered his brief apology as he accidentally hit the side of a table when he tried to abruptly leave. "I didn't know anyone would be in here. I just needed to get one of the record books."

The deacon couldn't speak. He stared at the man as though seeing him for the first time. As he rose, he kept staring and it took a few more seconds before he could speak. "It's okay, Brother Jessie. I just needed some alone time with the Master."

"It's not a problem. I've felt the need for some alone time in His presence quite often, especially since Cindy's passing."

"We all miss your wife. But I'm sure it's nothing compared to how you and Tamara must feel."

Jessie's wife, Cindy, had passed away almost six months ago. A very attractive, plus-size woman with an enormous voice, she'd sung her heart out at one of the church's anniversary services one Sunday morning. By that night New Hope's beloved soloist, Cindy Jewel, was gone. At the age of forty-five, she'd died of a heart attack.

"Well, I need to get back to the fellowship hall," Jessie whispered. He was still grieving and willed his tears not to fall. He quickly pulled from his pockets a pair of tinted reading glasses that hid his hazel eyes. "The sooner I give some information to the other trustees, for the meeting, the sooner I can grab Tamara and go home."

"You go on ahead, Jessie. I'll be just fine." The deacon could only hope he sounded convincing. "I'll see you and baby girl later on this evening."

There was no denying Jessie's grief was still fresh. His voice choked when he said, "Just be sure to show up in time for dinner. I'm cooking. And you know she'll be real upset if her favorite deacon doesn't join us at the supper table like he does on most Sunday evenings."

The deacon's heart was about to break as he watched Jessie struggle to act normal. "You two got me spoiled, and that's why I love living upstairs over you." He managed a weak smile and he was certain Jessie knew it was for his benefit.

Jessie was almost out the door when he slowly turned and managed a smile of his own, too. "Don't know what I would've done without you these last few years, Deacon Pillar. You've been a God-send." He didn't wait for the deacon to answer before he closed the door behind him.

It'd been almost five minutes since Deacon Pillar had watched Jessie leave and yet he hadn't moved an inch.

As hard as he'd prayed—not just that day but for so many years—he never thought he'd see this day come. And although he'd played his guitar in church that morning and led his signature song, "No Ways Tired," suddenly, he was.

"Father God." The deacon stood this time and continued his earlier prayer. He'd begun as though God waited on him to get back to it. "I'm forever grateful that You let me find my son after so many years of searching. And, Heavenly Father, I thank You for Your grace and Your mercy that Jessie can't hate me because he doesn't know I'm his daddy. But Lord, I just looked into Jessie's eyes. Exotic eyes like Delilah's, but his are beautiful and kind. I'm afraid that the light's gonna leave them dull and lifeless, if he's hurt. But he walks just like I used to walk; You know, Lord, with just enough of a swagger to let this world know it's lucky to have police like him in it." Suddenly Deacon Pillar managed a smile before he continued, "You know, Lord, that Jessie's confidence has a lot of humility wrapped around it. Jessie's not conceited, like his daddy once was."

The smile slid from the deacon's face as he implored, "Now, Father, I have just one more thing I need to ask. What are you gonna do about Delilah? Father God, You said in Your Word, You're not the author of confusion. That Delilah is about as confused as one gets." Suddenly the deacon started babbling. "Too much is happening today. Are You trying to reveal something to me? Father, I feel so convicted. I know my hands are not clean. . . ."

The deacon unclasped his hands and let them fall to his sides. Today was a little too close. He remembered that she now knew where he worshipped.

"If I remember right, she's sure not a God-fearing woman. She don't really attend church. Today must've been an accident or coincidence," the deacon murmured.

Yet somehow the old man knew better. After all, there were no coincidences with God. He suddenly remembered her saying that there were *other churches.* "Sweet Jesus," he said aloud.

He plopped down upon the sofa again and allowed his heavy head to fall forward, as though all the strength had gone from his neck. Here he was, in his seventies, if he ever told the truth about his age; and for most of his life he'd slid by on God's mercy and grace even as he pimped and hustled his way along. And now, the way he figured, since he'd turned his life around he must've done something wrong to displease God. What the wrong was, he didn't know.

What he did know was that Delilah Dupree Jewel and Old Karma had swept down upon him that day. They both were calling upon him and they aimed to collect what he owed. And as sure as his name was Thurgood Pillar, he knew that all his old street chickens were racing back home. That could only mean that his proverbial goose was cooked. He needed to find a way to keep Delilah out of the way before she ruined everything for him and the two people he loved more than his own life.

"Well, God helps those who help themselves," the deacon murmured, and rose. He slapped his thigh for reinforcement. Just that quick he'd forgotten that earlier when he ran his big mouth and got ahead of God, it brought him to where he was.

If the deacon got in God's way when God got around to finally checkmating Delilah, then there'd be a checkmate waiting for him, too.

Chapter 5

It'd been three weeks since Delilah ran into the deacon in New Hope Assembly Church's parking lot. She'd since attended the parking lot services at two other churches in the Bronx and Harlem, with no sighting of him.

And yet every morning, noon, and night inside the posh Garden City rental, which she couldn't afford, she thought about Thurgood Pillar. She couldn't forget running into him, nor could she forgive herself for not asking about her son. But then he hadn't mentioned him, either. Had they both forgotten about Jessie?

But this particular Saturday morning, she was going to give it her best shot to put aside any thoughts of him, Jessie, or anything negative. Today, her small Social Security check should arrive. The Social Security folks were the only ones who knew her true age was sixty-three.

"Ain't too many ways for a woman of a certain age to make money," she'd decided just before she filed.

"Enough traveling down memory lane," Delilah muttered as she waved her hands as though shooing the memories away. Besides, she wanted to refocus on what should be waiting for her. Having money always lifted her spirits. It let her temporarily rebuke poverty, even if a short time later it still left her broke.

Although it was July and the humidity was almost visible, that Saturday Delilah stepped out her door and went to her mailbox wearing a pale yellow silk Japanese kimono. A little eye candy was her treat for the nosy neighbors. "Please, Jesus," she whispered, "let there be a check and none of those annoying collection or late notices."

Opening the metal lid, a smile stretched across her face and her large gray eyes twinkled as she let out a sigh of relief. *Thank goodness.* Nothing she saw looked like a bill, overdue or otherwise. However, there was a blue envelope, which she quickly ignored as she strolled back up the walkway and inside her home. The beige envelope with the government seal made her a bit more sure-footed.

Delilah ripped off her sunglasses, plopped down on the sofa, and began to eagerly open the envelope. It didn't matter that it was two days late; it had arrived, so it was time to hit the streets where she'd shop, miles away from Garden City. After all, how many of her neighbors shopped at the Dollar Store?

Later that afternoon Delilah returned home. All her shopping was done and her hair as well. Yet again, Delilah decided to spend more money she didn't have on something she didn't need.

She sat at the kitchen table and perused the *Amsterdam News.* It was a Harlem-based newspaper she subscribed to. Her connection to the old days.

The Baby Grand presents the Sarah Vaughan Review tonight at 8 p.m. . . .

That's it. Delilah smiled and reread the announcement. It was at moments like this when she realized she'd have to go to an event alone. And she'd have to pay her own way. She'd tried to keep a few female friends around for just such occasions, but it never worked out. The clutch of hens always cackled about something. One of the women couldn't hold her liquor, or another couldn't hold a man, and none of them could hold a candle to her good looks.

Then she did something she hadn't done in the past few weeks. Delilah laughed and said aloud, "Have mercy. I wonder how many people knew Sarah Vaughan always carried that towel around because she knew she was going on stage after me. I made ole Sassy sweat with fear. Menopause, my foot! She and I both knew better; just like she knew I could sing rings around her version of 'Lover Man' and 'My Funny Valentine.' "

Self-praise always lifted her spirits, but it didn't take but a phone call to deflate them. Her hopes collapsed when she called the Baby Grand. "I'm sorry, ma'am. If you'd called a little sooner instead of a couple of hours before showtime, you might've been able to get in. We're completely sold out for tonight's show. The last tickets sold about five minutes ago."

Delilah slammed down the phone. She took it personally that someone would buy the last tickets and deny her a night out on the town. All she could do was hiss, "Selfish bastard . . ."

And then Delilah's face lit up. She had an idea. Tapping out a rhythm with one finger on the newspaper, she continued, "If I can't see Sarah Vaughan Review in Harlem, I'll get a taste of her in Brooklyn."

Delilah rushed into her bedroom and started rummaging through her closet. "I got a taste for some salmon anyway. I can get in a little karaoke as well, and the Blue Fish is the only place I trust for that. I'm sure it's still there where I left it three years ago."

Delilah wasn't concerned about whether they had Sarah Vaughan tracks or not. She had a vast collection of karaoke jazz, gospel, and rhythm and blues. She'd always carry a few with her whenever she wanted to sing. "I can still be back in plenty of time to rest up for church," she muttered. "In fact, tomorrow I'll go back to Brooklyn. I think I'll see what the choir's up to at First Corinthian over on Lafayette Avenue. I'll try their eleven o'clock service and then maybe drive through St. Stephen's and hear Keith Wonderboy. Now that young man knows how to throw down a song."

Delilah acted as though she were choosing her salvation, one from column A and one from column B.

Chapter 6

Three weeks and Deacon Pillar had not seen another sign of Delilah around New Hope. Saturday he awoke with the hope that perhaps she didn't want to have anything to do with him, any more than he with her.

Later that Saturday afternoon, Deacon Pillar stepped refreshed from his shower, and dressed. He was renowned for his fashion sense, or lack of it. He had no problem with wearing polka dots and stripes together or seersucker jumpsuits if he felt like it. As long as his conk looked tight, he was alright.

That Saturday he wore what he called a Pillar Design special: a green and blue polka-dot tie, a black shirt open to mid chest with a dagger-style collar and green, skinny-leg pants. To complete his Pillar-style outfit, he snapped on a pair of neon blue suspenders. He used one hand and slicked back his conk.

That conked salt-and-pepper hair, despite the huge bald spot on the top of his skull, hadn't moved in weeks, and needed a touch-up badly. But until he could get it done, he reached for his old standby remedy: a jar of clear hair goo, applied two layers thick so it'd blend in with the conk and smooth the frizzy new growth.

"Now, if I don't make the pig beg me to take his oink," the deacon said with another laugh, "then a sausage came from a parrot."

Yet a few days ago the deacon wasn't quite so confident, and he sure wasn't laughing as much. Running into Delilah had set his peace meter almost back to zero. But turning his life over to Christ hadn't rendered him a complete fool either, especially where Delilah was concerned. He still had some residual "street" left in his system. So he met the problem head-on and had already taken a precaution or two. It was just in case age hadn't slowed hurricane Delilah down none. Anyone who'd ever crossed her path soon learned that summer storms left a smaller trail than Delilah Dupree Jewel when she was in her season. She was never out of season.

Consequently, he'd called in a favor from a longtime connection he had with a local homicide detective who worked at Jessie's precinct. He gave the detective the name on her license plate.

As soon as Deacon Pillar had explained the situation, the detective replied, "I see the women in Pillar Land are still giving you headaches?"

"Only if I let them." Deacon Pillar had let out a nervous laugh. "And I don't intend to let them."

Soon after the detective left, he reappeared with the information. "According to the DMV, she lives in Garden City, New York, and there're enough outstanding tickets to plug a hole in Hoover Dam. It also looks like there's a suspension involved. You want me to see what it is?"

The deacon had cut the detective off. He'd gotten what he felt he needed. "Garden City isn't all that far, but perhaps it's far enough to keep her out of my neighborhood and she can deal with her own traffic tickets, suspension, or whatever."

Now, just knowing that he knew more about Delilah than she knew about him, put a little extra pep in the deacon's step. He was ready for prayer meeting. The deacon checked his watch. It was four o'clock.

Two Saturdays out of the month, whenever possible, the deacon came together with Jessie, Tamara, and, of course, Cindy, before she passed away. They held their own Bible study, complete with testimony and songs of praise. Either Cindy or Tamara would be on the piano and the deacon and Jessie would bring out their guitar and bass. They'd tried to keep up the tradition since Cindy's passing, and tonight was another effort.

Tonight's Bible study would be extra special as it always was when Sister Marty was able to join them. She was a huge part of all their lives and had a great voice, too.

Marty was in her early sixties and despite their age difference had been Cindy's closest confidante and Tamara's godmother. And Marty was the head of the nurses' unit at New Hope as well as a registered surgical nurse at Downstate Hospital. She was also the last foster mother Jessie'd had. She and her late husband rescued Jessie from the system when he was twelve years old. Childless, they'd given him all the love they had, which was a great deal more than he'd received in his other three foster homes. He didn't leave Marty's house until he was in his twenties and married Cindy. When Marty's husband died, Jessie bought the house two doors down. Even more importantly, she was the first woman the deacon let get close to reviving any interest in a serious relationship.

It was almost six o'clock that same evening by the time the deacon had decided that he was enough of a good thing and fit for Bible study. Depending on how the evening went, he was glad he'd earlier asked Sister Marty if, after she finished work, she would like to take in a late movie, or just spend some quiet time together. The thought of the woman brought another broad grin to his chocolate face as he stood in his living room.

"My goodness, that's a fine-looking woman." The deacon smiled and sang aloud, "She wears the sexiest looking pitch-black weave I've ever seen. A petite little thing with large brown eyes, a shape most women her age would pay extra tithes to have. If that gal plays her cards right . . ."

"Deacon Pillar," a voice through the hallway intercom called out, interrupting his made-up song, "I've got the list for dinner. It's your turn to get it."

The deacon shook his head and laughed before pressing the intercom button to respond. "Okay, Tamara. I'll stop in and get your list."

Tamara was Jessie's twenty-one-year-old daughter. There wasn't anything the deacon wouldn't do for her. In the almost four years since he'd moved into the upstairs apartment he'd watched her blossom into a gorgeous young woman. Tamara was smart, a singing superstar in the making, and already headed into her second year of college at Juilliard. Those were her good parts.

The bad part was that since he'd run into Delilah, he realized just how much the two looked alike. He needed to do everything he could to keep Delilah from tarnishing Tamara.

"Okay, baby girl," the deacon called out as he peeked inside the downstairs apartment at Tamara. "Let's see how much you gonna take me for this time."

"Oh, please, Deacon Pillar. You know you got more money than you know what to do with. I'm just trying to help you spend it before you forget where you hid it." Tamara's gray eyes sparkled as she laughed and teased the deacon.

"If that's the case, then I need to spend more money on buying something with more calories to put some more meat on your bones. I'm still trying to recover from trying to find a size two petite when you graduated from high school."

Although a couple of generations apart, Deacon Pillar and Tamara had a bond neither could explain. Almost immediately after he'd moved in, he was always available to play referee whenever she couldn't get her way with her parents. He'd go out of his way to buy her little things that cost big money. To most, Deacon Pillar acted more like Tamara's kindly old grandfather than just the upstairs tenant. And because he had no family he could claim, Deacon Pillar spoiled not only Tamara but Jessie. And he simply adored Cindy when she was alive. Coaxing her into singing while he strummed his guitar was his piece of heaven.

"Don't you worry about me and my weight, Deacon Pillar. As long as I don't go down to a size eighteen months, I'm cool."

Tamara always had an uncontrollable giggle, especially when she gave the deacon the same answer when he teased her about her weight. Her giggle was that carefree sound that'd caused him to nickname her "baby girl." "By the way," she continued, "since I'm spending up your money, would you like for me to go with you? Daddy's taking a shower, so he won't be ready for Bible study for at least another hour."

Deacon Pillar, as he sometimes did, touched Tamara's cheek and gave her a quick kiss. "Nope, you stay here and finish working on that tune I taught you. You didn't hit that G-flat and resolve it like you should. I'm gonna walk to the restaurant to use up some of that extra time and I can get my exercise in, too. Besides, the ladies on Putnam Avenue haven't gotten their Pillar fix for today."

"Okay, Deacon Playa, you do that. But you call me if you get a charley horse or something, or if Sister Marty catches you trying to *fix* something."

She giggled again as she left the room, but that time the deacon didn't laugh quite as hard.

If only Tamara didn't look so much like that treacherous Delilah. There was no denying their resemblance now, and it made him sadder not being able to tell Tamara that he was her natural grandfather. It hadn't bothered him nearly as much in the past as it had over the past three weeks. He was glad Tamara had turned away and couldn't see his face. *Damn you, Delilah!* When he stepped out of the apartment into the sunlight, he looked at the palms of his hands. They'd always had a dusty color to them. Right now, in the brightness of the sunlight, they looked dark and dirty; just like his past with Delilah. He quickly shoved the list and his hands into his pockets and walked away.

And much like real life, it wouldn't take long before he'd have to show those hands. Even though he believed that God wouldn't place any more on him than he could stand, and that the Almighty had forgiven his sins, he suddenly wasn't as confident. He wasn't ready for any trial or test that would reveal a past he'd avoided for so long. Just living in his small apartment above Jessie and his family was all he needed. Was God going to snatch it away? Would He use Delilah to do it?

Chapter 7

Delilah parked her Navigator a little ways from the front door of the Blue Fish Restaurant. She'd worn a bright yellow, sleeveless cotton top and a skirt that stopped about midcalf. Her walk was easy, not like the little hops that most women her age moved with. Each step permitted the high split to show creamy thighs with no cottage cheese curse. With her bag of karaoke tunes in her hand and her head raised as though she were above the surroundings, she walked toward the door.

Not a lot had changed in the many years since she'd been there. There was still the ghetto décor of burnt building frames dotted along Fulton Street, a few crackheads crossing against the traffic while they laughed and searched the ground, snatching at anything tiny and white. Of course, there were still not enough cops on each corner. There was what looked like a new shade of blue on the brick-and-mortar one-story building, and a larger sign that carried the name of its new owner. But it wasn't until she'd actually gotten closer to the door that she realized that the sign no longer listed karaoke as entertainment.

"When did they stop having karaoke?" Delilah threw one

hand up in surrender. "Okay," she snapped. "I give up. Let me get something to eat. It's their loss." She stepped inside and told the server she only needed a table for one. The server led her to a small table for two near the front window. He removed one of the place settings and handed her a menu.

She hadn't sat for a good five minutes, poring over what she could afford and what she was going to order, when she heard it.

"Dammit, Delilah."

Delilah didn't bother to look up. She knew it was Thurgood Pillar calling her name, again.

Just that quick, with just that one outburst, Deacon Pillar had erased his three weeks of peace and quiet. As soon as the letter *D* left his mouth, he'd lost the battle.

He stood there in his black seersucker shirt and pants, not two feet away from her, and wheezed. It was all he could do. His hands filled with the bags of food he'd ordered for the Bible study were the only things that kept him from choking her.

Delilah still didn't bother to look around. Although there was no doubt the sizzling sound heard through the din in the restaurant came from the kitchen nearby, she was so mad it could've just as well been her wig crackling. She was just that angry. "Just when I thought there was somewhere I could go without seeing you, here you are."

He'd walked the ten blocks to the restaurant praising God and humming. The deacon, though tired from the walk, had no more than a few moments ago resolved to walk happily back. The sight of her had erased all of that. He'd lost it and his mouth was now in overdrive.

Despite the chances of someone in the place knowing him, and that he was a church deacon, he blasted her. "You can go to hell! Now that's someplace you won't see me."

Delilah shot up from the table. She turned around so fast

she almost pulled off the tablecloth. With both hands now on the table, she glared. "Your old ass will be giving the welcome address while the devil ushers you in."

From all over the Blue Fish, inquiring and surprised eyes turned in their direction. The server put his experience to work. He sprinted over and yanked another chair from one of the nearby empty tables. He shoved the chair by the deacon and almost at the same time a second place setting appeared on the table. The server almost slapped the deacon on the cheek as he forced a menu into the old man's hands. "Have a seat, sir, where you can continue your overanimated conversation in private."

"I don't want him seated with me," Delilah said quickly as she slumped back down onto her chair.

"You don't get to tell me what I can do and where I can go. You gave up that right years ago when you decided the name Pillar wasn't good enough for you." Whatever else the deacon was thinking didn't require common sense or a lot of thought, evidenced by the way he then slammed the bags down to the floor and plopped down onto the chair. He sat opposite Delilah and let his glare show he wasn't finished. "If you had any sense of decency, you'd have divorced me first. Or at the very least divorced me from wherever you've been hiding all this time."

"Well, awrighty now. I'll be back." The server announced his lie with an air of authority. He'd done his job. Combat duty was not in his job description.

"The real question is why haven't *you* gotten a divorce?" Delilah snapped. She couldn't decide between giving the deacon hell and being nice so she could get her way. But he still hadn't mentioned Jessie. Perhaps she could throw him off track and get him angry enough to spill something.

The deacon's eyes became slits as he pondered his next step. *I don't care if it has been about forty years, she's hiding some-*

thing. I know her. She hasn't mentioned his name at all. I wonder if she knows that Jessie lives right here in Brooklyn and that's the real reason she's haunting so far from Garden City.

The minutes seemed an eternity as the staring contest continued while each marinated in thought and plotted. But the time continued with no sign of either mule giving in, until another server appeared with a basket of bread sticks and a saucer overflowing with pats of butter. Much like the first server, he didn't need a fortune-teller to tell him there was anger in the air.

Neither the deacon nor Delilah had any real plans beyond the stare-down. It took the loud sounds of their stomachs growling to break the ice.

Delilah was the first to reach for one of the bread sticks. After all, it was her table. He, on the other hand, was an uninvited and unwanted intruder. She studied him for a moment while she buttered the bread. He still said nothing, but she could've sworn he looked like he was about to pass out from hunger.

"Either grab a bread stick and go, Thurgood, or go without it. I don't much care." Delilah crammed the bread stick into her mouth without breaking it in half. Being nice was proving harder than she'd like.

"I don't know what good you think it will do to shove that whole bread stick down your mouth. That doesn't do anything for my juices anymore." *Lord, help keep me from lying. That's one demon act I ain't overcome yet.*

"What in the hell are you talking about? Are you having a senility moment or something? If you are, please have it someplace else."

The deacon's eyes widened with embarrassment, and he would've stood and left if his manhood hadn't grown at the same time. *She's still the same ole Delilah, a tease even in her old age.*

Delilah watched the deacon in amusement. She hadn't tried to do anything but eat a bread stick because she was hungry. He obviously wasn't as angry at her as she'd thought.

But could she risk asking him about Jessie, with so much hostility present? Delilah clasped her hands together and hung her head slightly. Whether the deacon took it as her ignoring him, she didn't know. When she needed to consult God, she didn't care where she was or who she was with.

Okay, Lord God Jehovah, give me a sign. I've been praying and asking for a while that I find my husband and my son. You put Thurgood in my face first, but I didn't necessarily mean it in that order, plus I'm sorry, but this old man pushes my buttons. And I've prayed hard to find Jessie, ever since I read the news about him losing his wife. You know I tried the telephone book and the crazy Internet, but Brooklyn is a big place, and I can't find out nothing. Please give me a sign if I should ask this old fool about my son.

"Amen." No sooner had she lifted her head than her eyes met his. The deacon was still staring.

"You surprised me, seeing you pray for a couple of seconds. I didn't know that you and God had met." Again, his mouth spouted what he should have kept to himself.

"From the way you keep putting me down, perhaps I should take a moment and reintroduce Him to you." *Jehovah, he's making it so hard to be civil.*

"Well, since you're in such a good mood, while we discuss God's Word, why don't we also go back to the subject of our fake marital status." The deacon thought he saw her shake. Perhaps he still caused a spark. He wasn't sure if that would be a good thing or not.

Delilah clasped her hands together. Her gray eyes turned almost black, but she was actually very cool and deliberate as she spoke. "Perhaps you need to reread that Bible. You can't get rid of me with a divorce unless you can prove I cheated on you first. I doubt if you can."

Deacon Pillar's fist hit the table. She'd pulled the old

Matthew 19:9 card on him. She knew he couldn't divorce her just because she had a death grip around his last good nerve, unless she'd been servicing outside the marriage. If he did divorce her and remarried, then he'd be the adulterer without a legal marriage before God.

"Damn!" The deacon slapped the table again and sputtered through teeth long turned beige from tobacco abuse in middle age. He tried to bluff. "You left me. I can get one based just on that."

"Well, why haven't you then?"

"How do you know I didn't just think you were dead and didn't need one to move on?"

"You could've had me declared dead, but as you can see, I'm not dead. . . ." Delilah stopped and leaned across the table. "Hold up. What do you mean, move on? You got an understudy waiting in the wings to play my part?"

"Trust me"—the deacon leaned back and folded his hands and laughed—"she's no understudy. She's a star!"

Delilah's mind started racing. *If this old coot is really ready to move on to someone else and I'm standing in the way . . .* "Tell me something," Delilah said nonchalantly, "what if I gave you that divorce? Would you do something for me in return?"

The deacon sat up straight. "I've got exactly eighty dollars on me. I can get a little more if it's money you need. Oh hell, I'll pay for the divorce and a ticket for you to go anywhere on the other side of the earth you want to go."

"Oh, don't start doing the happy dance. I haven't told you what I want yet."

Deacon Pillar suddenly looked puzzled. *She doesn't seem to want money. The Delilah I know would stampede a buffalo to get it off its nickel. She's up to something. . . .*

"I know it's a long shot and I know you probably won't believe me."

"Let's not go there, Dee Dee."

"Don't push, Pillar." Delilah was about to get loud, but

she hadn't gotten what she wanted yet. She remained calm. "I need you to help me find Jessie."

"Say what? Jessie—you want to find Jessie? Why?"

"I don't know how you could ask such a question. He's my son. I would think that you'd want to know where he is and how he is doing, too."

"Don't pack a bag for me, because I ain't going on a guilt trip with you. I've always wanted what was best for him. In fact, I looked for years to find the two of you. I just stopped looking for you before I stopped looking for him. The better question is, why now? After all these years, Delilah, why do you choose now?"

"He needs me." Delilah hoped she sounded convincing. She wasn't certain how a mother would say something like that. The truth was, she needed her son. One had become the lonely number for her. She pulled a folded piece of newspaper from her pocketbook. "Read this."

The deacon slowly took the newspaper clipping from Delilah's hand. As soon as he saw the date on the top and the word *obituary*, he knew. He knew that she knew, too. Seeing Cindy's death announcement sent a chill through him. He'd helped Jessie write it. But he scanned over the clipping anyway, hoping he'd not given anything away as he handed it back to Delilah.

Deacon Pillar wasn't ready for that revelation. Delilah obviously knew Cindy was dead and she was asking him to trade their son's whereabouts in return for a divorce. He'd need time to think it over. Hopefully, she'd give it to him.

"I don't know what to say. Are you sure this is our Jessie?"

"I'm even more convinced, since you don't look shocked. Why is that, Thurgood?"

"Trust me. I've been in a state of shock for the last three weeks. I need to think this over and figure out what to do and how to do it. I haven't read the *Amsterdam News* in quite some time, so you've got a head start on me. Please give me a little time to check and see if this is our Jessie. Why don't you give me your telephone number?" He pulled out a pen and gave it to her. "I'll call you in a couple of weeks and, if it's him—then, well, we'll see where to go from there."

"I've got a better idea," Delilah replied as she wrote her number on a paper napkin and handed it back. "It's a beautiful day and we've done nothing but argue. Let's try and be more civil. We need one another, so let's start there."

She gave her best happy grin and winked. "Why don't we just exchange numbers? That way it'll build mutual trust. . . ."

She tried to continue and failed. All she could do was throw her hands up and laugh.

He didn't want to join her, but he couldn't help but laugh at the absurdity of it all. When their love fled, it took trust as a hostage.

Suddenly the deacon's cell phone vibrated in his pocket. He continued laughing until he pulled it out and looked at the name displayed. And that's when his entire body tensed up.

It was Jessie. "Thank you, Jesus," he murmured. Normally the phone vibrating in his pocket annoyed him. This time he was thankful that he'd left it that way. If he hadn't, the automated voice would have announced, *Jessie Jewel calling.*

"Gotta run . . . I'll be in touch, and keep away from New Hope." The deacon leapt from his seat and grabbed the bags he'd left on the floor.

She'd tried *nice* and *reason,* but she wasn't about to let him leave without her having the last word. "Please tell whoever that is that just called you, especially if it's your woman, that I said thank you. They called just in time."

Delilah held the glass of water in her hands and smiled while she sipped. *Jehovah, I thank you for giving me some of that grace and mercy you keep handy. Now all I need to do is stay calm. I can keep Thurgood occupied, with me promising that divorce; that is, if he can help me find our son.*

Delilah smiled again. She was proud of the advice she'd just given God. And then, just as she was about to summon the server and order her meal, she was distracted by noises outside the restaurant window. The smile slid from her face faster than a raging mud slide.

The deacon hadn't left the table quick enough to suit him. The last thing he needed was for Delilah to know he'd already found Jessie several years ago. He zigzagged between tables as he struggled to keep the phone pressed against his ear, using his chin, while he spoke and carried the bags to the restaurant door. "I know I'm late but I'm on my way. Tell baby girl to hold tight. I've got the crab cakes and I didn't forget the special remoulade sauce she wanted. . . . . No, Jessie, I didn't forget your tilapia with dill sauce, either. . . . See you shortly. . . . Marty called? What did she say? Did she say how long she would have to stay at work? Okay . . . I'm walking back as fast as I can. . . . No! Please don't you come get me!"

Deacon Pillar had barely gotten the restaurant door open when Delilah sped past, knocking one bag from his hand and slapping his cell phone to the floor.

She didn't even look back. That ended their truce.

"Oh, you have lost your doggone mind for sure. . . ." The deacon was about to add something more, but instead he scooped up his phone and the dropped bag and took off after Delilah. "You won't hit and run this time, Delilah." And even as his spirit screamed to let it go, the deacon pursued her. Bible study or no Bible study, he wanted her to pay; there was a forty-year payment due.

By the time Deacon Pillar caught up with Delilah, she was standing on the curb. Her body shook as though she stood in the middle of an earthquake, and there were tears streaming down her face.

As soon as he reached her side he saw a tow truck. "Dee

Dee, what's going on? Isn't that your car that's booted?" He hadn't meant to call her by that old pet name. Whatever harsh words he was about to use seemed to evaporate when he'd seen her cry. And then he saw her morph right before his eyes. Delilah turned from a helpless female into a pint-sized praying mantis.

Delilah was hot. Her face turned red and her tears dried up. "You know I could just slap the black off you, Thurgood."

"I guess you could try to carry through on some of those empty threats if your Alzheimer's and arthritis didn't ride for free on your arse."

"If you hadn't taken up so much of my time back there, I could've been paying attention and gotten out here sooner."

Meanwhile the reasons for the noise that had caught her attention stood. There were folks on the sidewalk who laughed until they cried outside the Blue Fish. Most were just happy it wasn't them, that time. The other reason for the laughter stood next to Delilah. It wasn't unusual for the young people to see the repo man place a boot on a car so the driver couldn't drive it away. But most of the young folks had never seen a jacked-up conk; at least not in the twenty-first century, unless it was in an old movie.

One second she stood on the curb, the next she was climbing up the back of a big, muscular black man. He looked like a ghetto Hulk in filthy coveralls with a chain in one hand and fighting off Delilah with his other.

And then someone in the crowd screamed, "Oh damn, look at pops. He's going to help his woman."

More applause and even louder laughter erupted again. The gawkers slapped five. "Crack his head, old playa," another voice shouted.

But as much as the deacon didn't want to get any further involved, he found himself butting in again. One minute he was threatening Delilah and the next he was hyperventilating and fighting a definite heart attack as he struggled to keep

Delilah, with her wig now flipped out, from whipping the repo man's behind, or vice versa.

"I'll kill you if you don't take that damn boot off my car!" Delilah was clawing and scratching with no apparent effect on the repo man.

"I'm just doing my job, lady. You've got three days to come up with the money, and next time pay your damn car note!" He was much quicker than Delilah. In seconds, he'd gently shoved her off and not so gently knocked the deacon off his feet. Before Delilah or Deacon Pillar could string two words together, the man had her car in neutral. With the crowd still laughing, he got into his tow truck and drove off with Delilah's car bumping up and down as it gave off sparks along the street.

"Delilah," the deacon pleaded with what quickly seemed like his last breath, "it's no use. If you keep it up the police will come."

"Let 'em!" But all Delilah got for her effort was a sad last look at the back of her car. All she could do was stand on the sidewalk wearing her wig lopsided. The sight of it made her look more like a Phyllis Diller than a Farrah Fawcett. She looked a hot mess.

"Jesus, please get me outta here. . . ." Deacon Pillar had barely gotten to the *amen* of his prayer when it was answered, sorta.

"Hey, Deacon Pillar. You need a ride?" A Crown Victoria Black Pearl cab pulled up to the curb. "I thought it was you, but I ain't never seen you fight befo', so I couldn't be sho'," the almond-colored elderly man called out as he leaned farther out the car window and waved for the deacon to come over. "I was about to head into the garage, but I can take you home if that's where you're going. It looks like you've torn your bags."

Deacon Pillar sighed as he looked down and saw that the

second bag had burst, too. *Have mercy, Jesus. Can this day get any worse?* There wasn't much the deacon could do but accept the offer. "Thank you, Brother Libby. I guess I'll take you up on the ride. I may need to make a stop before then, but it's along the way."

"Well, c'mon then. I'll only charge you ten dollars instead of the regular fifteen."

If the deacon had to explain his next move on Judgment Day to keep from going to hell, then hell would be his eternal home. It began when Delilah suddenly started cussing and throwing punches in the air at invisible demons. The next thing he knew, he'd somehow shoved Delilah, albeit as gently as he could, inside the cab.

Of course Delilah didn't say thank you. She was too busy yelling, "Damn, damn, damn!" Delilah wept as she glared out the cab window and stared at the spot where her Navigator had stood. "All I needed was another couple of weeks and at least a heads-up. I could've probably come up with some of the money."

Delilah's tears suddenly dried up again. Her mouth clamped shut. She'd said more than she'd meant to. After all, she was still acting the part of a diva and a diva wasn't supposed to be on a budget.

"Dee Dee." There it was. He'd said her pet name again. This time the deacon's voice took on an authoritative tone. "Why didn't you just say something?"

"Say what, Thurgood? What did you want me to say, and when was I supposed to say it?" She turned and faced the deacon with her hands balled into what looked like two golf balls. "Was I supposed to tell you while you cussed me out two seconds after you laid eyes on me?"

"Stop exaggerating, Delilah!"

"Oh, I'm sorry. Perhaps it was three or five seconds after you hadn't seen me in almost four decades."

"Okay, we're here," Brother Libby announced louder than he needed. "Don't worry about the fare. Y'all just go ahead and get out. Now!"

"I'm so sorry, Brother Libby." The deacon wanted to explain what wasn't explainable. "I'd meant for you to make that other stop before we got here."

"Well, there are cabs going in the other direction, too." Brother Libby wasn't about to drive another inch with the deacon and the irritated woman battling in his leased cab.

Delilah looked about the neighborhood. The sun had already begun to set, so she couldn't get a real sense of where they were. All she knew for certain was that they were still in Brooklyn. She needed to find a way to get her car back as well as return home.

Brother Libby's cab sped away, leaving them on the sidewalk. Delilah kept quiet, although she couldn't figure out why she should.

"Just wait here," the deacon said nicely. "Let me take these things inside and I'll take you where you need to go." He paused, suddenly proud that he hadn't said more. *At least I didn't say Garden City.*

"As if I have a choice," Delilah muttered. "Just hurry up. For the next two weeks I want to get as far away from you as you need to get from me."

Delilah fought the tears just as hard as she'd fought the deacon's kindness. She wouldn't allow herself the comfort of accepting something as simple as a car ride.

Deacon Pillar gripped the bags by the ends that weren't torn and climbed the porch steps. He'd already made up his mind to hurry inside and make some type of apology to Jessie and Tamara before leaving again. And if God was truly in the plan, the Master would keep Sister Marty away, too.

Father, please help me to get Delilah away from here before it's too late. I just need a little more time, Jesus.

And while the deacon prayed his prayer, Delilah stood resting against the porch stoop and began to advise her God.

Well, Heavenly Father Jehovah, this has been one joke of a day. If this is one of those tests, then I sure hope I passed. I can't take another one. If I need to be praying another kind of way, I wish You'd show me how. I asked You to lead me to my husband, and to my son. Instead, You take away my ride and leave me in the hands of Thurgood. As bad as he's trying to get rid of me and get a divorce, he'd have said something about Jessie if he knew anything. Why do the tables keep turning on me? Or, if Thurgood does know something, You wouldn't let him get a head start and turn Jessie against me, would You?

Delilah suddenly stopped calling on God because nature was calling on her.

As put-out as she was, she still wasn't too proud to ask the deacon to use his bathroom.

Chapter 8

"You don't look too bad, and at least the food didn't spill out of the containers." Jessie stifled an urge to laugh. The deacon's story of unwittingly getting involved in a stranger's situation that left him less than blessed was funny.

"If you really want a story, you should've been out on a call with me last night. I'm telling you, if I have another night like last night, I'm taking off my badge and going upside some heads over there in Crown Heights. Hot as it is and young folks running all over the place over on Lincoln, turning on fire hydrants and slashing tires. Don't make sense." Jessie had almost fifteen years on the police force and every other week he threatened to take off his badge.

"Listen, something came up and I got to handle it quickly. I promise it shouldn't take more than a couple of hours. Go ahead and start eating. If I'm not back in time, then start the Bible study." Deacon Pillar tried to say everything in a way where it wasn't a complete lie; a little deceptive, but not a complete lie.

"I guess it's okay," Tamara said as she gathered the food to take to the kitchen. "Sister Marty's working late anyhow. And, as usual, I don't have a date. Actually, I could have one—I just don't want one. . . ."

The deacon tuned Tamara out. His mind had gone else-where. *Have mercy. I'd almost forgotten about Marty.* And then the deacon realized he'd left Delilah alone for a little too long.

The hair on Deacon Pillar's neck suddenly rose and he knew why. He raced to close the door just as Delilah came barreling against it. It was almost a head-on collision.

"Stop with the games, Thurgood," Delilah barked as she started to knock on the door. "I need to use your bathroom and there's no negotiation."

"Deacon," Jessie asked slowly, "who is that? What's going on?"

"Uhhhh . . ." That's as far as the deacon got before Deli-lah, encouraged by the urgency of her situation, pushed the door open.

Delilah didn't bother to check out whether there were others there or not. She hadn't thought that far.

"I don't need this crap!" Delilah almost tripped when the heel of one of her latest knockoffs became stuck as she tried to cross over the threshold.

Delilah wanted to move out of the doorway, but couldn't get the heel of her shoe to twist back into place. So she sim-ply took it off. With one tiny foot bare, Delilah entered and stood defiant and lopsided.

She and the deacon had shared a lot in the past, but none of it compared to the *Twilight Zone* moment they shared then.

Delilah took one look around the living room and fainted, which was also something the deacon wanted to do but couldn't.

As Delilah slowly came around she peeked through heavy false eyelashes and found she couldn't see as clearly as she could hear.

Jessie folded his arms and stared. It took him a moment to

believe his eyes and another moment to find his voice. "What the hell is she doing here?" Jessie's angry question shot around the room, and if it had been a loaded gun, Delilah would've been dead. "Lord, please help me. I don't believe this is happening. And you've laid her on my sofa."

If Delilah had wanted to pretend she was still unconscious, she couldn't have. Deacon Pillar, the bald-faced liar, was literally water-boarding her as he wrung a soaking wet cloth over her face. He looked as though he enjoyed it.

"I just don't know what to say, Brother Jessie. This is the woman I tried to help. I had no idea you were so against me bringing another woman here unless it was Sister Marty. . . ."

Delilah ignored the deacon's feeble attempt to throw her under the bus. Instead, she watched her son with curiosity as Jessie's eyes glared in her direction. She was sure she could almost see—no, *feel*—his anxiety and pure hatred. Then again, she wasn't sure if she knew it was hatred for certain. She wasn't even sure if what she was feeling was some sort of maternal feeling. Could it be that God had thrown some mother wit into the mess?

"Deacon, this has nothing to do with who you bring or don't bring to where you pay rent. But do you know who you just let into my home?" Jessie's voice sounded as though he spoke from within a cave. It was just that loud and seemed to reverberate around the room.

The deacon realized that he needed to remain calm during what was certainly turning into a very dangerous verbal showdown. He'd have to chew crow and get Delilah out of there and back to Garden City before his own mess went on display.

With one hand fingering his suspenders, he replied simply, "Yes, I know her. Pretty much—"

At that moment Jessie needed more than simplicity. He needed something to throw, much the same way he needed to believe he'd misheard the deacon. "You're standing here in my home telling me that you actually know this woman?"

Deacon Pillar nodded toward Delilah. He needed to quickly turn things around. So he tried to sound more confident. "More than forty years, I believe. We used to run in the same crowds back in Harlem where she sang in a few bands. I even played in some of them, too." Deacon Pillar stopped. He was sure to tell a bigger lie if he spoke another word. It was bad enough tiptoeing across a thick carpet of lies.

It took Delilah's inability to shut up when she should to break her awkward silence. She didn't care if it saved the deacon from himself or not. But she did enjoy a conversation about her that was positive, and she'd not heard anything positive. She raised her head and barked with indignation, "Are you two gonna stand here and talk all over my head like I can't hear?"

Whether he meant to do it or not, Jessie used his hand to hit a nearby wall. The hand immediately started to swell and turned from a pecan color to almost blue right before their eyes.

"This demon dressed up like a woman . . ." Jessie's mouth began to twist. He felt almost dizzy as the pain in his hand shot up his arm and landed upon his tongue.

Oh, Lord, he's recognized her. The deacon shuffled a little closer to the door. He hadn't meant to do that. He'd done it on instinct.

"Repeat that, Jessie." Delilah leapt off the couch and now stood with her hands on her small hips. This was not how she'd envisioned their first meeting, but she'd be damned if he was gonna come at her in such a manner. Now it was her time to glare and she used it to the maximum. "I'm a little older and perhaps I don't hear so good anymore." Delilah stopped and yanked her hands off her hips and shook them at

Jessie. "Now when the child I birthed, after more than forty hours of damn hard labor, tries sassing me—"

"Deacon Pillar," Jessie interrupted, ignoring his pain as his anger mounted. Jessie's eyes narrowed and issued a silent warning to the deacon before he turned back around. He was saving his next words of rebuke for Delilah.

At that moment his need to put Delilah in her place outweighed his pain. "Maybe you are hard of hearing, 'cause you sure ain't no kind of mother."

From across the room Tamara stood with her arms dangling by her side. She'd been in the basement and heard all the yelling. After racing upstairs it was as though she'd flipped to a bad movie on television and couldn't change the channel. It took another moment before she could speak. "Daddy, what's going on?"

Waves of spasms attacked Jessie's mouth, causing it to twist even more as he ignored Tamara's question. Since he'd buried Cindy he'd kept all his sane and insane emotions simmering. His grief pot was about to boil over. At that very moment all he wanted to do was just lash out, and a conveniently placed punching bag or two stood gift wrapped in his living room.

While the others in the room stared at him as though he'd truly lost his mind, which he was about to, Jessie's anger soared. Without apology Jessie gave in to his need to lay his salvation down at an invisible altar. He would leave it there just long enough to punch both Deacon Pillar and Delilah in their mouths. But Jessie was still Delilah's son, and the apple hadn't fallen too far from the tree. He just couldn't make up his mind as to whom to start with. He knew he'd possibly broken his hand, which meant he'd have to take time off from the job. But a possible broken hand be damned.

"Go to hell!" Delilah suddenly shot back at Jessie. "I know what you're thinking, and if you ever live to see a hundred I'll still be older than you and I'll still be your mama. Come at me, and I'll whip you until I can't no more."

"Who are you gonna whip? And who are you to tell me to go to hell? Join me, because I'm in it now." Mama or no mama, he was more than a foot taller than Delilah and he'd bend over and hit her if he had to. Jessie wanted to say something even more vicious, but words wouldn't come again.

Yet in that *Twilight Zone* moment, as she looked to where Tamara stood, it all became clear to Delilah. *What a mighty God I serve.* She saw Tamara and almost folded again. "You've worked a miracle, Father, and it was here all along. . . ."

"You've lost your damn mind." The pain that shot up Jessie's arm again seemed more like a punishment; a hindrance to keep him from stopping what was about to unfold.

Delilah's eyes moistened again as she finally realized that God had indeed delivered. Why in such a crazy manner, she didn't know.

An easy smile crept across her face when she turned from Jessie and looked at Tamara once more. "God brought me here, Jessie. He truly did."

The observation had not escaped the deacon. "That's Tamara, your grandbaby," Deacon Pillar said, as though the previous conversation had gone smoothly instead of a mother-son cuss out. His move was more to keep her mind temporarily off retribution where he was concerned.

Delilah allowed Deacon Pillar to walk over and take her by one arm to escort her across the room. It was the least he could do after his brazen performance earlier. She'd come back to him later.

He'd gotten her halfway across the room before he realized he had to pass Jessie to get to Tamara. He saw the anger in Jessie's eyes and almost felt the heat coming off his head. Deacon Pillar wasn't certain he'd make it. It was a lot safer upstairs in his apartment, for sure.

"Thurgood Pillar, you idiot." When the deacon stopped just short of Jessie, Delilah shook her arm loose from his grip with ease. "I know who she is."

"Oh, I ain't gonna be too many more idiots—" Deacon Pillar wanted to finish the threat, bad grammar and all, but he was caught off guard by the strength she showed when she snatched her skinny arm from his firm grip.

"Just shut up, Thurgood," Delilah warned, her eyes turned into slits to back up the implied threat. Then, without missing a beat, she turned back to Tamara, saying sweetly with her eyes now loaded with sympathy, "I'm sorry I wasn't here for your mama's funeral. I did read about it and tried to find y'all. I guess by now you know I'm your grandma—"

Delilah started to cough, which quickly turned into more of a hacking sound. The word *grandma* stuck in her throat like a fishbone and was just as uncomfortable. Not even her beautiful granddaughter could make her feel at ease enough to say the word *grandmother*. Instead she corrected herself. "I'm Delilah, your father's mother."

"Damn, Delilah," Deacon Pillar barked, "you couldn't even say grandma? That's cold even for that refrigerator you call a heart."

Delilah turned slightly and looked up at Deacon Pillar. "Mind your business. It's my last warning, daddy-o." She'd placed emphasis on the *daddy* part.

Whatever she was thinking was enough to cause him to move a few steps back.

"Don't even think about speaking to my daughter," Jessie warned her as his girth seemed to double with the threat. "She doesn't even know you. You won't be tiptoeing around her life like you used to do mine."

The deacon's conked head turned quickly in Delilah's direction. He pointed toward her and then turned back to speak to Jessie. "You mean you recognized her because this is not the first time you've seen her in years?" The deacon glanced quickly again at Delilah. He'd not known that little bit of information.

"Yes," Jessie hissed, "I saw this mother impersonator for the first time since I was a toddler when I was about ten years old. She had the nerve to show up at"—Jessie stopped and started to count on his fingers before he continued—"I believe it might've been at the second or third foster home I was placed in."

"It was when . . . ?" Deacon Pillar suddenly felt dizzy, but he couldn't move and there was no place to fall that was comfortable. That had to be just before Marty's involvement. Six degrees of separation would always have a special meaning for him.

"Oh, it gets better," Jessie continued. "She told me—no, she promised me—that she'd go to court and get me back. She told me she'd been on the road with a couple of groups in Europe, to make money because my father had abandoned us."

"*Abandoned* you?" Strength returned to the deacon's legs. He started to move toward Delilah. There was no mistaking his intention.

"Go ahead," Delilah said as her fingers clutched her purse hard enough to leave fingerprints. "Hurry and get it all out in the open, Jessie."

"What I'd like to do is split you open," Jessie hissed.

Perspiration broke out on Jessie's face and he began to shake as he turned to face the deacon. "This so-called old friend of yours—well, she never returned. And then when I saw her again, Tamara was about three years old. I was a grown man with a wife and child. I didn't need a mother. So I left her and her lies standing on Forty-second Street in front of Grand Central Station."

"Daddy—" Tamara felt helpless. Too much was happening

and whatever it was, it raced past her at warp speed and it was hurting her father.

Delilah saw the anguish upon Tamara's face. She took a few steps toward her.

"Don't even think about it!" Deacon Pillar hadn't quite reached her yet, as he was suddenly haunted by Jessie's revelation. He was learning that Delilah—the same old Delilah—hadn't changed at all.

"Touch my daughter and I swear . . ." Jessie threatened.

Delilah was quicker than Jessie's threats and certainly quicker than the deacon's feeble attempt to stop her. By the time the men got it together to block Delilah, she was already inches away from Tamara.

Delilah's gray eyes never looked away as she honed in on every inch of Tamara. "She's beautiful. She's even my height and size and she's got my gray eyes instead of her father's light brown ones."

Suddenly all the ghosts from the past invaded Jessie's huge living room and discovered even then there wasn't enough room for all of them and the truth.

"Don't touch me," Tamara snapped as she jumped aside when Delilah reached out to touch her. "I don't know you, and if my father says I don't need to know you, then I don't want to know you."

Delilah knew she shouldn't be surprised, but Tamara's words were a punch in her gut. She lifted her head as though it would make her superior by doing so. "Is this supposed to be a room full of Christian folks?"

"She must be kidding." Tamara inched away from Delilah. She spun around and headed toward the front door. "I gotta get out of here."

"Forget about this old witch," Jessie called out to Tamara. "You don't have to leave, but she does."

Delilah stood with her arms still outstretched as she watched

Tamara race from the living room while ignoring Jessie's pleas to return. There was nothing more Delilah could do but continue to watch in amazement as her granddaughter raced from the room.

Tamara stumbled a bit, but she kept going until she reached her front door. She left the door wide open as she raced through the front gate and sprinted up the block.

"Damn you, Delilah," Jessie snarled as he turned around and began to dump more pent-up rage onto his mother. "Get the hell out of my life. I don't need a prodigal mother. I won't ever need you."

"I see how well you have your house under control." Delilah didn't wait for Jessie to respond, and she certainly didn't need to hear further details of what a bad mother she'd been. She'd be the first to say guilty to whatever the charges.

The heaviness Delilah suddenly felt in her heart for her son was as foreign to her as the notion she wanted to take out after Tamara and just hold her. She wanted to hold both of them and never let them go again.

Jessie's shoulders turned spastic as he glared at Delilah. With one swollen fist clenched in pain, he turned to the deacon.

"Deacon Pillar, I know I told you that I wanted to go to the ManPower conference in Dallas, even though it was so soon after Cindy's death. I think I'm gonna use my vacation time and hang around. I need to stay close to home until things get sorted out."

Torn, Delilah's eyes still clung to the image of Tamara leaving, and at that moment, she didn't care what Jessie said or how much he hated her.

Jessie pointed toward Delilah as he continued speaking to the deacon. "Thanks to you, she now knows where I live. I can't take any more stress. . . ." Jessie couldn't finish.

"I understand, Brother Jewel." The deacon really did

understand. If there were ever two people that could cause an explosion if placed together, it was Delilah and anyone unlucky enough to be in her presence. "I'm so sorry to bring all this pain to your door. Please forgive me."

"I'm not really blaming you, Deacon. You're an honorable man. I'm sure she lied to you."

The deacon could barely respond above a whisper. Guilt became a steel trap around his spirit and lips that'd seemed to lie more in the past three weeks than before he knew Christ. *What kind of man am I,* the deacon thought, *to let Delilah take all the blame? I deserve some, too. Lord, please don't let me turn into that kind of man.* Yet he still didn't say or do anything to make things right. Instead, he did the next best thing; he would offer to do what he'd always done for Jessie since he came to live there. "You go and take care of that hand. Don't worry about Tamara. I'll stay here until you get it taken care of. I'll wait on her to get back."

"Thank you, Deacon Pillar, but it's not necessary. I believe she probably went for a walk. She'll be back." Jessie turned back to face Delilah. He nodded her way and admonished the deacon, "Just make sure you take out the trash when you leave."

"That's mighty Christian of you." Delilah turned away from Jessie and with her head held high, as usual, added, "I need some fresh air." Delilah announced it as though Jessie had begged her to stay instead of ordering her to leave.

Defiant as always, she spun around and looked Jessie straight in his face while saying to the deacon, "C'mon, Thurgood, let's go." Sheer stubborness replaced her need to use the bathroom.

Delilah took a few steps back without taking her eyes off Jessie. She grabbed the deacon by one elbow and started to lead him out of the room. She wasn't waiting for the deacon to respond or to recover from the shock of her deciding that they needed to leave because she said so.

"You just hold up a moment, Delilah!" Jessie's eyes narrowed and sweat poured from his face and neck. "In the precious name of Jesus"—in an instant Jessie went from threatening and almost cussing to praying—"Delilah, I'll not let you take away my testimony."

"C'mon, Brother Jewel." The deacon gently moved Delilah aside. He stepped to Jessie and put an arm around his shoulder. "That's right, you pray. You let God use you."

"Why are you two acting like y'all the only ones God can use?" Delilah wasn't certain if she liked the spontaneous change in Jessie. She was sure she didn't trust it coming from the deacon.

"Delilah," Jessie said softly, as though she were a child and not his mother, "I'm beyond angry and conflicted. Yet I can feel a stirring deep down in my soul. The Bible says that I shouldn't let my good works be spoken evil of. . . ."

"Preach it and make it plain." The deacon relaxed his arm around Jessie. The way he did so looked as though he'd really placed his arm there to hold Jessie back from jumping on Delilah. "God is not an author of confusion."

"Ain't nobody confused but you, Thurgood. Everybody knows the Bible says not to let the moon show up and you still mad."

She needed something to show that she was not intimidated and knew a little something about God's Word.

"The Bible says not to let the sun go down on your anger," the deacon murmured and turned back to Jessie. "She does try, though."

"For Pete's sake, be quiet, Thurgood." Delilah shifted her pocketbook from one hand to her other and stared directly at Jessie. "I'm not saying that you don't have a reason to be upset with me, because you do. But I am saying that you don't have all the facts, so before you give the devil your testimony, you might get to know me a little better."

"I'm not blaming the devil for this." Jessie continued to speak softly yet his mouth still looked a bit twisted. And the perspiration now poured from his head and down around his ears. "I am saying that I just watched the one good remaining part of me and Cindy bolt from her home. I'm saying that the Bible says that I am to forgive my enemies and those who spitefully use me."

Delilah's mask of composure slipped and she didn't try to hide it. Her son's words had confused her and she wasn't sure where he was heading. "I'm not your enemy and I've never used you."

Deacon Pillar, as usual, shot off a word or two from the sidelines. "I can bear witness to that." Then he remembered he wasn't supposed to have known that Delilah was Jessie's mother, so he added, "I've never known her to use any children for nothing. . . ."

"Thurgood, will you please just keep quiet."

"This time you're right, Dee Dee. I shouldn't interfere."

Jessie used the deacon's interruption as a chance to pick up a Bible off the coffee table. "It's true," Jessie said as he began to flip through the pages of the Bible using his good hand. "You're not my enemy in the way the Bible describes such, and I don't recall you ever using me."

"I haven't," Delilah replied. "I can promise you that." She wanted to add more, but was drawn to the many pictures on the wall and almost everywhere else in the room. They were of Jessie, Tamara, and Cindy. There were even a few that had the deacon posing with them. Delilah's heart raced and her blood boiled. The deacon had enjoyed what she'd given up. All this time, and her family was so close and yet so far away. *I shouldn't be the only one Jessie's mad at.* Delilah turned to the side and glared at the deacon, who'd already turned away.

"But you see"—Jessie stopped thumbing the pages as he apparently found what he sought—"this is the scripture that the Spirit brought to my mind after Tamara left and when I'd just used language that I hadn't in years. The Word says in Proverbs 23:22, 'Listen to your father who gave you life, and do not despise your mother when she is old.'"

Both the deacon and Delilah were completely dumbfounded. Neither dared to breathe or to speak, each for a different reason.

"Now, I haven't used the term *mother* in quite a long time, unless I referred to Cindy or to my last foster mother. And I don't know who my father is, and at this point, I'm not sure I'd believe you if you told me. I do know beyond a shadow of a doubt that at this moment it is easier for me to forgive my enemies than it is for me to forgive you. So I'm going to now do what me and Cindy always did when we confronted the devil."

"So now I'm the devil?" Delilah's face produced a frown that made her look very much like something she didn't like—she looked her age.

Jessie ignored Delilah's question and continued. His voice remained calm despite the pain that still engulfed the hand he used to point to a room off to the side. "I'm going to go into my prayer closet. I'll fast and talk to God. I don't know how long it will take, but I do know this: My God will fight my battles and He'll lead me to the place in His will where I'm to be and where He is, too."

"Then you need to pray for Jehovah-shammah's grace," Delilah whispered. It took all the strength she possessed not to reach out to him. She'd do anything to have it all back again.

For a brief second both Deacon Pillar and Jessie were stunned, but Jessie recovered first. "What do you know about Jehovah-shammah?"

As Jessie asked the question, the deacon pondered the same thing. *I thought I knew all of God's nicknames.*

"Jehovah-shammah means 'the Lord is there.' " Delilah's voice was reverent as she said the name Jehovah. No matter how she prayed, it was always something about the name Jehovah that gave her the most comfort.

"I know what it means," Jessie replied. "I'm just surprised that you would."

Still confused, Delilah decided to take what Jessie said as something positive. "I'm so sorry you're in this state, but you being a man of God, I know you will find it in your heart to forgive me."

"I certainly hope so, too, Delilah, because right now I can't stand to look at you; I can't stand to hear your excuses. To be truthful, I'm not certain I even care where you've been all these years, and that's not of God, nor is it the person I truly am."

"I'm sure you've raised Tamara to never have a reason to look at you like that. . . ." Delilah's eyes swelled with tears, preventing her from explaining further, but she refused to let one drop fall. Perhaps, if she hadn't given in to her stubbornness instead of pushing the deacon out the door ahead of her, she would've seen the flood of tears that'd begun to soak her son's face.

Jessie remained silent as his tears poured. He looked like an adult who'd suddenly had to grow up and didn't want to. All his life he'd wanted to experience the beautiful flower of a natural mother's love. Now it came delivered in person and he'd treated it like poison ivy.

But like Delilah, who hadn't seen her son's tears, he, too, had turned and walked away and hadn't seen hers.

All those tears wasted.

★ ★ ★

In the darkness, with only a glimmer of light provided by the street lamp, Tamara rested against the coolness of the metal chain fence for almost twenty minutes, and she was hot. Emotions of anger, confusion, and the need to pray collided.

"Tamara?"

Tamara's face swung around toward Sister Marty's voice. The proud walk, the pure white nurse's uniform—she'd know the woman anywhere, even if she'd not called out. Sister Marty was the sort of godmother who'd laughed, sung, prayed, cooked, and was the one who answered yes when her mother often said no. Although Sister Marty, a petite woman, was a size five to Cindy's tall size eighteen, some folks wouldn't believe that Marty wasn't somehow Cindy's lost sister. And because Cindy loved Marty for the way she'd loved Jessie when he was in her foster care, the two remained inseparable until Cindy's death did the parting.

"Hi, sweetheart," Sister Marty called out again as she came toward Tamara lugging two heavy plastic bags. Her usually smiling, pecan-colored, heart-shaped face looked confused. "What are you doing outside my door by yourself? You have my spare key. Why didn't you go on inside and wait for me?"

By the time Tamara could think of an answer, Sister Marty was standing next to her.

"I haven't been here but for a minute," Tamara replied, not wanting Sister Marty to worry. "It was such a nice evening I thought I'd come down and chat for a moment."

"Oh, now really . . . ?" Sister Marty handed one of the bags to Tamara and started up the porch steps. "Didn't your father tell you that I was working late and couldn't make the Bible study? I certainly hope he told the deacon. . . ."

And that's when Tamara happened to turn and look up the block. She saw Delilah appear to drag the deacon along as the two of them headed toward the deacon's truck. The truck was parked just a few doors down from Sister Marty's.

"I don't know how you carried these heavy bags," Tamara said as she almost threw Sister Marty through the open door. "Whew! I need to hurry and set this thing down."

Sister Marty was too surprised to answer. And she'd have been even more surprised if she'd seen what Tamara had.

Chapter 9

It was Monday, and two days had passed since the deacon had driven Delilah home from Jessie's house. She couldn't believe she'd finally seen her son and met her granddaughter. But now she'd grown tired of being stuck at home.

And yet she still couldn't wrap her mind around how her only family lived an hour or so away, and that she'd had her car repossessed. She'd have to take three buses just to get to a train that would take her to Brooklyn. She needed her beloved Navigator to get around, and back into their good graces. Delilah was at her wits' end. *Knowing where Jessie lives ain't doing me a bit of good if I can't get to him. And what about getting to a church service? I certainly need a car for that.*

So over the past forty-eight hours she'd often fallen to her knees or just stood in the middle of the floor and prayed.

Delilah looked at the clock in her living room. It was almost twelve noon. She'd heard it mentioned that God was always available for extra heavy lifting at twelve, three, six, and nine o'clock. So she went for it.

"Jehovah, one and only . . ." Delilah began with what she felt was the solid truth. Everything she'd had was her one and only: the deacon, the only man she'd ever married or truly loved; Jessie and Tamara, her only son and granddaughter;

even her career—she'd never done anything but sing and model. She needed to start there because at the moment, none of her life made sense except her one and only great Jehovah.

And so there she was. Even at the end of praying for two days, the sense of family she'd seen on display in Jessie's living room gnawed away at her. Where was that homey feeling inside her home? And why should the deacon be free to remarry, if she went through with the divorce plans? Did she really need to go through with the divorce after the deacon hadn't been honest about knowing where Jessie was? It was beginning to look as though everyone would end up with a family except her.

She'd gone from room to room, inside her large rented house in affluent Garden City. And yet Delilah felt as abandoned and as poor as a church mouse. Suddenly none of her mementos displayed throughout the house meant a thing.

Pictures of her and Ella Fitzgerald should've been of her and perhaps her daughter-in-law, Cindy. The ones of her and jazz great Arthur Prysock, whom she'd met when she spent a short time in South Carolina—that should've been Jessie standing proudly next to her. Even her precious autographed pictures of her and Lena Horne became almost irrelevant. Lena had written on one of them, *To Delilah, my sister from another mother.* It should've been of her and Tamara. After all, if she could pass for Lena, then so could her one and only granddaughter.

Delilah had also waited for the deacon to call. When he'd brought her home the other night she could tell he'd softened a bit toward her. Besides, she could've spilled the beans about him back at Jessie's and she hadn't. Before he'd driven away she'd exploited his unspoken guilt and gotten him to promise to help her get her car back. Of course, she had to also promise not to drive it anywhere on Jessie's block. She'd only made the promise because she had to. Delilah also had to get her family back, and if that meant she had to park around the corner from Jessie's block to keep her word, she would.

But just when she thought the deacon wasn't going to come through with his promise to call, he finally did. He called that afternoon. But all he seemed to want to talk about was making an appointment to see a divorce lawyer. Every time she asked, "What about my car?" he'd respond with, "What about that divorce?" Finally she'd slammed down the phone out of frustration.

To her credit, she did want to call him back. She'd sacrifice and be the bigger person, but she couldn't. She should've insisted on getting his telephone number, too. *Doggone cable folks would have to keep their subscribers' numbers unlisted.* She'd gotten that tidbit from the deacon when she told him how hard she'd tried to find Jessie and couldn't.

But all she could do was go inside her living room and wait. Waiting wasn't something she was good at or used to, so she hoped the deacon was still anxious for his divorce and would call back.

At the same time that a frustrated Delilah waited inside her Long Island home, anger brewed over in Brooklyn, New York.

Upstairs inside his comfortable one-bedroom apartment, Deacon Thurgood Pillar was pissed. He slammed down the black phone, which looked almost pale compared to the deep ebony hue his already dark skin took on.

"That witch Delilah just hung up on me. She's fussing about where I've been, like I was supposed to be at her beck and call."

So Deacon Pillar did what any proud man, who'd always bragged he'd given the cat its meow, would do in a situation like that. He got dressed in a multicolored, striped shirt, polka-dot suspenders, and khaki pants, which like all his pants were an ill fit for his height.

Once he got inside, he ignored the sound of his bony butt slapping against the leather seats of the truck he called Old Lemon. His gnarly long fingers yanked the gears hard enough to create a new gear. Then he tore out of Brooklyn for the long drive out to Long Island.

By the time Deacon Pillar reached Garden City, it was well into the late afternoon. Most of the residents on Delilah's street were absent from their front yards. It didn't mean they weren't home, it was just that they preferred to lounge in their backyards, on patios, or in swimming pools. Hanging out in the front of one's home was so low class.

Deacon Pillar searched the block until he found Delilah's address. It was dark when he'd driven her home the other night. This was his first opportunity to see it in the daytime. "No wonder this woman stays broke and can't pay a car note."

He pulled up to Delilah's house and turned off the engine, which always barked like a mad dog and caused cats and squirrels to scatter. Accustomed to parking in his crime-filled area of Brooklyn, he took a moment to wrap a club device around the steering column, and got out. No sooner had he rung the doorbell and she finally opened it a bit than he received the welcome he'd figured he'd get from Delilah.

"What the hell took you so long?"

"Don't talk trash to me," Deacon Pillar ordered loudly before he pushed past her and entered. And before she could protest, he marched toward her living room as though he'd been there many times before.

"Damn." Delilah looked out the door to make sure no one saw what'd happened and called the cops. She followed a few seconds later. Her face was still a mask of irritation. "Don't bother to sit 'cause we need to get started."

"I don't intend on staying too long. I guess we must've had a bad connection. I'm sure a classy woman such as you wouldn't hang up on someone who's trying to help her out."

"I reserve my class for them that has some."

"Not *has some,* it's *have it.*"

Like an old habit he just couldn't get rid of, the deacon wanted to reprimand Delilah further about her bad English, but decided to stick to the plan.

"Look, Delilah." Deacon Pillar began to speak, and with a quick wave of his hand he cut off whatever nastiness Delilah was about to spew. "I know I was less than honest about Jessie's whereabouts. But hell, I wasn't all that thrilled when I ran into you a few weeks back, and neither have I walked on cloud nine during our brief encounters since. For all I knew you could've just wanted to make his life a living hell, 'cause that's what you do to folks." He stopped and paused for a quick breath. "Okay, I'll say it again, just like I said it the other night. I thank you for not telling Jessie everything you know about me."

"I probably should have. You looking down on me the way you do."

"Looking down on you? I'm just happy I haven't had to look across a mattress at you for the past forty-something years. It was more of a blessing than I'd thought."

"You wasn't no taste of sunshine, either, when I ran into your jacked-up self."

Delilah abruptly stopped her impending barrage. *I need to stick to my plan,* she thought. *If this is the way Jehovah has things set up, I can wait a little longer—but not much.* "You know what, Thurgood . . ."

The deacon clasped his hands and this time he spoke slowly, cutting Delilah off before she could say something even nastier than before. He had already made plans to see Marty later that night, so the sooner he helped Delilah, the sooner they'd be divorced and the quicker he could get back to his life. "Forget all this. It's not about me or you. It's about family; Jessie and Tamara. They need peace in their lives, and if helping you get your car back so you can terrorize some other family, well so be it."

Delilah didn't respond. She chose to hold her head a little higher. This time it was her way of letting him know that whatever he had to say was beneath her. Yet it didn't mean she wasn't listening or didn't know what the deacon implied.

"Look, Dee Dee—" Deacon Pillar caught himself. *Why do I keep calling her that?*

But that time he wasn't quick enough to stop Delilah from interrupting and ripping into him.

"Look at what, Thur-no-good?" Delilah's eyes darted around the room as she wrung her hands. Help or no help, Navigator or no Navigator . . . She didn't try to hide her feelings. If she got her hands on something heavy, she'd knock him out. Frustrated, Delilah threatened, "What else you got to say?"

The deacon didn't flinch. He ignored her question and asked one of his own. "Why do you have to refer to my former street name, Thur-no-good, because you're antsy?"

"And I see you didn't forget what you used to call me, either, when you're trying to annoy me. You know I never liked that pet name, Dee Dee."

"Don't you fret none, it doesn't have the same meaning as it did back then, when I'd come off the road from driving that old truck, or gigging, and want some special attention." Deacon Pillar winked and allowed a smile to relax his face. "I mean it in a more affectionate but less sexy way now."

"You'd better," Delilah replied as she searched his face to see if he was lying. "Okay, I promise only to call you Thur-no-good when you work my last nerve."

The deacon nodded slightly to signal he accepted the compromise.

But that was before Delilah added, without smiling and

with just a hint of agitation, "I'm sure you'll be working my nerves just as bad as you have in the past."

They went at it again. Delilah and Thurgood, old enough to be closer to a dirt nap than to a sky-high calling, quickly forgot what they'd each asked from God and needed from one another.

"Give me an aspirin," Deacon Pillar finally ordered as he held his head in his hands. "As usual, whenever I'm within two feet of you I get a headache."

And as if there'd been no separation of time, or animosity between them, Delilah didn't hesitate to move. On her way out of the room, she looked over her shoulder and asked softly, "You still chase your aspirin with your cousin Jack?"

That broke the ice as each began to smile and let their guard down. The two, without saying so, had again agreed to disagree.

Delilah shook her head and chuckled as she left the room to get the aspirin. She thought it was funny how she remembered their drink of choice. Even back then it was still whiskey. Within a few minutes she returned with the pills and an unopened bottle of Jack Daniel's.

"You still know how to treat your man, I see." The deacon licked his lips and wrung his hands, a sign of anticipation as he playfully snatched the bottle from her hand.

Delilah didn't respond, choosing to ignore the reference to him being *her man*. Instead she watched in amusement as Deacon Pillar took two aspirins from the plastic bottle and laid them to the side. He then twisted the cap on the Jack Daniel's top until the wrapper came off and poured some of the dark liquid into a glass. She resisted an urge to smile as he threw back his head, his conk surrounding his bald spot like a halo. With what seemed like a blur, he'd quickly taken the pills and drunk the whiskey chaser.

"You still think you're the cat's first and last meow, don't you?" Delilah finally asked, with just a hint of fun in her voice. "Still can't believe you're a church deacon now. Old Thur-no-good Pillar working for the Lord while guzzling whiskey and aspirin. At least you keep it real and don't blame the devil for your little revisit to the drink. Maybe that's why that crazy concoction ain't ever killed you."

"I never said anything about blaming the devil for the way I take care of a headache," the deacon replied. "Besides, the Bible says you should take a little wine for the stomach's sake."

"You're drinking whiskey," Delilah reminded him.

"Do you have any wine?"

Delilah shook her head and conceded, "No."

"Then you should remember the old saying that if you're a lioness who ate an entire bull, don't chastise or roar—"

"What are you talking about, Thurgood?"

"A hunter might shoot you if you roar, so just shut up when you're full of bulls—"

The truce ended, again.

It'd taken another thirty minutes before Deacon Pillar and Delilah calmed down enough to step outside her home without flailing at one another, and into his old truck.

They'd driven along the Long Island Expressway, hardly speaking, when suddenly the deacon broke the silence.

Out of the blue he said, "I'm still trying to figure out if God has a hand in all this sudden craziness. After all these years, and you're sitting beside me in an old truck like we just came back from a show in Manhattan or something."

"Well, if you can't figure it out, you know I can't." Delilah wanted to get her car, not chat.

"All I can say is that it's a good thing for you that I'm not broke, Dee Dee." Deacon Pillar laughed softly before adding, "Since not having you in my life over the last forty years, pissing away my money, I've managed to save a little something."

As hard as Delilah tried, she couldn't help but laugh at his feeble attempt to have a rational discussion. "I was a financial drain on your wallet, wasn't I?"

"Like a hungry newborn baby on a tit." And much like his other uncontrollable urges, the old deacon smiled, reached across the seat, and took Delilah's hand. "Don't worry, Dee Dee. God's gonna turn everything around for you."

"God," Delilah blurted as she yanked her hand out of the deacon's grasp. "I thought *you* had the money! I thought *you* were gonna help me."

"Calm down, woman," the deacon snapped back. "I am gonna help you. I'm gonna also give you the address to another church up in the Bronx. Just because you can't come around Jessie or back to New Hope Assembly don't mean you can't continue seeking God. I sorta like the way you're trying to get to know Him. Trinity Baptist Church up there on 224th Street in the Bronx is a praying church." He stopped and laughed. "I still can't get over how you knew some of God's nicknames."

Without hesitation both the deacon and Delilah laughed at one another. The deacon laughed because whether she went to church or not, at the end of the day, he would give her the money to reclaim her car.

Delilah laughed for the same reason.

Two hours later Delilah and her insane dramas kept repeating like bad reruns. It was all the deacon could do to keep one hand on the steering wheel. The other he placed against his forehead to keep it from choking Delilah's neck.

Delilah sat hunched in the corner of the passenger's side, cussing. "Dayum, dayum, dayum."

"Stop acting like a low budget Esther Rolle, Dee Dee. You do realize that you are still in my truck and you didn't get your car, right?"

"I'm not crazy, Thurgood. I'm mad."

"I can see and hear that you're mad. We disagree on the crazy part."

"Not now, Thurgood Pillar, not now."

"Dee Dee, trying to pick up your car was a complete waste of time. What made you think you could drive it out of there with no insurance, even if you'd paid off the entire car note? You know you're supposed to keep insurance on your vehicle. It's the law. What if you have an accident or something?"

"Just shut up, Thurgood, please. I need to think."

"You need to think. . . . You need to think? Well, Dee Dee, how's that working out for you?"

He stopped pressing her. He still couldn't get used to seeing her so defeated, despite the fact that he'd wanted to kill her earlier. "I'm sorry. It's too late to try and get insurance today. Maybe tomorrow will be a better day."

"Forget about it, Thurgood. You can take me to my own home. I won't be coming back here tomorrow or any other day."

"Why not, Dee Dee?"

"I don't get my social security check until next month, and I'm broke."

"Delilah Dupree Jewel!" Deacon Pillar swerved and almost lost control of his truck. "What is wrong with you? You can buy all sorts of fancy clothes, and I'm sure you still wear pretty drawers, but you can't insure your car?"

Delilah swung around with one of her tiny fists headed straight toward the deacon's face.

The deacon's street instincts from his old days of dodging bullets and fists after some outrageous gigs helped him to catch her fist in the palm of his hand while he managed to control his truck.

"Whoa," the deacon snapped, "what's it gonna be, car insurance money or bail money? I ain't got both."

So since Delilah couldn't hit the deacon, she had to do something else. She grabbed the cup of Pepsi she'd been sipping and threw it in the deacon's direction. The dark liquid spilled all over his beige and orange striped pants and left a stain that looked like he'd crapped all over hisself or had his pants on backwards.

After he screamed out several words which he was certain negated any recent prayer requests, he had to make a decision. There were too many cars on the highway and that meant too many witnesses. So he couldn't toss Delilah out and leave her. She certainly didn't have any men's clothing at her place; at least none that he'd want to wear. The only thing he could do was turn the truck off at the next exit and head west, toward Brooklyn.

He'd driven only a few miles in blissful silence and red-hot anger and was about another twenty minutes from his home when it happened. The sticky soda had also seeped down and into the gearshift. In no time the gears had become a sticky mess.

For the first time in a long time, the deacon's conk moved as his head bobbed and weaved in frustration. He finally pulled over, got out his phone, and called for road service. He was so mad he didn't realize how loud and angry he sounded as his voice rose. The AAA road-service representative hung up on him twice before the deacon got the message.

The deacon became even angrier when he realized that in order for AAA to get to him he needed to get his truck off the highway and onto a public street.

He placed a second call to a highway towing company that'd tow him the five hundred feet off the highway. And then he sat back in the driver's seat, angrily hitting his shoes against the pedals. His shoes sounded like he was clicking them three times and wishing Delilah back to Kansas.

Delilah, on the other hand, said nothing throughout his

entire tirade. It was almost pitch-black by the time the second tow truck arrived. The deacon was still livid but not Delilah. He'd had no choice but to bring her back with him, and she was already plotting a way to hopefully run into Jessie and Tamara. She'd make use of any opportunity no matter how strangely it came her way.

Chapter 10

"Thurgood, is that you, dear?" The voice was almost a whisper yet had a little extra sweetness to the greeting. "I was just coming home from work and I thought it was you getting out of that tow truck," Sister Marty said as she approached Deacon Pillar on the sidewalk outside of Jesse's house. She saw the shadow of a second person and added, "I guess the Lord's work is never done where you're concerned."

"Praise the Lord, honey." The deacon looked at Sister Marty and the peaceful aura she always carried calmed him immediately. It also reminded him of the hellcat he'd left seated inside the tow truck.

He quickly glanced back toward the cab of the tow truck as its driver began to lower Old Lemon. And then, as though he were taking his last breath, he blurted to Sister Marty, "Honey, if you're just getting home, I know you must be tired. We'll get together some other time. I'll let you go on inside your house and get some rest."

He was thankful for the cover of darkness. He couldn't have explained the stain on his pants nor did he want to.

Without waiting for Marty to respond to his strange behavior or see her shocked look, the deacon turned away. He'd done it just in time to see and feel the climate change in his life. Without a doubt he knew that Hurricane Delilah was about a level five and one minute away from a becoming a full-blown cyclone.

Delilah hadn't missed a beat. She was too far away to see the woman and determine the threat level. It didn't matter; a female standing so close to Thurgood wasn't good. She needed him focused and available to help her get back into her son's life. So Delilah did what Delilah always did when her upper hand was threatened. She lowered the boom.

One moment she was sitting in the tow truck acting like a stubborn old she-ass. The next moment, Delilah the she-ass broke out from the cab's gate at a gallop.

When she arrived within a yard or two, Delilah slowed her gallop and changed it into a sexy slink. She slinked until she finally reached the deacon's side.

"I'm so sorry, precious," she purred to the deacon. "I thought I'd dropped that extra key to your apartment inside the truck." Delilah then stood real close to the deacon, making them look almost like Siamese twins.

However, the deacon's neighbor and current girlfriend was just as much female as Delilah, and then some. Just because she didn't bust out cussing or swinging didn't mean she wasn't wise to what was happening.

It seemed Sister Marty had one-upped both of them. She'd been a little troubled by Tamara's sudden visit the other night. When she later spoke to Jessie, he'd told her of the latest development involving the sudden appearance of his mother, Delilah. He'd also mentioned that his mother and the deacon went way back and might've had a real close relationship. And yet her supposedly saved boyfriend stood flat-footed in front of her while the low-budget Lena Horne wannabe felt him up. And he hadn't said a word, nor did he look like he would.

Sister Marty just smiled at Delilah and then extended her

hand. "Hello," she said before quickly retracting her hand. She'd made it seem as though she'd just seen cooties on Delilah. "Thurgood never mentioned he had an older sister or an aunt."

She didn't give Delilah a chance to recover. Instead, she turned toward the deacon and smiled again. "Listen, Thurgood, honey, I'm certain you'll let me know in time if our plans have changed."

And that's when old playa Deacon Pillar finally learned the true meaning of standing between a rock and a hard place.

And of course Delilah wasn't a rock, she was a boulder. And she wasn't a hard place, but she did carry around her own brand of hell, which she freely shared.

"I didn't quite catch your name." Delilah didn't move an inch from the deacon's side. Her gray eyes seemed to turn demon red and glow in the dark. "If Thurgood mentioned it before, I didn't catch it. I guess we've been too busy."

Sister Marty smiled. She wasn't taking the bait. "You say you didn't hear it clearly? Well, I'm certain Thurgood must've mentioned me—but they do say sometimes the ears and reality are the first things to go."

"Well, you know what they also say," Delilah said slowly. "The lion and the lamb shall lie down together. . . ." She blew a kiss the deacon's way.

"I've heard that before," Sister Marty smiled and replied. "Of course, when the lion sleeps with the lamb on my turf, the lion never closes his eyes." *Oh, enough with the games . . .* Sister Marty smiled again and never flinched as she looked the deacon straight in the eye. "Thurgood Pillar, when you're done with whatever this is, please come by and let's chat, honey. If we're to continue doing what we do, then I expect your word to be your bond."

For the second time that night, Delilah's wig felt the blast from her volcanic emotions.

And for the umpteenth time within the past few weeks, the deacon thought he'd heard God calling his name and saying, "Pillar, come on home where you'll be safe."

Before the deacon could gather his wits, the two women had gone their separate ways and left him standing on the sidewalk. He had one hand holding a chunk of his conk and the other his head, as he wished a migraine would just kill him before Delilah did.

Of course, there was always the possibility that either Jessie or Tamara would kill him first if they found out he'd brought Delilah back there.

Even if the deacon wanted to, he didn't need to rush to catch up to Delilah. Like a lion crouching in the bushes for her prey, she waited in the shadows on the front porch. Delilah wasn't going anywhere and she wasn't saying anything.

Still giving him the silent treatment, Delilah waited for the deacon to open the front door.

"Let's not wake anyone," he whispered.

Delilah glared and continued the silence while they tiptoed up the stairs to his apartment.

No sooner had the deacon stuck his key in the door and opened it than Delilah entered ahead of him and stopped short. She curled her lips and glared.

The deacon was all set to tell Delilah about his relationship with Sister Marty and how he'd get Delilah a hotel room after he changed, but the words never came.

It didn't matter. Delilah had moved on from that concern. She'd only wanted to block whatever would've happened with the woman if Delilah hadn't attached herself to the deacon. She'd accomplished that.

To the deacon's surprise, Delilah pointed through an open door toward a small room where he had a twin bed. Beige striped sheets covered the bed and a deep brown comforter lay folded at the foot.

"It's been a long day and I need my beauty sleep. I'm turning in. I only see one bed, so just where are you supposed to sleep?" Impatience was Delilah's middle name. So of course she didn't wait for an answer. "Whatever happened to your sense of style, Thurgood? I'm surprised you took up with that overweight woman, whatever her name is. I don't even see how the two of you could fit on that little mattress." She always used sarcasm when it was available.

"Oh, you mean Sister Marty. . . ." The deacon stopped. It was his home—why should he explain?

"Marty, Cathy, Sasquatch; I really don't care."

With her tiny, childlike feet she swiftly kicked aside a couple of magazines and with a frown on her face she wiped her finger across the dusty leaves of an artificial plant.

Houseguest or not, Delilah didn't try to hide her disapproval as she maneuvered her way through the small living room with its furniture almost piled one upon the other, until she arrived inside the bedroom.

While Delilah performed her uninvited home inspection, the deacon slipped into the bathroom. It hadn't taken Delilah two minutes to return him to headache hell. *Lord, please help me get that woman to a hotel somewhere.* When he came back she was still complaining almost as though she hadn't noticed he'd left.

"How do you sleep with your long legs in this small bed? Do you sleep balled up?" The bed occupied a space between a small dresser and a nightstand. "One thing's for sure," Delilah added while pointing back toward the living room, "I'm definitely not going to sleep all crumpled up in that recliner." She'd barely finished her complaint before she'd added another as she sniffed the air. "And what's that smell?"

The deacon lifted the small Dixie cup to his mouth as he threw back his head to swallow his special headache medicine dissolved in a small amount of whiskey. When he finished he remained in the bedroom doorway. He sneered and took his time as he wiped his wet mouth with the back of his hand.

Although the medicine concoction hadn't had a chance to work, the deacon replied nonchalantly, "I haven't slept anyplace other than my own bed for years. And if you notice," the deacon said as he pointed to the wall over the bed, "that's my picture hanging there, too, so why don't you guess where I'll be sleeping tonight?"

Delilah's lips tightened as she scowled. She was just about to reply when the deacon cut her off.

"Hush your face, Dee Dee. Don't you ask another dumb question and take away the buzz these pills are about to lay on me."

By the time the deacon finished giving Delilah the dos and the don'ts, he was holding his head in his hands again. And, he had drunk the last of his whiskey.

However, he did manage to call two nearby hotels that wouldn't cost him an arm and a leg in cab fare, but neither had a vacancy.

"It looks like getting you a hotel room for tonight is out." Deacon Pillar threw up his arms. His lips seemed to curl as he gave Delilah more rules of his house. "So whether you like it or not, you *will* sleep on that recliner or the couch, or you can sleep standing up—makes no difference to me."

The deacon inched toward his kitchen. He stood now with his hands on his hips and announced, "And as for that smell, I was cleaning some tripe and chitlins earlier and I forgot to take out the garbage. Of course, this smell is nothing compared to the scent you'll get on the subway if you keep trying to have things your way when it ain't your home."

"You finished?" Delilah had already stepped past the deacon and was laying down her pocketbook on the bed as though he'd said nothing. "Now, just let me tell you something—"

"No, let me finish telling you something," the deacon interrupted, "before you say or do something else akin to mule-like behavior; remember we need to get your car insurance so you can get your car from the repo man tomorrow. They only gave you a one-day extension. Now, go ahead, say something else!"

Not more than thirty minutes later, after the deacon had tried repeatedly to call Sister Marty with no success he was sleeping in his own bed. He could've picked all the cotton out of his sheets, he was just that mad.

In the meanwhile Delilah had traded in her usual classy outfit for one of the deacon's old shirts. Minutes after she'd complained about the color, the ever classy Delilah was moaning and passing gas while balled up on the recliner.

But then it was hardly another hour later before both the deacon and Delilah lay in that same small bed. They snuggled together like two spoons or a couple of old potato chips. And although they grinned like two babies, happily fed and burped, they snored like truck drivers on speed.

Chapter 11

The foreign buzzing sound of an alarm clock filtered through whatever dream state Delilah was in and caused her to bolt straight up in the bed. Her head wobbled side to side while her blond wig rocked somewhere between her shoulders and her ears. Both her white locks and the wig tresses were damp; no doubt a result of either sleeping in an un-air-conditioned room where the humidity was in abundance, or night sweats from her menopause.

"It's about time you woke up. Come on, there's no time to waste."

Deacon Pillar stood by one of the three windows in his apartment. He was already dressed and about to open the venetian blinds just before Delilah finally awoke.

"Thurgood Pillar," Delilah snapped, "what in the world are you doing up so early?" She was about to say something more, but she realized she was lying in the bed and not the recliner. Naturally, Delilah thought she'd won the battle of the beds.

"I see you are a gentleman after all." She peeked under the sheets and saw she was still wearing the old nightshirt the deacon gave her. "I knew you'd let me sleep in the bed instead of the recliner."

"You know I'm a true gentleman," the deacon replied slowly. "I certainly let you sleep in the bed. And I'd probably still be asleep in it, too, if I didn't have to avoid your little hands groping all over me last night, trying to find the key to open your happy door."

And that's when Delilah flipped. She jumped straight up and bolted from the bed. Delilah hadn't moved that fast from a bed since she was in her thirties. For sure, the brick in the hand of her last man's wife had been her inspiration.

With the nightshirt barely covering what she affectionately referred to as her moneymaking pocketbook, she rushed toward the window where the deacon stood, now bent over in laughter.

"You old degenerate!" Delilah balled up her small fists and threw one hand back like she was about to throw out the first pitch.

"Sweet degenerate is what you called me last night."

Words wouldn't come to her, so before Delilah left the room she threw the nearest thing she could find. It was a mayonnaise jar, one the deacon kept his loose change in.

Jumping was the word of the day, because old Deacon Pillar jumped faster than he had in quite some time. That jar hit the wall and loose change sank into the deep carpet. Whether he tripped over a quarter or his ottoman didn't matter; hitting the floor on his bony behind wasn't an option. He reached out to grab on to something. Unfortunately, the closest thing was his small desk with one of its legs propped up by an old, thick telephone book. The book gave way and then he and it hit the floor with a loud thump.

And that's when his doorbell rang.

It was all the deacon could do to stop a flood of un-Christian-like words from flying off his lips. He'd barely gotten to his feet to answer the door when it flew open. Of course, Jessie stood dumbfounded in the doorway.

The deacon tried to explain for a second time why

Delilah was in his apartment. But Jessie was too angry to listen so he bolted out of the deacon's apartment with the deacon in pursuit, and rushed down the steps. Jessie slammed the hall door, barely missing the deacon's foot, and walked quickly into his living room. He paced back and forth. "Have you lost your mind, Deacon Pillar?" He wanted to take his bandaged hand and slap some sense into the old man. "Of all the places in Brooklyn, why would you bring that woman back here?"

"I already told you why, Jessie. My truck broke down on me. My pants looked like I'd crapped on myself. I couldn't find a vacant hotel room to toss her in, so I had to bring her back here. I can't drive your automatic, you know that. Which reminds me, I need for you to take us to get this insurance. She can get her car back and drive on about her business."

"There's something you're leaving out," Jessie said slowly, as he eyed the deacon up and down. "You could call a cab to take you to get insurance." Jessie sat down on the sofa. He pointed to the love seat and indicated the deacon should sit there. "I'm concerned that you're becoming a little too involved with a woman who you claimed you haven't seen in almost forty years."

"Stop being so suspicious, Jessie." Deacon Pillar didn't know if he sounded convincing or not, but he was giving it his best. "Brother Jessie," the deacon implored, "forget that she's your deadbeat, absentee mother. Think about what Jesus would do."

Jessie leaned forward and looked the deacon right in the eyes. "Do you see a crown of thorns on my head?"

The voices filtered up the stairs to the deacon's apartment and through the bedroom door she'd left slightly ajar.

Delilah hadn't bothered to return to the scene of her hysteria, where she'd let go on the deacon with the mayonnaise jar filled with change. She would've, but she heard Jessie's angry voice. Her son started arguing with the deacon as soon as he'd stepped through the door. As much as she wanted to see Jessie, she was smart enough to stay out of his way.

About fifteen minutes later, when the deacon hadn't returned and she could still hear their angry voices, she got dressed and waited for his return.

At first she couldn't figure out why the voices no longer filtered through the door yet she could still hear them. She looked around the living room where the voices seemed the strongest. She didn't see any pipes or even a radiator where the sound could travel through. But as soon as she sat down by the window she heard them clear as day. Her eyes followed the sound and it was coming through the floor heating vent.

And, of course, Delilah wasn't happy with what she heard. "I shouldn't have bothered. . . ." She stopped complaining. It didn't make sense to complain to herself when she could grab God's ear.

"Great Jehovah," she whispered, "perhaps this wasn't such a great idea. Maybe I wasn't supposed to have a family. You know my mama and her own mama didn't want children. It seems like I probably didn't either. . . ." She stopped and allowed her voice to become even lower and a little more reverent. "Now, Father Jehovah, since I do have a child and I did ask for Your help in finding him—if it's not meant to be, and You only did it because You took a liking to me, please stop this madness. Please just let me go on about my business and grow old with a little dignity. Just give me a sign or something. Amen."

It wasn't exactly a sign. It was more of a loud tapping on the half-open door. "Grab your purse or whatever and let's get this over with. I don't need conversation, I just need you to move on with your life and out of mine. So I'm helping with that."

Delilah looked up from her prayer just in time to see the deacon standing behind Jessie. He'd placed a finger across his lips, a signal for her to shut her mouth and move it while Jessie was in a good mood.

And Delilah pretended she didn't know what the deacon was trying to say or that Jessie had forbade any conversation between the two of them. "Thank you, Jessie. I truly appreciate your generosity."

"Since you're gonna speak anyway, it's not generosity. I'm not paying for it."

Jessie quickly turned around. "Deacon Pillar, I'll be waiting downstairs."

The deacon waited until Jessie left before he felt it was safe enough to speak. "At least this is a start," Deacon Pillar said nervously. "He didn't say he was going to run you over or anything like that."

"Whatever." Delilah frowned. *There's got to be a way to turn this around. I need an ally and it certainly can't be Thurgood.*

"Let's go, Delilah. Jessie ain't gonna wait all day. He's got to take Tamara somewhere, too."

Delilah suddenly got a burst of energy. Tamara was her key. It wouldn't be easy, but she'd find a way to get to her granddaughter. It wasn't that she didn't want Tamara; Jessie and Tamara were a family package deal that Delilah wanted. She'd just never thought about winning Tamara over first.

In no time Delilah's smile vanished. No sooner had she stepped onto the front porch and looked toward the street than her blood began to boil.

The deacon came out behind her and had just locked the front door before turning around. He almost had a heart attack. Seated inside the car with Jessie were Tamara and Sister Marty. The three of them were laughing up a storm.

Chapter 12

When Delilah and the deacon entered the car, everyone greeted him with a loud hello. Delilah got deafening silence.

It was a tight squeeze inside the car as the five tried to get comfortable. Jessie had asked Tamara to sit up front with him. He purposely put Deacon Pillar in the backseat between Delilah and Marty. *I wanna see the old playa play his way outta this one.*

"Hello, honey." Deacon Pillar's dark skin looked ghostly. "You look gorgeous, as usual. I didn't know you were coming along . . . not that I didn't want you to."

"Well, when you called me from Jessie's earlier, you sounded a little strange. . . ."

"Oh yes. I did call you from Jessie's because that's where I was. I was with Jessie."

Sister Marty sank farther into the car seat and looked straight ahead. From the corner of her eye she saw a smirk on Delilah's face. But she would bide her time. "Don't worry, darling," she told the deacon. "Love means never having to explain. Besides, I was off today and going to choir rehearsal anyway."

Before Marty could get the last word out of her mouth, Jessie and Tamara smiled. Each thought Deacon Pillar was dumber than a bag of rocks if he believed all that Sister Marty had said.

"So, Jessie"—Sister Marty's frown quickly gave way to a smile—"Tamara tells me that she's expecting a huge blessing in the near future."

"We've claimed it, for sure." Jessie's face broke out into a smile, too. "My daughter is going to be a star. I just know it."

"I always knew she would be." The deacon couldn't control himself as he reached over and squeezed Sister Marty's hand.

That action and none of the conversation included Delilah, but it didn't mean she wasn't parsing through it to see what she could glean. She pretended to focus on whatever was happening outside the car.

"That's right," Tamara chimed in. "In a month or so I'm auditioning and they're talking about coming to the church to check me out. In fact, the A&R rep mentioned that they may visit my home. Now, that doesn't always happen, does it, Daddy?"

"No, it doesn't. But when God is in control," Jessie replied, "ordinary has to take a backseat. You know I'm on pins and needles—and Cindy would've been beside herself." Sadness crept into his voice and cloaked the joy. Would he ever get over his wife's passing?

With no prompting at all, Tamara broke out singing. She didn't want to see her father sad when she was about to cry, too. By the time she'd gotten to the chorus, Jessie, Sister Marty, and Deacon Pillar had all joined in. They took quartet singing up to another level.

They were about to go into another song when suddenly Jessie looked through his rearview mirror. He thought he saw a look of defeat on Delilah's face. It made him a little sad, and sad was not what he wanted to feel when she was involved.

"Daddy, what kind of note was that?"

"It was flat, Jessie. I don't recall ever hearing you sing flat."

The deacon looked at Marty and hunched his shoulders to indicate he didn't know what was suddenly wrong. "Don't worry about my flat note, Tamara," Jessie teased. "You just make sure you don't sing one." The spell was broken. The rest of the ride, no one said a word or sang a note.

No one was happier than Jessie when he pulled up in front of New Hope Assembly. Peeking at Delilah each time he needed to use his rearview mirror was unsettling. No matter how long he'd prayed in the last few days, he still wanted to remain distant, if not angry, with her. "Okay, we're here. Tamara, you make sure that you call me when the choir rehearsal is over."

"I will, but I still don't think you should keep driving with just one hand." Tamara leaned over and kissed her father's cheek. "I love you."

All that love in the car and none of it for Delilah.

At that moment Deacon Pillar couldn't have looked at Delilah or Sister Marty with a straight face if he'd wanted to. One by one, his plans to get his divorce and keep Delilah away from New Hope for as long as he could were unraveling. It looked as though if she didn't kill him, then Marty would. Now she knew that Tamara could sing well enough to have an audition at her own home. He tried to control his nervousness and agitation by tapping his foot and using one hand to rub a kneecap. Delilah was getting everything she'd wanted, so why should she help him?

"I'll talk to you later, Thurgood."

The sound of Sister Marty's voice broke his train of thought. "Okay, Marty." Because he'd sat in the middle he couldn't get out and open the door for her. Before he could say anything or move, Jessie did the honors.

"We'll chat later, Mama." Jessie leaned over and gave Sister Marty a big hug. "I love ya."

Jessie couldn't have hurt Delilah any more than if he'd dropped a boulder upon her head. Why was he calling the deacon's girlfriend Mama? She turned once more and glared at the deacon before she looked back out the window.

Delilah turned just in time to see Tamara and Sister Marty wave back at the car. A wave she was certain was not meant for her. They then walked arm in arm and resumed laughing.

If Delilah looked confused, she wasn't. Moment by moment things became clearer. *This is why Thurgood didn't want me to come around New Hope. He knew all the time that Jessie came here. And he never said a word about Tamara's singing. I didn't even read about that in Cindy's obituary. He should've told me.* Delilah turned and looked at the deacon. It took every ounce of strength she had to make the next move. She smiled.

The deacon mistook it for a look of concern. "If you're worried about paying me back for this insurance and the car notes, Dee Dee, you don't have to do that."

"Oh, but I want to pay you back, Thurgood." Delilah turned away and looked out the window once more. *Once I get my car back then it's the big payback.*

Chapter 13

Jessie drove while the deacon led the prayer. They'd hoped to simply buy car insurance that would allow Delilah to take back possession of her car and give them back their lives. But Delilah was like a bad rash that was more than skin deep. It was rooted to the bone.

Deacon Pillar had just finished praying for grace, mercy, and strength when he saw Jessie's good hand gripping the steering wheel so tight the veins were about to pop. "Should I pray again?"

"Please do."

"Y'all acting like it's my fault. How was I supposed to remember every little accident, speeding ticket, or HOV violation?" Up to that point Delilah hadn't said much since they'd left the insurance agency. But she'd finally had enough of pretending not to hear their accusations and prayers to God to save "her lying soul," as if she weren't His child, too.

"I know it's their prerogative, but how did you manage to get your credit so messed up that the dealership decided not to let you retake the car, even with insurance?" Jessie didn't want to ask but he felt compelled.

"I guess I was doing too much with Peter and Paul."

"This isn't the time to talk about your nasty love life," Deacon Pillar snapped.

"Shut up, Thurgood," Delilah replied. "I was robbing one to pay the other."

"So what are you going to do now, Delilah?"

"I'm not sure, Jessie. Just drop me back at my house and I'll figure out something."

Jessie looked at his watch. "It's gonna have to be later. I need to pick up the women."

As if he'd already read Jessie's mind, the deacon said, "I'm supposed to get a tow to take my truck over on Northern Boulevard tomorrow for repairs. They're gonna need to either change those gears or use some type of solvent to get the goop out."

"It's almost five o'clock and I've got a board meeting tonight. Family and Friends celebration is coming up shortly, and I'm in charge of putting the program together."

"Well, since I have no transportation, I was gonna ride with Marty tonight to a movie or something. . . ." He stopped speaking, knowing he probably had given Delilah ammunition for something. What that something was, he didn't know.

"Hmmmm, I doubt if she'll want to take a ride out to Garden City for any reason." Jessie shook his head. How many wrenches could his mother throw into his life and those around him?

It didn't really matter that Jessie and the deacon's back-and-forth wouldn't get Delilah back to Garden City. Each knew she'd be with them for another night.

All they needed to figure out was where and how to break the news to Tamara and Sister Marty. Hopefully, Sister Marty wouldn't break the deacon's neck.

Delilah, meanwhile, laid her head against the comfort and coolness of the leather backseat. *Jehovah. Either You playing Ping-Pong with my situation, or You've got something up Your sleeve. Either way, I thank You for allowing me another opportunity* to get to *Tamara*. She lifted her head and her eyes looked directly onto the back of the deacon's woolly-edged conk. She dropped her head and added, *I want to thank You also for giving me a chance to block whatever Thurgood had planned tonight. After I've made him pay for his lying, You and that Madge, Martha, or whatever her name is, can have him back.* "Amen."

"Were you praying?" Jessie hadn't meant to ask but it'd come out.

"Yes."

"I've seen her do that a time or two recently." Deacon Pillar winked at Jessie. "I'm sure she's thanking the Lord for your kindness."

"Oh, I'm thanking Jehovah for a lot of things." Delilah smiled and she meant it that time.

Chapter 14

"So do you want to tell me where she's gonna sleep tonight?"

As she spoke, Sister Marty's black weave bobbed around like it, too, wanted to fight. It'd been that way ever since she and Tamara heard about the latest impending Delilah storm. Enough with the kindness—she was going to speak her mind in her own house.

"I don't know what kind of fool you think I am," Sister Marty ranted on, "but me having the *S* word won't matter in this situation."

"The *S* word?" Deacon Pillar had been trying to catch up ever since she leapt from the car and he'd had to chase her home. "I don't understand what you mean."

"It means that because I have Salvation don't mean I'm stupid." She was tossing her handmade doilies all over her living room and that wasn't a good sign. It took a lot to get her angry. In this instance all it took was one word: *Delilah.*

"I'd never take you for stupid." Deacon Pillar wasn't in a position to be offended but he truly was. "Why would you think that?"

And that's when Sister Marty used another *S* word. She

schooled the deacon right then and there. She ran down her road-to-Christianity fight resume and compared it to what she supposed was Delilah's still-a-hussy one. And then she told him what he needed to do to get rid of Delilah and just how long he had to do it. "It shouldn't be that hard, Thurgood. Neither Tamara nor Jessie wants her around. Hell, buy her a used car if you need to be so kind to her. And if there's nothing between the two of you, what could she possibly have that you need?" When she finished, a smile spread across her face as though she'd just preached the Word to him. "That's all I have to say about this crazy situation." But it really wasn't because she quickly added, "I've been there for Jessie and Tamara all these years. That she-hussy can't just walk in here and interrupt that."

That's when the deacon realized why she reminded him of Delilah. Marty was Delilah-lite. Both women were the type that would knock your teeth out and then make you wanna chew a piece of caramel with your gums. And yet he was attracted to that type, and Marty had never said she loved him.

The deacon simply hung his head. He swore in his spirit he heard God speaking to him again: *Pillar, I told you over a week ago to come on home, son, where you'd be safe.*

Deacon Pillar allowed Sister Marty to give him a few more of the dos and the don'ts of a one-sided relationship before he'd had enough.

"Sit down, Marty." Deacon Pillar collapsed onto a nearby chair. He suddenly looked older and more tired than his years. His eyes moistened and he again beckoned Marty to him.

"Thurgood, what's wrong?" Her anger disappeared. She couldn't fight him when he looked already defeated.

"I've got to tell you something. If I don't, I'm going to be a nervous wreck."

"What?"

"Please," the deacon pleaded, "as a child of God, you've got to keep this to yourself until I can fix things."

"Thurgood, are you on a wanted list or something?"

"No, but it would be better than where I am now."

The deacon finally got Sister Marty to sit. He poured his heart out. He held almost nothing back as he told her about him and Delilah.

By the time the deacon finished his confession, Sister Marty looked older than he was. "My God, Thurgood. Delilah's your estranged wife?"

"I'm afraid so. I married that demon under duress a little more than forty years ago."

Marty rose. There was no way she could sit after hearing that kind of news. "What about Jessie?" She hesitated, not knowing if she really wanted to know the answer.

Deacon Pillar could've blurted out the complete truth as he had a moment before. He didn't. Instead, he gave her the Thurgood Pillar version. "Jessie was about two years old when I married his mama." He hadn't totally lied.

"So she'd already had Jessie when you married?"

"Yep, they were my ready-made family." *A family I'd helped to make.*

"Damn, Thurgood. Why didn't you say something to Jessie when you moved in there?"

"I swear, Marty, I had no idea until he showed up at New Hope. I gave up trying to find him and Delilah years before. And then when I looked for an apartment and it was right in the same house, I just kept quiet."

"Why?"

"By then Jessie was a grown man with his own family. Except for my best friend, Earl Athens, I had no family. I believed it was God who led me to Jessie—if God wanted Jessie to know everything, then God would've let the beans spill right then and there."

"We're Christians, Thurgood."

"I know."

"And what you just said amounts to nothing more than a cop-out and don't make a lick of sense."

"I know."

"So what are you going to do?"

"I don't know."

"Well, now you've laid this burden on me. I know I promised not to say anything. . . ."

The deacon got up and put his arms around her shoulders. "I'm sorry, honey. I'm in a fix."

"But this is not all about you, Thurgood. You've got to tell Jessie and Tamara the truth. They deserve better than what you've given them. Jessie believes that his mother is just someone you may have had a fling with years ago."

"I just didn't want you thinking that Delilah had some kind of hold on me. . . ."

"Thurgood, she does. She's got the wifey-thing noose tightly wound around your neck."

"Well, that's temporary. I know I wasn't completely honest when I didn't tell her from the beginning about Jessie. I explained to you that helping her find him was the way to my quick divorce. I was going to try and outlast her, but that card's been trumped. I need to find another way to make her give me that divorce so I can move on."

"Who's moving on with you?"

"Hopefully, you will."

"I don't like any of this, Thurgood. If I believed Delilah truly had Jessie's best interests at heart, I could understand telling him. He's a grown man who can make his own decisions, but he's just lost his wife." Sister Marty lifted her head and silently prayed. "I've always protected him, and with Cindy now gone, I've got to step up again. Just tell me what you need me to do."

"Isn't there someplace in that equation for me?" The deacon began to wonder why he'd needed to ask. Better yet, why did he?

"Of course there's a place in my heart for you, Thurgood. Like I just said, tell me what to do."

"I need you to get along with her for a start."

"Say what! How is that supposed to happen? I'm not using up all my salvation capital on your wife. What else you got?"

"That's it to start off. The rest I haven't worked out yet."

With the framework of their battle plan laid, the two walked back to the sofa. They continued to sit, for what seemed like forever, in silence. It was finally the deacon who made the first move.

"I'm suddenly not in the mood for a movie," the deacon said as he turned and kissed her on her cheek. They walked to her door, still hand in hand. "I'm not looking forward to jumping through any of Delilah's hoops, but whatever challenges lie ahead, I won't let them hurt us."

"I'm depending on you to do the right thing, Thurgood."

"You can depend on me, Marty."

"That's a good thing," she said playfully, poking him in his chest, "because you still have only six weeks to get it together. Or the deal's off."

"Which deal, honey—me or Jessie?"

"That's entirely up to you, Thurgood."

No sooner had the deacon put the key in the front hall door after he'd walked home from Sister Marty's than Tamara rushed out into the hallway. She held a phone to her ear and was signaling the deacon to wait.

". . . But Daddy, I didn't know she was gonna do that. . . . You told me to let her use the spare room in the basement. . . . Deacon Pillar just came in the door. . . . Well, hurry home, please."

Deacon Pillar's mind barely had a chance to regroup from

trying to salvage his relationship with Marty, and now *this*. And whatever *this* was, it could only be more Delilah drama.

"Baby girl, what's going on?"

Tamara began by telling the deacon her father had stayed longer at the church to handle some business. In the meantime, it was so awkward with just her and Delilah alone in the house, and she really didn't have anything to say to Delilah, so she went ahead and showed Delilah the spare room where she'd spend the night.

"Deacon Pillar, I truly believe she did it on purpose."

"Did what?"

"She managed to stop up the toilet and break off the showerhead."

"That's no problem. Let me grab my tool kit and I'll fix it."

"Well, good luck with that. I told her to wait until I came out of the shower upstairs and she could use it. Delilah didn't want to wait."

"Where is she now?" Somehow the deacon already knew the answer. All he could do was shake his head. "Is she still up there? I've got to start locking my door."

"Yes. She's been up there long enough to take a couple of showers. Make sure you count your loose change and silverware. But wait—I have something else to tell you."

"What is it?" He really hoped it wasn't something that would take all day. He needed to see what Delilah was up to in his apartment.

"I found out some stuff about Delilah," Tamara began. "Did you know if you look up her information online in Wikipedia that she's got a pretty scandalous background?"

The deacon folded his arms. It was an indication that Tamara should continue.

"It says that she was once connected with a producer named Croc Duggan. . . ."

"Go on. . . ." The deacon was pretty sure what Tamara

was about to say, but he wasn't going to divulge it in case he was wrong.

"Delilah almost slept her way through the music industry, and it was Croc Duggan who provided the music she danced to, if you know what I mean."

"Tamara Jewel." Deacon Pillar was shocked and angry. "You're gonna talk about something you read and don't know if it's true or not? If you'd read that about Sister Marty, would you have believed or repeated it?"

"No, I wouldn't. But I know Sister Marty. I don't know Delilah like that. . . ."

"And yet, you'd repeat it when you don't even know if she knows anyone by that name or reputation. . . ."

"I'm sorry." She didn't want to hear any more. She didn't have to know Delilah too well to believe the woman who gave up her father was scandalous.

The deacon left Tamara as well chastised as he could with a straight face. She was becoming almost as bad as her grandmother.

As soon as the deacon flung open his door, he saw Delilah. She was straddling a chair with her feet up on his couch while she painted her toenails. It was apparent she was wearing one of Tamara's outfits, which meant it should've been much too young for her. Though he was angry, he still thought she looked good in it. She was also without her wig, which allowed her natural white tresses to fall somewhere between her shoulder blades and her waist. The dress material was flimsy and yellow. And when he finished ogling, he realized Delilah wasn't wearing a bra. Nor from her profile did she look like she needed to.

Without saying a word, the deacon walked into his kitchen and poured something to drink. Within a few moments he returned to his living room.

Delilah said nothing, either, as she continued to watch with eagle eyes from her perch. The reaction from the deacon didn't sit well with her.

"Enough is enough," Deacon Pillar said sharply. "Blow on them toes to dry them or whatever. You're going home this night."

"You ain't in charge." Delilah rose slowly from the chair, no doubt looking for another mayonnaise jar full of change. "My son said I could stay here tonight."

"What would you know about staying put somewhere?"

Delilah put her head down and continued polishing her toenails as she answered. "I know it was a good thing when I left you."

Whether she meant it or not, Delilah's words cut through him. They ripped out feelings of any peaceful coexistence on a smooth road to a divorce. He also wanted to pray a moment, but the moment was killed by Delilah's edited version of the truth. It was now Deacon Pillar's turn to put the *T* in truth, something he hadn't fully told in a long time.

"You didn't leave, you fled." He moved back on the sofa and pointed a finger at Delilah. "I stayed and took a rap and a two-year prison sentence for you, Delilah Dupree Jewel. You stabbed that gangster, Jimmy James Lanier. I took the hit."

"I know, dammit, and if you want me to say I'm sorry about it, again, I will. I'm sorry, Thurgood."

"Sorry won't cut it."

Peace had left and civility was shattered quicker than a lead anchor dropped in a fish tank.

"I loved you, Delilah. Hell, I even loved your dead mama's drawers and I'd never met her."

"I . . . I." Delilah found it hard to speak to the truth, so she didn't.

The deacon's already dark complexion grew darker as he pressed, "There was a two-year-old child involved, Delilah. I didn't want him to be without a mama so I married you. At that age a boy needs his mama. I gave up my freedom for Jessie."

Delilah felt trapped as she watched a sudden indignation and something akin to a feeling of deep dislike flood over Deacon Pillar's face. He looked as though he was gulping for air and her presence was sucking it all out of the room.

"I gave up my freedom for the boy." The deacon's voice rose with each accusation. "And you gave him up for *yours*. You didn't nurture that boy, but you for damn sure nurtured your career."

Delilah's heart raced. So much she wanted and needed to tell him, but her pride would not allow it.

Deacon Pillar wasn't finished and it seemed as though he never would be. "It don't matter that you never wrote or visited while I did without in jail. I was a hustler, a musician who played the street game and lost, but that boy, Jessie, he wasn't supposed to get hurt."

The deacon fought tears as he struggled to retain his composure. "I didn't find Jessie until almost four years ago." Deacon Pillar began to wring his hands. "Imagine how I felt when my place of worship became the same place of worship for Jessie. And then when I needed a place to live—oh my God. My God, I wound up on Jessie's doorstep. When I saw him up close . . . I . . . I would've known him anywhere."

Delilah didn't know when it happened, but she'd turned completely around to face him. Still, all she could say was, "I'm so sorry. . . ."

"Shut up! I know now it was only the Lord that led me to him, but I didn't know it then. And now I still don't have the courage to tell him everything because after all these years I'm not sure if I truly know *everything* except what you told me back then."

Deacon Pillar couldn't hold back his tears. He was almost completely wiped out as he continued. "And Tamara, his daughter, she looks just like you. It is as if Cindy gave birth to Jessie's mama."

The deacon continued his outrage. Delilah's sense of self diminished with every accusation.

". . . And I didn't know what to do, Delilah, because I didn't have you, Jessie's mama, to discuss nothing with."

Delilah's eyes widened as each word from the deacon continued to pierce her soul. Yet she was unable to defend herself with her own words, only her thoughts. *I thought I needed fame to prove I was worth something. I had a baby and I had a dream, too. I just couldn't hold on to both.*

As the deacon continued being her judge and jury, Delilah winced at the thought of how she'd become unable to take care of herself, much less Jessie, after Thurgood had been sent off to prison.

How she'd spent so many years running after singing and modeling jobs between Los Angeles and Atlanta. And she'd gone from Washington, DC, and back to Los Angeles until she finally ended up back in New York. All that time she was always so close to what her soul thought it needed, when what it really needed she'd left in foster care. For now she'd have to take his outbursts.

Deacon Pillar finally wiped the tears from his eyes with the palms of his hands and stood next to Delilah, this time blocking her escape.

"Here it is, forty-something years later, Delilah, and nothing much has changed at all."

One thing was certain—their trip down memory lane had too many potholes. It was amazing neither of them broke a leg during the trip.

And just that quick, Delilah went into survivor mode. That meant whatever he'd just said, she'd get back to it later. "Look, Thurgood, I probably shouldn't have used your shower. I did. I probably shouldn't be sitting here painting my toes, which seems to have either turned you on or made you lose your mind, but I did. I'm not about to say sorry again, and I'm not leaving when my son has invited me to stay."

Deacon Pillar was so outdone. "Lord, please help me maintain my sanity." He was ready to leave his own apartment.

As soon as Jessie parked and got out the car, he smelled it. "Tamara," Jessie called out as he entered the house, "what's that burning?"

"I'm in the kitchen, Daddy." Tamara walked slowly from the kitchen carrying a pot that was still smoking and sooty on its bottom. "I'm sorry. I tried to heat up something to eat and I let it burn."

"What is it?" Jessie was surprised because the one thing Tamara never learned was how to cook. He or Cindy always cooked. Since Cindy's death they'd relied on mostly takeout, or ordered in, even though he kept freezer and shelves stocked. "What was it supposed to be?"

"It was baked pork chops, mustard greens, and macaroni and cheese. I've pretty much ruined most of it and I'm starving. If I weren't so hungry I wouldn't have touched it."

Jessie took the pot from Tamara's hands and headed back to the kitchen. "Why would you not eat it?"

"Delilah cooked it." Tamara made a face that showed how much she detested her newly found grandmother. "I don't like her, but it smelled so good. She sure can burn in the kitchen."

"It looks more like you did the burning." Jessie shook his head, smiling as he emptied the charred food into the garbage and set the pot in the sink. "So where's mommy dearest?"

Tamara explained again how Delilah wouldn't wait until their shower was available and had insisted upon taking a shower in the deacon's apartment. "You know I called Sister Marty to tell her to haul her sanctified behind down here before Delilah laid hands on the deacon."

Jessie didn't try to hide his annoyance. "Why would you do that?"

"Are you taking her side?" His reaction wasn't what she'd expected.

"We can't let her jeopardize our walk with the Lord. I know your mother wouldn't have acted that way. You see how I had to flip things around. I don't know the last time I've fasted and prayed so hard."

"You think Mama would've met a scandalous mother-in-law halfway, too?"

"Cindy wouldn't have let anyone or anything steal her testimony or her joy. Not even if Delilah was Lizzie Borden."

"You're right. Mama would've dragged Delilah's little butt to church, drizzled some blessed oil over her, and let prayer burn out those demons." Tamara started the dishwasher and began to smile. "Anyway, I've not heard any noises from up-stairs—no yelling, no screaming, no bed springs creaking . . ."

"Tamara!" Jessie had never heard his daughter talk that way. She'd always kept her adult conversation PG. "I'm too tired to get into it, but you and I need to revisit boundaries."

"I'm sorry, Daddy. I only meant that since Sister Marty didn't answer, it's a good thing I didn't bother to leave a message about the deacon and Delilah on her answering machine."

"Thank God."

Their feet sounded like an army running down the stairs. "Hey, who's trying to burn down the place?" Deacon Pillar rushed into the kitchen with Delilah almost fused to his heels.

"Is everyone okay?" Delilah's eyes swept over the stove where the remnants of the dinner she'd cooked lay about.

"I'm sorry, Jessie." Delilah's eyes looked quickly at Tamara. Not that she wouldn't have taken the blame, but here was an opportunity to get closer to her granddaughter. "It's my fault. I must've left the stove on while I showered. . . ."

"Tamara's already told me what really happened." Jessie wanted to say that it was okay. Instead he scolded Delilah. "Is a lie always the first thing to pop out of your mouth rather than the truth?" Jessie didn't wait for an answer. He slammed another pot into the sink and left the kitchen. He shut his bedroom door so hard glasses in the kitchen cupboard rattled.

If Delilah was floored, then Tamara and the deacon were doubly so.

Tamara jerked the switch to the range fan so it would disperse the rest of the smoke and the odor. "I didn't ask you to take up for me like I'm some poor little toddler who can't make a mistake and accept consequences." Tamara's show of gratitude was completely lacking. "I don't need you trying to be a grandmother. You just need to spend the night and then move on and out."

Like her father, Tamara left the kitchen in a huff. She didn't even bother to say good night to the deacon.

Delilah became as still as a corpse. Her mouth gaped as Tamara fled the kitchen.

"Damn, girl, you still got it," Deacon Pillar said to Delilah as he chuckled and watched Tamara rush out. "First it was your only son, and now it's your only granddaughter. Like magic, *poof* they're gone. I have to hand it to you. I don't know anybody that can piss off foes, friends, and family alike, quicker than you can."

Jessie turned on the air-conditioner in his bedroom. Even as he changed out of his clothes and sprayed the room with Cindy's favorite deodorizer, lavender, to cover the smell of burnt food, he felt chastened. "Lord, all this fasting and praying and still I can't let it go. Father, I need to let it go, but I don't know if I want to."

Since Cindy's death the ghosts of their life together

moved in and took him over. He was hurt, but he didn't want anger to enter into a room where it'd not existed during his marriage. There were disagreements between him and Cindy, as with all couples. But there was no space in that room for anger. They wouldn't allow it. Only love was invited in to stay.

And try as hard as he had since she died, everywhere Jessie looked in the home he and Cindy shared for more than twenty years, her essence lingered.

Cindy's handmade potholders hung on the kitchen wall; a flat-screen television she gave him last Father's Day. Sometimes he swore he heard her strong, Aretha-like voice in the spare basement room. She'd turned it into her music room and added a sofa bed for houseguests, or for when she just wanted some quiet time with her God.

Nighttime was the worst. He knew she was gone, but could still feel and smell her Red Door cologne. He reached across their king-size bed, imagining her next to him as he lay there. For the first few weeks after the funeral, he hadn't even changed the sheets for fear of losing what part of her that remained. He'd completely broken down.

"Why, Lord?" Jessie sighed. "When I can finally take a guilt-free breath, and accept your will for Cindy, another death comes to my door."

Delilah was his mother and when he had needed her she wasn't there. He was a grown man before he had accepted that it wasn't his fault. It took Cindy to make him believe that he was worth something. It took God to make him a man who no longer hated and could have compassion. And yet, every once in a while, his resentment surfaced and he'd have to go to God all over again because it was easier to believe Delilah was dead, than just gone away.

I'm so angry with the deacon, but I can't stay mad. How would the deacon know that Delilah was my mother?

And then another thought came to Jessie. *I wonder if the*

deacon knows who else Delilah was involved with. His long-held feelings of not wanting to know the identity of his natural father took a sudden turn. It was a long shot. *I know I can't rely on Delilah to tell me the truth. The deacon won't lie. He'll tell me if there was someone who could be my father.*

And with that thought in mind, Jessie found rest. And tomorrow he'd find a way to get along with Delilah. "I can do all things through Christ who strengthens me," he repeated several times. How much trouble could she be, staying away from him and living in Garden City?

Chapter 15

Marty fingered through her Bible as she sat on her sofa and listened to the messages on her phone. She'd not answered her phone or door since the deacon left the other night. He'd called her several times. She just wouldn't pick up the phone. She wasn't sure if he'd gotten his truck back from the repair shop or not and she didn't try to find out. And she'd not returned Tamara's call either. And that was something she'd never done before.

"Cindy," Marty began again for the umpteenth time in two days, "girl, I don't know what to do." She didn't have another friend as close as they'd been and she'd not tried to find one.

Have mercy, I'm sitting around here trying to discuss the problems of the living with the dead.

The deacon had a lot of nerve putting her in this position. She could be nice to Delilah if need be—she was somewhat okay with that. The question that haunted her was the possibility of the deacon being Jessie's real father.

Marty replayed the conversation over and over in her mind. *Why didn't he just come on out and answer my question about Jessie's age and his marriage to Delilah? I was in such shock it just didn't hit me right then to press him about it.*

He didn't seem too concerned about who might be Jessie's natural father was one thought she'd had. And then she thought, *Perhaps he knows and just doesn't want to get involved.*

One thing she knew for certain, ever since the deacon had moved into Jessie's home, she'd come to view him as a part of Jessie's family. Although she'd known the deacon in passing, there were five thousand members in that congregation, so they'd never really connected. Now they had, and she wasn't about to deliver her family into Delilah's hands. Her hands weren't worthy as far as Marty was concerned. Plus she wasn't in love with the deacon, but she was on her way. But life was short, too. She wasn't waiting beyond the six-week deadline she'd set.

Two days after Jessie, accompanied by the deacon, delivered Delilah all in one piece, with no scorn or scolding, to her Garden City home, she was still smiling. She went from room to room singing at the top of her still powerful lungs, *God bless the child . . .*

No matter how the change in their attitudes started, she was thrilled it'd finally begun, after she'd spent a night in her son's home. She would never have believed it would happen after she'd heard the cruel accusation of Thurgood that her best talent was to piss off foe, friend, and family alike.

She recalled that later the other night, once settled in the spare room in Jessie's basement, Delilah saw with her own eyes even more evidence of what she'd missed over the years. There were several photo albums of pictures taken on a cruise, which showed laughing, kayaking, and playful Jessie, Cindy, and Tamara. And when she saw smiling pictures of the deacon on the ship with them, she became sad. She wasn't angry, just sad.

And then it all came together for Delilah. She found a few DVDs of Cindy and Tamara which also featured, sometimes, Jessie and the deacon. They were singing and clowning around, having a great time singing gospel, jazz, and R & B. And their harmonies were sweet and their improvisations and riffs blew her away.

Now here she was, two days later, happy as a clam in her home with nothing but hope in mind. She'd just picked up her *Daily Word* and was about to pray again when her doorbell rang. "I'm not expecting company. Lord, please don't let it be a certified letter from some collection agency." So imagine her surprise when she found the deacon standing in her doorway. He leaned against the door frame, grinning like he thought he was Denzel Washington.

And it all changed once he set foot across the threshold. Peaceful means of coexistence magically disappeared once they laid eyes upon one another. And like champagne and chitlins, they didn't match but seemed to end up on the same menu regardless.

"Well now," the deacon said as entered and spied the book of Bible verses she held. "I'm glad you're in a prayerful mood." Without asking if he could, he sat down on the sofa.

"Hold up, Thurgood!" Delilah let her voice rise to show who was really in control. "Before you come in acting like you're still better than somebody, this is still my home. I do pray from time to time. So if you gonna cuss, fuss, or insinuate, please don't do it in my living room. This is the room I pray in."

"Woman, now I know you've completely lost your mind." Her shudder was almost invisible, but it'd happened. Delilah struggled to keep a composed look upon her face at the mention of her mental state. *He better hope I don't flip out on him and show him what real crazy looks like.*

Any reaction by Delilah was lost upon the deacon as he leaned back on the sofa and chuckled. "I shouldn't reprimand you for the way you pray. I guess I'm still adjusting to the fact that you actually allow God to come into this spotless living room and hear your dirty little secrets."

"Like I said, I do pray and the how and the when ain't none of your business. But since you insist on knowing," Delilah insisted as she sat down in her recliner and let it out, "I do it right here."

"You can't confine God to any one place, Dee Dee. You think he don't know what devilish things you're doing throughout the rest of this house?" Laughing—he just couldn't help himself—he decided to take it a step further and teased, "Dee Dee, tell me that you still do one 'devilish' thing. I'd sure hate to think that's gone to waste."

Despite her need to remain in charge, Delilah almost lost control of her bladder. She laughed until she cried. "Thurno-good Pillar, you still ain't got the sense God gave a cricket. Some things are just like riding a bicycle." She stopped and patted her hips. "But right now I ain't offering no rides. Besides," she said as she pointed to his head, "you're still wearing a conk, which means your *bicycle* might still have training wheels on it."

"Yes, I do ride a bike without training wheels and yes, I am wearing a conk. Conked hair or not, I can still ride that bicycle and I still know when to switch gears. Hell, it don't take a genius to spot a dog in the midst of a litter of kittens."

"If that's true, then how in the world did you end up with that Macy character?"

"Her name is Marty, and you know that." The deacon regretted teasing Delilah because he suddenly felt guilty. It was like he was cheating on Marty. Why did he always allow Delilah to push his buttons? Yet he'd been the one who started it.

Deacon Pillar needed to get back to the business of why he was there.

"Listen, Dee Dee," the deacon began, "I think I might have a solution to your transportation problems."

"What are you talking about, Thurgood?" As usual, she was suspicious of any act of unsought kindness. Her bells and whistles where the deacon was concerned fired off and almost brought her to her knees.

"As a divorce gift I'm going to buy you a car."

Chapter 16

"My goodness, Thurgood, you could've at least taken her out to dinner or brought some flowers."

Sister Marty shook her head. She'd never have imagined she'd come to Delilah's defense. "I'm about to revoke your Christian playa card."

Marty had jumped on his case almost as soon as he'd come inside her house. He'd had her sympathy until he mentioned why Delilah had almost physically tossed him out onto the street.

"But it was your idea, honey. You told me to buy her a car if I had to."

"Look, Deacon, you've got about three weeks before I pull the plug on us. I told you when we started dating that I live in a drama-free zone. Jesus don't like this mess, Pillar."

"Marty, you don't even like Delilah."

"Yes, that's true."

"I guess I'll just let her cool down before I try again."

Suddenly Marty started laughing. "Pillar, I believe I got the answer."

"Lay it on me. I'm fresh out of ideas."

"Why not let Jessie buy her the car?"

"Jessie don't like her, either."

"But he doesn't have to like her to use your money to buy a car."

"That's true."

The deacon thought he'd finally found a reason to relax. But somehow he knew better.

No sooner had the deacon gotten the words out of his mouth than regrets nibbled at his spirit. "Brother Jessie, I'm trying to help you out. You said it was my fault that Delilah's playing havoc with all your lives."

Jessie poured a cup of coffee and sat back down at the kitchen table. Before the deacon revealed his latest plot to rid them of Delilah, he'd been leaning against the counter. He'd finally gone to a doctor two weeks before. He was astonished that he'd actually fractured his hand when the sight of Delilah had caused him to slam it against a wall. "I'm not going to buy Delilah a car with anyone's money."

That wasn't the answer the deacon expected. Had he misread Jessie?

"You missed a spot by the edge over there, Deacon."

"I got it covered." The deacon moved a sponge across the molding around the kitchen sink. He was cleaning up after he'd finally stained several wood items in the kitchen. It was something he'd promised to do before Delilah disrupted things. "I guess you're right, Jessie. I'm just trying to rectify a mistake."

"Speaking of mistakes, Deacon," Jessie said as he took another sip, "I want to ask you something."

Deacon Pillar laid the sponge down and closed the lid on the can of stain. "What can I do for you?"

"I pray I'm doing the right thing, but I don't want you to get Delilah a car yet. I want you to get close enough to her to find out something for me."

"Define 'close enough' and 'something.' " The deacon walked over to the table to sit down.

"Since Delilah's shown up and continues to do so, I can't figure out her true intentions. I'm just not getting this 'I wanna be your mama' reason. I'm thinking rather that she's really sick and needs a kidney or something. You know, something straight out of *Grey's Anatomy*. I sure hope she's not looking to use one of mine."

Deacon Pillar's butt missed the chair. He fell on his butt harder than he had when he tried to avoid the flying mayonnaise jar Delilah threw. And then he landed on the same hip bone.

"Are you alright, Deacon?" Jessie tried to use his one good hand to help the old man off the floor.

"I'm fine. I guess I should've been doing just as much looking as I was listening."

"I didn't mean to throw that at you like that."

"Didn't mean to throw what, Daddy?" Tamara had just walked into the kitchen when she saw her father helping the deacon up.

"I don't know if you'll agree with this, but I'm asking the deacon to help me learn more about Delilah. Why is she really coming back into my life?"

"Too bad we can't sometimes pick our parents," Tamara said as she sat in one of the other chairs. "I'm surely blessed in that regard. Well, if that's what you feel you need to do, then I would do it."

"I'm glad you understand. I feel better about it already. No matter how it turns out, I'm keeping my insides."

"What do you mean, no matter how it turns out?" the deacon asked as he rose to touch up another spot he'd missed.

"I mean if I give it my best shot and I find out she just wanted to use me and she hasn't changed at all over the years, well, then I'm blessed with a loving family anyhow." Jessie smiled at Tamara. "And if Delilah can't be a stand-up grandma, we've got you, Deacon Pillar, to keep on spoiling this brat like a grandpa. And if you ever hang up your playa card and make Sister Marty an honest woman, we can make it an official and legal family."

"I don't need nothing official," Tamara said with a wink. "Ain't no natural grandfather gonna spoil me more than Deacon Pillar. So I'm sticking with the deacon I love to love."

If Jessie and Tamara never wanted to see a grown man weep, then they should've kept their feelings quiet. One moment the deacon was staining a counter molding and the next he was hugged by them and sobbing.

Since the kitchen weep-fest, for a day or so, Marty kept dropping little reminders of the impending deadline. At least she'd amended it a little and said she'd be happy if the divorce was at least in the works by that time. Of course, the deacon had not reached out to Delilah at all.

And during that time, whenever he looked at Jessie he'd run to God and sought help. In his spirit he knew that he should've told Jessie the truth. But he was a coward and God didn't need any cowards in His army.

After the deacon had stayed away for a couple of days, by that Friday Delilah wasn't surprised when she heard from him. He was so predictable. It seemed the worse she treated him, the better he behaved. Delilah didn't bother to don her signature wig and she wore no makeup, but the lavender and white floral housedress and matching sandals had the young look she favored. She also tossed aside her idea of making life nice for him.

She'd spent those couple of Pillar-free days in Garden City praying and going over some recipes she felt Tamara would like. She'd overheard Tamara mention that Cindy and Marty got together sometimes and made special dishes for the church's various events. She'd also learned that New Hope was having a Family and Friends Day celebration soon.

*I think it would be great if Tamara and I cooked something in
Cindy's honor for that day.*

Delilah hadn't considered that Tamara still hadn't shown
any signs of welcoming her into the family or even wanting
to be in the same room. That wasn't going to stop Delilah.

So by the time the deacon showed up that Friday at
noon, looking like something the cat pushed out and flung at
the dog, her mood had changed dramatically. "What in the
world happened? Did I mess you up this bad?" He either
couldn't or wouldn't answer, but she took pity on him and
decided being nasty could wait for some other time. No matter what, she still didn't have transportation and he did. She
wanted to stick to her plan.

"What are you doing?" Deacon Pillar asked her, although
he didn't resist as she led him quickly into the living room.
And because he definitely looked like he needed it, she went
into the kitchen and fixed a plate of lasagna, along with garlic
bread and a glass of cold lemonade. When she returned, she
placed it on the coffee table where he could get to it.

"Thank you, Dee Dee." Deacon Pillar watched Delilah
fuss over him instead of at him. He liked this Delilah better.

While he ate she began to sing. Suddenly she got up and
danced over to her record player.

"Dee Dee, that was delicious." The deacon felt much
better with his stomach full. He wiped his mouth and licked
his lips. He leaned forward off the sofa and then smiled,
showing his approval at what she was about to do. "Woman,
you still have a working record player in this day and age? I
didn't know you could still find a spindle for those things."

"Not only do I have spindles," Delilah replied, "I have a
quarter taped to the arm to keep the weight steady on the
record."

Just like Delilah and the deacon and many their age, their
favorite music served many purposes. That afternoon the

music was the balm he needed. "Have mercy! Dee Dee, please take me back. Take me back to the sixties—and even further back if you can. What you got from back then?"

For the next hour, instead of getting back to the sad business at hand, which was why the deacon drove there, he listened to Delilah play her records and deejay the soundtrack to their past history.

And then the deacon rose off the sofa and even surprised himself. He did the last thing he'd ever think of doing with Delilah. He hadn't even done it with Marty. He reached out and he pulled Delilah's small body into his long arms. He put an ole-skool hump in his back and they began to dance.

"Thurgood," Delilah whispered. She hadn't seen this coming when she thought about playing some of her old 45s. She was quickly losing control over the situation as they swayed, clinging like they'd done when young and in love. It was an old blue-lights-in-the basement, grind-'em-up moment. And Delilah wasn't having it. Not yet.

Delilah pushed away just in time. A loud hissing sound came from the record player as the spindle arm returned to its cradle. The song was finished and the deacon had come close to the same conclusion. Delilah wrung her hands as she watched him.

"You still got it, gal!" He breathed harder than he had in years as he quickly placed a hand inside one pants pocket. He adjusted what needed adjusting.

Delilah suddenly felt something she'd not felt in quite some time. She felt embarrassed. She pushed a stray strand of white hair from her face and smoothed the front of her dress. She'd have said more, but she, too, needed to regain control. The one dance had taken her to a place with the deacon she hadn't considered; not consciously anyway. He hadn't lost his touch, and probably could give some of her past, younger lovers a run for it.

Delilah sat down. She let her head fall back against her love seat, opposite the sofa, and spoke aloud what she was thinking.

"You know, Thurgood," Delilah said as she slowly closed her eyes and allowed her feet to tap the carpet as another record dropped on the record player. The tapping turned rhythmic as she continued to speak. "I know you came here to talk about Jessie, but I need to tell you something while it's on my mind."

"Okay, what is it?"

"I can't say it enough. I owe a lot of people, especially you and Jessie, an apology. I chased stardom like it was a runaway slave I'd always owned. Only I was its slave. There was nothing out of bounds that I wouldn't do to get a gig or a print job. A lot of times it was with the sleaziest modeling agency or in the raunchiest dive. Lord knows I lowered myself just to get ahead. I don't want that for Tamara. I just hope she has more smarts than I did."

Deacon Pillar leaned forward and with compassion tried to say something encouraging. "Don't you worry about Tamara, and I still say you were better than those who did make it."

"Those who made it?" Delilah's voice rose slightly, and suddenly with the air of a college professor she added, "That's an odd thing to say because back then they only let Negroes through the gates of stardom one or two at a time, and sometimes only a decade at a time. I must've been number three in line each time."

Delilah stopped. "You know I haven't even asked what you've been up to all these years. I see you still love to drive a . truck and you've joined the church. What else did I miss?"

Her question caught him off guard, as had most of what'd happened since he'd arrived. Deacon Pillar regaled Delilah with the best parts of how he'd fared since leaving prison.

"You mean to tell me that you got involved with the church almost as soon as you got freed? And you hooked back up with old Earl Athens and he brought you to the Lord. If that don't beat all, I don't know what does. Sorry he's gone now, but I remember his scandalous self. He was your running buddy for quite a while and used to smoke like a chimney."

They let the taste of the good time they'd just shared linger on the lips of time just a little longer. Neither one wanted to bring up what needed saying.

Delilah refilled the deacon's glass. "Thurgood, do you hate me?"

"Not quite as much as I did a few weeks ago." He didn't know why he chose that moment to be quite so blunt.

Delilah laughed. "That's a good place to start. I'm starting to stomach you a little better, too."

"Are you still going to blackmail me?"

"Of course, Thurgood. You should know that. But I have another question for you."

"What?"

"How in the world did you ever get hooked up with that woman, Madelyn?"

"It's Marty. Why do I have to keep reminding you?"

"Whatever."

"Well, if you weren't so mule headed I might've told you sooner. I know you're going to be just as surprised as I was."

"I don't want a speech, just an answer."

"Stop being so bossy, will you? Do you remember Tight Ben Madison, that cheap, whale-looking something that owned Tightfisted Records up in New Rochelle back in the day?"

Surprise crept across Delilah's face. "Of course, I remember that no-good son of a monkey! He used to go around ripping off folks after they'd sing their hearts out for him.

What's he got to do with anything?" Suddenly she understood. "Don't tell me he was hooked up with that Marty woman? I thought she was so much into the church."

"She is and they were. Yep, he's the very same one," the deacon answered, and laughed. "But he got his comeuppance, because cousin Karma came back to visit his sorry arse and almost dragged him back, kicking and screaming, to the afterlife's family reunion."

"What do you mean, Thurgood?"

"I'm sure it was God who must've nudged him toward the church altar a bit, because soon after he'd beaten the charges of forgery and misappropriation of monies, the Almighty let a Mack truck kiss the rear end of Tight Ben's Pinto. It was all the emergency folks could do to extricate his huge, yellow butt, and his even bigger noggin from what was left of that car."

"He got hit by a Mack truck?" Delilah was truly surprised. "Did the truck survive?"

"That truck looked like Ben's head had used it for an accordion." The deacon stopped and snickered. "Have mercy, I tell you there was a hickey so wide on that skull that it required some brain surgery. That Mack truck busted his fat arse, from his tooter to his rooter. It surprised no one that after that accident no real pretty woman or even one who looked like a moose wanted his little five-foot-two-inch butt. He couldn't get a female gorilla to kiss him, not even with a wad of cash wrapped in a banana peel dangling from his zipper. So I suppose there was nothing left for him to do but finally marry Marty. I heard she seemed to be the only one who wanted him. Later on he truly found Jesus. He and Marty took Jessie in. Thank God they did. I only found out about it a couple of years ago when Cindy introduced me to Marty."

"I don't know quite what to say."

"You still want to go through with making my life miserable?"

"That hasn't changed."

"You might want to think about it some more when I tell you why I'm here."

"You want me to give you a divorce? And you know I want a relationship with Jessie and Tamara. So what's changed?"

The deacon sat down next to Delilah and explained Jessie's latest request. "Jessie wants me to get information from you." He watched her eyes glass over as she struggled with it. "He doesn't quite believe that you've turned maternal. He's a fan of that medical show, *Grey's Anatomy*. Jessie feels you really popped back into his life because you wanna use a kidney or one of his organs."

"Thurgood, you know none of that's true." Delilah couldn't believe what the deacon told her. "Besides, I doubt if he would give me a kidney if I needed one."

"Not if you needed it today, he wouldn't."

"What are we going to do? I just want my family; my son. He's my only child, Thurgood." Delilah plopped down onto the sofa. "Maybe I should have a heart-to-heart talk with him."

"And say what to him?" the deacon asked. " 'Oh, by the way, Jessie, not only do I love and need you and Tamara in my life, but that fella that's been living over you—well, he's my husband.' "

"We need to do something. You certainly can't be the one to tell him. If you do, then he might break off all ties with you, too. Neither of us will be in his life."

"Then I don't know what to do, Dee Dee. And for the life of me, I can't figure what's changed him over the past few weeks. Why he won't embrace the mother who's trying so hard to be in his life. He should do it, regardless. He's close enough to the Lord to forgive you. At least I think he is."

Delilah got up and stood by the living room window. She took her long hair and twisted it into a ponytail before pulling out a clasp seemingly from thin air to tie it back.

"I know why."

"You do? Well, I certainly wish you'd tell me. I don't have a clue that makes sense."

"It's that damn Marty Madison. She won't say or do nothing to my face, but I know she's the reason. Jessie don't need me because he's got her living within a rock's throw." Delilah looked at the deacon and added, "She wants everything that's mine."

"She was his foster mother, Delilah. Of course she feels a connection to him. She's also Tamara's godmother and was Cindy's best friend. There's history there."

Delilah began to unravel the hair she'd just pinned back. "Well, then I'll send her a thank-you card and some flowers, but I'll be damned if I let her keep me from my family." She stopped once more before adding, "And I mean my entire family."

Deacon Pillar once again was clueless. But he wasn't stupid. He didn't bother to mention the divorce. Yet he was dumb enough to ask, "I am his father, ain't I, Dee Dee?"

Within moments after asking his dumb question the deacon fled her house holding his mouth. And Delilah fled to her kitchen and went to work on her hand, which already had started to swell. She quickly thrust it into a bowl of ice. She didn't know she could still land a punch like that. *That fool almost caused me to fracture my hand. After all this time, how in the world could he ask me if he was Jessie's daddy? As far as I know, he is.*

Chapter 17

"Hold still, Thurgood. I can't get the swelling to go down if you don't stop squirming like a baby."

Sister Marty had raced over to the deacon's side as soon as Tamara had called. She'd sounded alarmed. "Somebody's mugged the deacon!" When Marty arrived, he lay in his apartment blubbering. His lips had swollen to almost twice their normal size. The deacon looked like he had two balloons taped between his nose and his chin. It didn't take her long to discover it was Delilah who'd beat him up again. And that's when Marty laid into the deacon for the second time.

"My goodness, Thurgood, maybe you should leave Delilah to deal with her anger on her own. You can't take too many more beatings like this at your age. At this rate she's not leaving much for you to divorce or for me to have."

Deacon Pillar wanted to speak, but it would have to wait. He'd driven home scared to open his mouth, as if he could without some teeth falling out, too. Delilah had hit him with something, but he didn't know what it was. He refused to believe it was her small fist that caused the damage; although he'd not seen anything in her hand. But then again, he hadn't seen the punch coming, either.

Shortly after Marty had begun working on Deacon Pillar,

Tamara walked into his apartment after going to get her father.

"Tamara told me what happened, Deacon. This is my fault. I shouldn't have asked you to do what I needed to do." Jessie put his hand on the old man's shoulder to comfort him as best he could. "I'll handle things from this point on. I'll just come out and ask her what she's really after."

"What are you going to do, Daddy?"

"Don't worry about it. God's got all this under control."

Jessie sat down and held an impromptu family meeting. He'd decided to share with them his need to find out all he could about Delilah. No matter how much he didn't trust her—or really like her, for that matter—they still shared blood. He just wanted to know, and then they could go their separate ways.

"I don't ever want you to feel that I don't appreciate all you and pop did for me," Jessie told Sister Marty. "Even Delilah showing up after all these years has not diminished one bit of love I have for you, and it never will. But I'm sure I didn't have to tell you that. You know where you stand in Tamara's and my heart."

Marty's spirit should've soared. It didn't. All the conspiracies and the lack of trust that ruled her actions over the last few weeks had pulled back a veil. She thought her salvation was more solid than it was. She wanted to tell him so bad that the deacon and Delilah were married. She couldn't. "I won't pretend to understand or particularly like Delilah. She wouldn't be my cup of friendship even if she weren't your mother—your natural mother. But that's something I'll have to pray about. It won't be for her sake but for my own."

Marty continued anointing the deacon's swollen lips with the ice pack. This time she bore down a little harder. She intended to send him a message that there was a new game on the table, called *truth*.

"Well, if you're about to confront Delilah," Sister Marty

continued, applying ice to the deacon's lips a little more gently since he'd almost leapt off the sofa a moment ago, "you'd better put on the whole armor of God and take a bat along with you."

"Mama Marty," Jessie said, laughing. He hadn't called her that in years. "I know it's going to take time. I think she and I need to get to a place where truth can't hide behind a lie. But I've got to start somewhere and sometime. I'm still fasting and praying about it."

If any of them saw the deacon's eyes go wild they never said a word. His body became stiff like a corpse. Time was running out for him. Delilah was already thinking about coming clean.

"I'm going with you," Tamara announced. "If you're going into enemy territory, I'm going, too."

"She's your grandmother. She's not the enemy!" Jessie barked. He was just as surprised as the others at his outburst. "I'm sorry, Tamara. I didn't mean to yell. But we cannot allow Delilah's issues to become ours and make us cynics." *Who am I kidding? I'm going over there because I'm already cynical. Father God, help me to rule over my tongue.*

"Don't worry about it, Daddy." Tamara was indeed hurt. In all her twenty-one years, her father had never raised his voice at her. Yet in the past several weeks since Delilah showed up, nothing was normal. Despite what her father said, she was beginning to not just dislike Delilah, she hated the woman. She couldn't wait to get Delilah told off. "I'll drive. You need to take better care of that hand."

Despite his protests, Tamara followed her father to the car and slid into the driver's side.

Since leaving Brooklyn, Tamara and Jessie hadn't said much to one another except to share information about the best route to Delilah's home and his cautioning that she slow down. And though she hadn't driven her father's car in quite some time, Tamara quickly found the "play" button on the CD changer. If they weren't going to share conversation, music was the next best thing.

From the very first eight bars Tamara knew she'd lost her battle plan to stay angry until they reached Delilah's house. She hadn't been prepared to hear the last album the church recorded earlier in the year. Her father hadn't removed it from the CD changer.

Jessie knew immediately how his daughter felt. He'd felt the same each time he played it. With a nervous laugh, he said, "Let's never forget that when your mama sang she took it straight to the Throne of Grace." He quickly turned his head away. *Speak to your daughter's heart, Cindy.* Jessie's eyes moistened but it wasn't the time to cry.

"I Go to the Rock" was not only one of her mother's favorite songs but Tamara's, too. Was her mother sending her a message? Tamara felt rebuked by the song's words and her mother's memory, and she didn't like it. Yet Cindy wasn't the type to get or stay mad. So Tamara kept on driving, a bit slower and a little less angry.

However, back inside the deacon's house anger was just getting started.

Sister Marty put away the ice pack. She looked over at the deacon. He looked as though the effects of the painkiller she'd given him were kicking in and the swelling was almost gone. So she leaned slightly over him. With her pocketbook swinging from side to side like a pitcher winding up, she eyeballed the deacon. The more she thought about the havoc he'd begun to play in her life, the angrier she became. She was like a dog with a fresh bone to pick and she was ready to gnaw.

Sister Marty opened her mouth and grinned. And that's when she took the first bite of his behind, knowing he could do nothing but listen. "When are you gonna come clean,

Thurgood? Huh? Besides being that woman's husband, are you Jessie's daddy?"

The deacon's head rolled over to the side. He imagined he was dreaming. What happened to the sweet thing who'd just bathed his lips?

Yet she'd thrown it out there.

"Say whaaa . . ." He couldn't answer without a prepared lie. *Damn Delilah.* His masculine Garden of Eden life was quickly disintegrating. Delilah had sowed seeds of discord at every turn. One thing he knew for certain, if he wanted to keep his garden peaceful, he'd need to retool his hoeing skills.

And he needed to do it quick because Marty now looked like the Queen of Winter, coldhearted.

Deacon Pillar managed to sit up on the sofa. "Listen, Marty," he said with a slight lisp. "I honestly can't say for sure."

"What does that mean?" She came over and took a seat. "Either you are or you're not. That routine you did the other night about you and Delilah getting married when Jessie was only two is not gonna work with me this time. What I should've asked was, when did you and Delilah hook up? Not when y'all got married."

"It was about a week after we met, honey. By the time I learned she was pregnant, we were head over heels in love. So we thought, anyway."

"So why didn't you marry her then?"

"Delilah wasn't sure if she could handle a baby. She'd even thought about an abortion." He grew more agitated as he tried to explain. "I don't believe in abortion!"

"Neither do I, Thurgood. What happened next?"

"I got arrested for some petty stuff. You don't need those details. By the time I got out of Upstate, she'd had the baby and Jessie was almost two."

"And you didn't marry her soon after you got out?"

"No. I didn't. It was another six months before I even

found them. By that time Delilah had moved on and hooked up with some pretty shady folks. . . ."

"More shady than you were?"

"That is possible, you know." She'd insulted him. And her pushy attitude was beginning to get on his nerves. He'd never seen this side of her. The deacon needed rest, not an inquisition. "The bottom line is that Delilah was about to get into some serious trouble when I finally found her and Jessie." The deacon's smile came easy and sudden. "I immediately fell in love with him. He was so handsome there was no way I'd believe he wasn't mine. . . ."

"Are you serious?"

"That's the way I felt back then. I'm not quite that conceited anymore. Anyway, she saw things my way and we ended up getting married on Jessie's second birthday."

"You really are serious." Sister Marty was about to set the deacon straight about his current level of conceit, but she needed him to stay focused.

"This pain is coming back," the deacon said quickly, "so here's the short version. Delilah had already started making quite a name for herself singing at different spots up in Harlem and eventually downtown, too. And just when it could've sent her star rising, she stabbed a gangster who tried to take what she didn't want to give. I'd just arrived at the club that night when it happened. I guess I was running on emotions because I got her out of there and we went and picked up Jessie. We left Harlem that same night and went up to Poughkeepsie, New York. Long story even shorter—the cops came knocking and I immediately took the rap. I couldn't have Delilah go to jail and I certainly wasn't able to take care of a two-year-old, and I already had a record. The one letter I received from her while I was doing her time said she'd placed Jessie in temporary foster care until she could get on her feet."

"My Lord, Thurgood. No wonder no one can stomach

the woman. She's a selfish—" Marty stopped herself. She was trying to reclaim her own status with the Kingdom. Her hands weren't all that clean, either.

Her outburst again caught him off guard. It was as though he'd begun to see Sister Marty with new eyes. Either that or his pain was returning with a vengeance.

He tried to rise off the sofa. "I sure hope I have some of those blue pills left."

"You take Viagra!" Sister Marty hadn't meant to shout at him. In all the time they'd been seeing one another, there was never an occasion to bring up sex.

"Hell no!" the deacon shot back out of embarrassment. "I was talking about Aleve. You're giving me a migraine."

Chapter 18

Jessie was impressed almost as soon as they'd turned onto Delilah's block. It was everything the deacon had described and more. Maples and hawthorn trees dotted the block, along with brightly colored annuals sprouting from well-kept lawns.

Tamara was still conflicted and she didn't know where to put her feelings of guilt. Every song her mother sang on the CD became a message meant especially for her.

Jessie, on the other hand, didn't hesitate once he parked the car. Instead of waiting for Tamara to get out, he walked around and opened the door for her. He was making his point because she'd insisted on coming. "Come on, Tamara, get out of the car."

Jessie rang Delilah's doorbell several times before he heard a shuffling sound.

If Delilah was shocked when she answered her door to the deacon earlier that day, she was now completely blown away to find Jessie and Tamara standing there. She asked them in and tried her best to hide her excitement. She'd been praying when she thought she heard the doorbell. *Thank you, Jehovah.*

"Sorry to just show up without a phone call first." That was the best apology he could give for coming without an invitation.

It's not like I came to you with an invite, either, Delilah thought. "You don't ever need one." She suddenly remembered what she'd done to the deacon. In case Jessie and Tamara had come to lay the blame at her feet, she needed them to see a different side of her. "Y'all follow me and come on in the living room. Please have a seat." Delilah slowly moved aside several of the Bibles on the arm of the recliner and offered that seat to Jessie. She was happy he'd at least seen that she could be a woman of peace despite all the butt kicking that happened in God's Word.

Tamara didn't sit down. She hadn't taken her eyes off Delilah's photo-decorated wall since she'd entered. She needed to see them up close. As she went from picture to picture, her plan to blast her grandmother again took a backseat.

Delilah couldn't suppress her smile as she watched Tamara examine the photographs. She didn't say anything when she saw Jessie pull one of the Bibles closer to him, either.

When Jessie saw how interested Tamara seemed in Delilah's photos, he mouthed to Delilah, "Can we go and talk?"

Jessie followed Delilah into her kitchen. Somehow he wasn't surprised to find it as spotless as the living room. But he did find it odd that someone who could wreak so much havoc could still have so much order about them.

Mother and son took a seat. Over glasses of lemonade they began to chat. But first Jessie prayed. That was something they had in common, although with different results.

While Jessie and Delilah were in the kitchen, Tamara studied the wall. Despite how Tamara felt personally about Delilah, all the star-studded, autographed photos on the wall caused her to admire the woman's gift. Even at her young age she knew about some of the jazz and rhythm and blues greats who grinned and laughed along with Delilah.

"How in the world did she hook up with Diana Ross? Delilah's wig is just as crazy as the Boss's." And there were others: Aretha, Smokey Robinson, Buddy Guy, and Shirley Caesar. It seemed Delilah had had a part in every music genre.

But then out of the corner of her eye Tamara saw the Roland E-600 keyboard and her heart pounded. A huge palm almost covered it. It was the exact keyboard she'd planned on asking her father to buy. She wanted to take it back to Juilliard when she returned in a few weeks.

"I wonder how Tamara's making out? Perhaps we shouldn't have left her alone." Delilah was sorry as soon as the words left her mouth. Hadn't she left him alone?

Although he hadn't said much to Delilah, she was glad the deacon had given her a heads-up. She might've had a chance to come up with a customized version of the truth, if Jessie had called first. But then she also appreciated that he'd laid aside his resentment and brought Tamara along.

"You want to know whether or not I want something from you. If you're willing to get to know me a little better, I think you'll see I don't." Delilah wanted to beg him to see her shame and her hurt from what she'd done. But she didn't.

Jessie smiled. "I think I know enough to believe God's Word when it says that I shouldn't hate my elderly mother. I'm also getting over the shell shock of seeing you, and my anger these days is tempered with a lot of prayer, but I need to know the truth."

"Jessie, I'll just have to show you that I've come to a place in my life where I've learned what's important. It certainly wasn't what I thought it was when I had you. I was young, ambitious, and selfish."

"For a few days now I've been consumed by this need to know the truth. And to be honest, even listening to what you're saying, I'm still not sure. I don't know if I'd want you in my life even if what you said was true. And that makes me even sadder and a little angry. But I still need to know who I am."

It wasn't exactly the answer she'd hoped to hear when she laid out her heart, but she'd take it for now. "Well, I can understand that," Delilah said softly, "but I need something, too."

Jessie's first thought was to say no to whatever she was going to ask, but then Tamara flew into the kitchen.

She was almost giddy, like when she was much younger and it was Christmas morning. "Daddy, I need to show you something."

"We're talking right now, Tamara."

"It'll only take a moment. I'm sure Delilah won't mind."

"Of course, I won't."

Neither Jessie nor Delilah spoke about it, but they knew the conversation was far from over.

By the time they got to the living room they found Tamara seated at the keyboard. "Like they used to say back in your day, this is the joint," Tamara said.

"Is that the Roland E-600?" Jessie walked over and with his good hand, he touched it. "This thing costs a lot of money."

"You'd better believe it." Delilah walked over to where Tamara sat and asked, "Do you play well?"

As soon as Tamara played one tune, Delilah got her to play another and then another.

Jessie watched their interaction. He still didn't fully trust Delilah when it came to his relationship with her, but he believed Delilah enjoyed listening to her talented granddaughter. He also believed Delilah would let Tamara play until the Rapture if it meant they didn't have to continue their discussion.

Tamara had played what he'd hoped was her last song. He was a patient man by nature, but his patience was growing short—and then Tamara asked Delilah the strangest question.

Tamara rose from the keyboard and took Delilah by the hand. Delilah didn't resist as Tamara led her to one of the pictures on the wall.

Tamara asked innocently, "Isn't this picture of the white man with the long blond hair, looking like Hulk Hogan, Croc Duggan?"

Jessie thought he saw a change in Delilah's cheerful mood.

"Yes, that's Croc." Delilah looked puzzled but she had to ask, "Tamara, do you know about the history of the music of the sixties?"

"Of course I do. Juilliard teaches a lot about music history—its good and its bad."

The answer threw Delilah a little bit. Obviously her granddaughter knew Croc Duggan's reputation as music management's biggest pimp, as well as the tainted reputations of the artists he represented. And there it was on her wall, for the world to see. Croc Duggan had his arms around her and it was obvious they were more than just manager and client. She'd never been ashamed of that picture. She was now.

"It's good to learn the positive and negative things about a business you're interested in. It can save you a lot of heartache."

"I guess there's not a lot you can advise me about because I don't intend to deal with the likes of a Croc. They might bite."

"I promise you. They will bite."

The granddaughter and the grandmother had a conversation that left little misunderstood.

"Am I missing something?" Jessie could feel the mood shift but couldn't figure out why. And he didn't have time to deal with it. "Delilah, can we continue?"

Delilah didn't want to ignore Jessie's question, but she wasn't quite finished with Tamara. "I'm really impressed with you. You sounded even better today than you did in the car. And you play excellently. You can take the keyboard with you, if you'd like."

"I'll have to think about it." Tamara wanted it and she was sure Delilah knew that. She might take her up on the offer, but she'd not make it easy for Delilah to buy her off.

Jessie knew Delilah was still stalling, but he wasn't going to let it go that easily. "Delilah, since you have such a great appreciation for all things harmonic, why not come with us to New Hope on Monday evening? There will be choirs rehearsing." He could wait a day or two more.

"Daddy . . ." Tamara appreciated her grandmother's music history, too, but to ask her to New Hope? She was going to say something more but she didn't. She'd had enough rebukes for one day.

"You want me to come to church with you? Why?"

"Can you give me a good reason why not?"

Long after Jessie and Tamara had left, Delilah still couldn't think of a valid reason not to go to church with them. She still appreciated listening to the choir as an outsider, parked outside the church. She'd never be able to explain it so they'd understand. And she didn't dare call the deacon so he could help, especially after she'd punched him in the mouth. She was on her own. Hadn't she prayed and asked Jehovah to help her get her family back? She had. And there she was, still looking for an excuse or a way out of telling Jessie the truth about her and the deacon; and that would truly lead up to the big question. She needed more time.

Still without a car the next day, Delilah prayed, watched religious shows on television, and then prayed some more that Jehovah would remove her own bitter cup.

And still Monday arrived.

Chapter 19

Just like Delilah, Tamara hadn't come up with a valid reason to keep her grandmother from attending the choir rehearsal with them, either. One thing was for certain—since visiting Delilah's home, Tamara had grown as conflicted as her father. There were things she'd learned to admire about Delilah, but there were also things to resent. There wasn't room for both emotions. Of course, in the end there was Sister Marty. At least that relationship was consistent.

When the time came, it was Tamara who once again drove to Delilah's house. Jessie had an emergency meeting and had left earlier. So she was glad the deacon's lips were back to normal. He didn't seem to harbor any resentment when she told him that her father had invited Delilah to church, although she'd not shared that with Sister Marty. In fact, he'd insisted on riding along with her to pick up Delilah. When they arrived in Garden City and Delilah came out, he held the door open so she could get into the backseat.

All during the drive from Delilah's house to the church, Tamara kept looking into her rearview mirror at Delilah. And every time she did, she found Delilah staring right back. Twice Tamara almost ran a light trying to rid the feeling of impending doom from her mind. *At least Delilah dressed properly,* Tamara thought. *Hussy chic is not a good church look.* It seemed the more she could find amusing about Delilah the more she relaxed.

Yet almost as soon as Tamara pulled into the number two parking lot at New Hope Assembly, a feeling of dread revisited. Tamara wished she could've put the car in reverse. Although earlier she'd made Delilah promise not to say anything about being her grandmother, Tamara didn't trust her.

"Okay, we're here," Deacon Pillar announced. "Are we all in one accord?"

"I didn't know this car was an Accord." Delilah chuckled and looked out the window to keep her nervousness from taking over. "I thought it was a Solaris."

"Good one, Dee Dee."

Delilah knew what the deacon meant. And it'd happened just the way she knew it would. She didn't want to actually go inside. She sat for a moment with one finger tapping the side of her head. "Just wait a moment, Thurgood. What's your rush? We still got another ten minutes before the rehearsal begins."

Without saying a word aloud, the way the deacon got out and slammed the car door said it all. He adjusted one of his suspenders, which had started to slide off one bony shoulder. With an extra little something in his step he held his head high and started to walk away. It was a walk less like John Wayne's and more like a penguin.

"Deacon Pillar," Tamara called out as she sprang from the driver's side. She'd turned off the engine but hadn't taken the keys out of the ignition. She had to almost sprint to catch up with him. "Hold up."

The deacon stopped long enough for Tamara to catch up. "Just follow my lead, baby girl." Never once did he act as though they'd just left Delilah still seated inside the car.

Tamara didn't say a word and did as the deacon asked. She shifted her purse from one hand to the other and got in step. They looked straight ahead and suddenly started laughing like they didn't have a care in this muddled world of Delilah's.

Watching the deacon and Tamara walk away didn't sit well with Delilah as she sat alone inside the hot car. They looked too giddy for her taste. She was starting to get in a bad mood.

The sounds of birds chirping drew her attention. She turned her head and watched them fly from branch to branch. And that's when a faint smile came over her face, then disappeared just as quick.

The sounds of the birds reminded her of the first time she'd been outside New Hope Assembly Church. It was on a visit back to New York that she'd not told anyone about. The deacon and Tamara would never understand what she was feeling. A church bell rang out and its clanging caused another memory.

However, this time what she remembered about New Hope was different than when weeks ago the deacon had surprised her. It was a time about which she could tell neither Jessie, the deacon, nor Tamara. Another event stuffed away in her overfilled closet of secrets.

It was 1988. Even with being the mother of a twenty-something-year-old, she'd maintained her hourglass shape, which made her look years younger.

Dressed in a yellow, formfitting, high-slit floral dress with matching hat and shoes, she'd sat in the church's parking lot wearing wide sunglasses that covered most of her face. And yet for all the color-coordinated dress and accessories, Delilah still looked like a lonely movie star as she sat inside a borrowed tan and black 1985 Cadillac.

Within moments of her arrival, she saw them. She hadn't seen her son, Jessie, in years; and when she'd seen him even back then she hadn't dared approach him. She'd preferred to watch him play foot-ball with some other boys in the school yard.

But she was still his mother, and although he was a young teenager and had filled out and wore a helmet, Delilah had still known her son.

But on this particular day in 1988, Delilah closely watched a grown-up Jessie. He was dressed in a black suit, a white shirt, and a black, skinny tie. His dark shoes shimmered in the sun. That made Delilah smile, knowing well-polished shoes spoke well of a man.

And then she saw Cindy. Cindy was very pretty in the face—a bit heavier than Delilah would've wanted for her son, but she looked fabulous in her crème-colored matching hat and flowing dress. And even from that distance she could see the love between them. How-ever, what really tugged at Delilah's heart and brought tears to her eyes was the little girl Jessie carried.

The baby was nestled in the fold of Jessie's arm, safe and secure. Jessie had his head held high as he carried his precious treasure. And the baby's long, brown, curly hair spilled over and onto his jacket sleeve. Using the binoculars she'd brought along, Delilah couldn't see the child's face or even tell whether the white christening dress was long or short, but it didn't matter. The picture she held in her hands, cut from the local newspaper announcement, was enough. The little girl named Tamara was absolutely beautiful. How could she not be?

Delilah was still deep in thought, and at first it wasn't clear whether she'd heard the strong rap on the car's window.

"I see you found your way to my church."

To the outside world as well as inside the church, Sister Marty always appeared shy and not up to any confrontation. And even on that hot day it was no different. She looked harmless enough, dressed in her choir's summer wear—a long, pale blue dress with a crocheted white cap. It was a complete turnaround from the spotless white uniform she'd worn earlier for work.

However, Delilah dismissed the unwanted interruption

by laying her head against the backseat and continuing to daydream.

Marty didn't like being ignored. So she rapped on the car window again and repeated, "I see you made it to the church."

This time, Delilah answered. "Say what . . ." She figured she must've gotten overheated and the woman was just her imagination. Delilah looked from side to side. She was still alone in the car. Neither Tamara nor the deacon had returned to see if she was okay.

Sister Marty's face, distorted by the glare from the sun, slowly came into focus. Immediately it caused a shift in Delilah's already salty attitude. "Did you think or wish I wouldn't make it here?" Delilah replied while she felt around inside her purse for her sunglasses. "I'll be just fine. I'm here for the rehearsal, so you can go on your way."

Sister Marty didn't respond right away; instead she stared at Delilah for another moment and finally replied, "Have it your way."

Sister Marty had turned to walk away when she pivoted suddenly and turned back to Delilah. "You know the Word of God says that in order for us to be known as a friend that we must first show ourselves to be friendly."

"Jehovah God is our best friend." Delilah didn't know and really didn't care about Marty's intentions. "What's your point?"

"My point is that I can be a good friend or I can come at you from another direction." She stopped to let the words settle onto Delilah and added as she turned to walk away, "It's entirely up to you, Mrs. Pillar, or whatever you care to call yourself. I really don't care about your marital status."

Sister Marty didn't wait for Delilah's response. She didn't have to. She was certain Delilah had understood that it wasn't all about the deacon. It was about much more. Neither was about to allow any claim jumping.

Delilah glared at Marty's back as the woman walked away from the car. Delilah wasn't stupid. This woman, church woman or not, was too much like her.

Was that why the deacon had reached out to Sister Marty? But why continue with an imitation when the real thing was now available?

The brief encounter with Marty Madison had only caused Delilah to dig in deeper. At that moment, she had never wanted the deacon more than when she thought Marty wanted him, too. And there wasn't enough of his lanky butt to share, particularly since that same woman was standing between her and her son. Delilah smiled and thought, *I swear it ain't nothing no worse than church trash that's willing to fight over a married man.*

The deacon had a change of mind. He'd returned and found Delilah still seated in the backseat where he'd left her, but this time she was smiling. The deacon looked around to see if there was someone who could've put the smile on her face. He saw no one.

"Dee Dee," the deacon said through the open window, "what's wrong with you?"

"Not a thing, Thurgood. I'm doing just fine. Thanks for caring enough to come back and see about me."

The deacon thought for a second before answering and setting her straight, but decided against it. There was something about Delilah sitting in the backseat of the car, smiling like the angel she wasn't, that disturbed him. He would never deny her a moment of happiness, but at that moment there was something inappropriate about it.

"Are you coming inside?" The deacon slowly opened the door, all the while wondering if it wouldn't be better if he just sat outside the church with her.

"Sure, why not?" Delilah answered as she pointed to the keys hanging from the ignition. "You might have to start this car up so I can raise this automatic window, unless you think folks inside the church won't break into Tamara's ride."

Without saying a word to defend or agree with what Delilah said about the church members, the deacon did what was necessary to secure all the car's windows and helped Delilah from the car.

Together they walked toward the church. Even though the door was only yards away, the closer they came, the more Delilah's usually proud walk weakened. It was to the point where he now almost dragged her toward the church.

The deacon stopped abruptly. "Okay, Dee Dee. What's wrong now? Why does it seem like you've turned into deadweight?"

"It must be this heat." Delilah began to fan herself with her purse. "I feel like I'm about to pass out."

Deacon Pillar shook his head and let her go. As usual he threw up his hands in surrender. "And yet, you sat in that hot car without the air-conditioning running."

Deacon Pillar stepped back and then quickly came within a few inches of Delilah's face. "You know what, Delilah. If you don't want to go inside, I'll take you back to the car."

"Thank you, Thurgood. I knew you'd understand." She quickly turned to head back toward the car.

The sight of Delilah walking off lit the deacon's short fuse. "Let me tell you what I actually do understand, Dee Dee."

Delilah didn't respond immediately, but she did stop walking away. She turned around to face the deacon. This time she had both hands on her hips. And then she extended one leg in front as though she was prepared to fight him again, but instead she suddenly crossed her arms and waited for him to speak.

And that's when the deacon released all he'd held since they reconnected. His anger felt like the weight of an elephant on his chest. Right there in the church's parking lot, in the presence of God and whoever listened, he prepared to spew all his hellish feelings. He was about to show Delilah a side of him she'd never seen nor heard. And when he'd finished, then he'd race to the nearest altar for forgiveness.

"You were about to say something?"

"Don't push me, heffa."

"Say wha—"

"Just shut up! I've not understood a lot since you came barreling back into my life like bad credit. But I do understand that you're throwing a major monkey wrench into plans I've made for my senior years."

Delilah's fist started to ball. And the action hadn't gone unnoticed by the deacon.

"I hope you try it. You got away with it the first couple of times. Now I've never hit a woman, unnecessarily, in my life, but there's always a first time." He waited only a second to see what she'd do and it was much longer than he wanted to wait. "I'm beginning to understand a lot just standing out here in this hot sun. I understand that I haven't attended church as regularly as is my habit in the last few weeks. I understand that a woman who left years ago and ripped my heart out is back, and brought her old funky habits with her. You take me to the edge and then you push me just enough to almost fall over, and then you snatch me back."

"Who are you yelling at?"

The deacon grabbed his head in his hands and lashed out even more. "I'm yelling at your funky arse because I ain't yo' damn yo-yo!"

The deacon must have really been into his angry sermonizing or brutal testifying, because by the time he finished fussing and using improper English and looked around, Delilah had walked away and was leaning against the car looking as though he'd punched her in the gut with a wrecking ball. Again, a look of defeat came upon his face.

From a distance Delilah watched the deacon with a confused look. What had she done? So what if she came to church and then changed her mind about going inside? Wasn't that a feminine prerogative? Where was the threat of violence against her coming from?

But whether she looked spanked like a little child or not, this time the deacon was not willing to give in to Delilah's feminine wiles.

The feeling of resentment he'd finally acknowledged and the vise grip Sister Marty had recently placed him into with her time limits and such, it went against all he held holy; and he'd blamed it all on Delilah's demons that started the bitterness ball rolling. All he'd ever preached and testified or witnessed to others—telling them nonstop to not think lesser of themselves than God does—soured. Delilah's sudden appearance had caused Jessie's unbearable pain and Tamara's total confusion.

His heart felt as though it pushed through his chest as he pounded it in anger. "What do you want from me, Dee Dee?" With determination, and despite several of the church members now looking on, the deacon hurried on toward Delilah. He was now on the verge of tears and his lack of decorum was on full display. "Where can I go to get away from you?"

Just as he neared Delilah, and before she could finally answer to his cold, hard facts, they heard a voice sing out. The sound stopped them cold.

It took her a moment, but Delilah rose slowly from off the hood of the car where she'd finally rested. She knew it had to be Tamara.

Although the deacon had heard Tamara's gifted voice on many occasions, there was something different this time. It was still spiritual and yet a bit sad; Tamara was singing a prayer and he knew it. She was singing Cindy's song, "I Go to the Rock."

And just for that moment in time, just long enough for

Tamara to finish her prayerful song of praise to God, Delilah and Deacon Pillar stood quiet and reverent.

Note for note, Tamara's soulful melody crept upon them. Their common love for her allowed a quiet peace to pick the lock to their stubborn hearts. Captured in that moment were unfulfilled promises they'd made decades ago, and it didn't matter.

From inside the church Tamara would never know how much she'd shamed them.

"I'm sorry, Thurgood. I never meant to bring that much pain back into your life."

"I know, Delilah Pillar." The deacon hadn't called her that for quite some time and the absurdity of it caused him to smile.

"You called me Delilah Pillar?"

"How about that." The deacon's laughter came easily and was welcome. "Calling you Delilah Pillar and me going off like that—I felt almost like I'd taken an enema." He stopped and patted his back pocket. "Gal, I feel relieved and pounds of frustration lighter."

"You sure have a romantic way of expressing yourself."

"I've always had a way with words. You should know that."

"So what are we going to do now?"

"Well, I'm sure some of these church gawkers who are still peeping at us and trying to act like they're not can't wait for us to go inside."

"I haven't changed my mind about not going inside. In fact, believe it or not, I'm a bit embarrassed. Aren't you?"

"Dee Dee, right now I've got so many emotions running through me I feel like I'd only bring spiritual confusion to Tamara's rehearsal. I certainly don't want to face Jessie right now. He's in the board room in a meeting."

Delilah nodded in agreement. "So then it's settled. We won't bring any more confusion to Tamara's rehearsal. But we can't just leave and not let her know what's going on."

"That wouldn't be right, so I'll call her."

The deacon called Tamara on her cell phone. He'd been right when he'd figured Tamara would turn it off during a rehearsal. So the deacon left a message. "Hey, baby girl, something's come up and I need to take your grandmother to handle some important business. Let your father know, too. We'll take a cab."

Of course, he wasn't about to leave a message that it was her beautiful voice that had kept him from doing another bit in jail. He'd never tell Tamara that he'd been about to beat her grandmother to a pulp.

"We still have the keys. How's she gonna drive?"

"Jessie keeps a spare with him. They'll be okay. Are you hungry?" Deacon Pillar asked. He thought he'd take Delilah somewhere quiet and they could talk. They might as well eat, too.

Delilah nodded her consent. "Are you paying?"

"Do you ever pay?"

They laughed as they walked to a nearby taxi stand where they grabbed a taxi and headed toward a Boulder Creek Steakhouse in the Gateway section of Brooklyn. It wasn't too far from the church, but they weren't going to walk it.

It was their second try at eating in a restaurant since the Blue Fish fiasco. This time it was different, except the deacon was still dressed like Christmas and Easter had collided with Halloween. They ordered their food and ate like two old folks with some sense. The deacon chewed a little slower because his mouth was a little sore. When they finished, they put their cards on the table.

"Thurgood," Delilah said, "we've got to come clean. I saw how much hurt Jessie is in. It's not right what we're doing."

"At least we agree about that." Deacon Pillar stopped and grabbed a toothpick from his shirt pocket. He took a moment to yank out a piece of steak before he continued. "What we have to do is find a way to break it so there's the least amount of collateral damage as well."

"Collateral damage—what do you mean?" Delilah wasn't too certain where he was going with his thoughts. "Explain it."

"I'm talking about the pain it's going to cause the others involved. Telling Jessie that you and I are married and that I'm his daddy . . ." The deacon winked, but he was serious when he added, "We did agree that I'm his daddy, right?"

Delilah almost broke her silverware in half. But she was cool. "Yes, Thur-no-good, we agree on that."

"That's good, because that means that I'm also Tamara's grandfather. I hope baby girl can forgive me. And then there's Marty. . . ."

"What about Marty?" Delilah let the venom drape each word.

"No matter how you feel about her," the deacon continued, "she loves them, too."

"She's not going to be hurt by this. What's she gonna lose—bragging rights?"

As if a lightbulb had gone off in her head, Delilah folded her hands and pointed at the deacon. "You haven't told her that Jessie's your son? I thought you two were so chummy, and almost ready to race down the wedding aisle once you got divorced."

"Can I get something else for you?" the waiter interrupted, asking in such a manner as to let them know that there were others waiting for the table. Delilah and Deacon Pillar didn't argue. He paid the bill. They caught another cab and went at it, back and forth, all the way to his apartment.

By early evening Delilah and the deacon hadn't reached

an agreement on how to handle their situation, but they were still at it. Only they weren't going at it the way Delilah had wanted, so she could finally get the upper hand by leading him around by his "old reliable," as he called it.

Even the heat from the blazing sun filtering through the venetian blinds in the deacon's bedroom couldn't compete with the heat Delilah gave off.

She sat, now fully dressed, on the edge of the bed. "Thurno-good Pillar," Delilah hissed, "I can't believe this."

"I'm sorry, Dee Dee." He'd come to apologize so often where she was concerned until he looked like a small child placed on punishment. He wanted to toss his failures out onto the sidewalk as he stood by the window. "I didn't plan for this to not happen."

"Apparently you did. Are you trying to tell me that you can't rise to the occasion? Is it because you go to church?"

"Hold your tongue, woman." He wasn't going to take another slap at his manhood. The deacon raced across the room to where Delilah sat. "Since you've been back, you saw for yourself that time we danced at your place, that I can still raise this soldier's flag."

"Well, then I guess I should assume that you couldn't complete the mission 'cause you don't have protection nowhere in this place."

She searched the deacon's face for a hint of guilt or an idea that she'd snooped through his medicine cabinet earlier while he'd taken a quick power nap. Instead, he acted like he didn't have a clue.

So Delilah tossed him another hint. "Why do you have a rubbers box in your medicine cabinet and yet earlier, you old fake, you pretended you didn't have any?"

"Condoms, Dee Dee. They're called condoms. With all the folks I know our age that's got that HIV, you think I sit up and just think only about sex? And besides, Miss Snoop, I keep money in that box."

"Say what?"

"That's right," the deacon replied, "I'm hoping most crooks, like you, will assume it's a condom box if they try and rob me. Nine out of ten they won't snatch a condom box."

"Whatever, Thurgood." Delilah turned away from him and added, "You ain't nothing but a tease. Ain't nothing worse than a supposed-to-be-all-that church fella that won't take care of his husbandly duties."

"Stop rewriting history, Delilah Dupree Jewel." The deacon bent over and turned Delilah back around by her shoulders before adding to her list of last names. "Pillar."

"Just shut up, Thurgood. For God's sake, just shut up."

"You're so ungrateful, Delilah. You were back then and I married you anyhow, and you still are now."

"Who's ungrateful?" Delilah hissed. "I gave you everything I had back then and you threw it away."

Just that quick she was in revision mode, and the deacon would not let it go. "How in the hell did I throw it away, Dee Dee? I married you, and then I went to prison so you wouldn't have to leave Jessie."

"You could've pled down, Pillar. You didn't have to accept the first sentence they offered you and leave me alone."

"Woman, are you listening to yourself? A plea down? How in the world was a black man supposed to plea down facing some white injustice?"

The deacon could feel his blood pressure rise. At a moment like this he needed to pray just about as much as he needed to get everything off his chest. Once more she'd brought him to the brink of laying his Christianity aside, but this time he wasn't trying to step back until he'd had his say again.

"Delilah, I'm telling you once more: You were supposed to stay with that boy. If you weren't gonna do it, then you should've told me. I would've kept Jessie and you could've gone to prison like you should have in the beginning."

"But you were my husband. You shouldn't have left me."

"And just like I said before, I was Jessie's daddy, too! Wasn't I supposed to protect him?"

Chapter 20

A little earlier Tamara, as usual, felt the pangs of hunger. She wasn't about to try cooking and burn down the house for real. The choir rehearsal had been both joy and pain. She'd found so much comfort when she'd sung her mother's favorite song. For a brief moment during the rehearsal, she could almost hear Cindy harmonizing along with her. In her mind, she'd pictured her mother performing in the background, like Nat King Cole had in his daughter Natalie's video.

Right now she wanted to keep that feeling for as long as she could, so she tried not to dwell on her hunger pangs. Tamara read through the latest issues of *Jet* and *Sister 2 Sister* magazines, while she waited for her father to return from the pizza shop. *How long could it take to pick up a pizza?*

She could've probably gone upstairs and waited around with the deacon, but she'd already heard Delilah's irritating voice earlier. With Delilah in the mix, that was out of the question. Delilah still brought out the worst in her, and she couldn't allow that to happen; not on this day. And if she knew anything, she knew God wouldn't be pleased with her feeling like that.

And then she heard them arguing upstairs. She knew better than to eavesdrop, but they were so loud. She tiptoed up the steps and barely laid her ear against the door when she heard their confessions; truths that made her head swim and her feet buckle. *"But you were my husband. You shouldn't have left me."* She'd clearly heard Delilah whine and make the accusation. But what did Delilah mean by it? *Protection, what protection? Husband, whose husband?* There was no one other than Delilah and the deacon inside. She was certain of it. But the deacon, what was he talking about? *"I was Jessie's daddy, too! Wasn't I supposed to protect him?"* he'd said. Those words and that declaration—they were his words. She'd know his voice anywhere.

Question upon question clawed at her. Her mind felt like it was in a vise and the deacon and Delilah kept tightening it.

There was only one conclusion she could think of. If Deacon Pillar and Delilah were married, was Deacon Pillar really her grandfather? A man who'd lived over their heads and hovered over her and her father. An old man so sweet and so loving, and yet wouldn't he say something if what she suspected was true? But he'd never said a word. A real grandparent wouldn't do that.

It was just another blow she didn't need. They must've been talking about something or someone else. Tamara decided to return to the tranquility of her apartment. She'd probably never know why she made the next move, but she did. At the same time she turned to tiptoe down the stairs, she tried to pull up the halter strap that'd slipped off her shoulder. She misjudged her step and tumbled down the stairs. In an instant she'd twisted one foot. "Ow!"

Her scream brought the deacon and Delilah spilling out into the hallway. They almost tripped up one another as they scrambled down the stairs to reach her.

Both Deacon Pillar and Delilah stood over her with obvious looks of panic fixed upon their faces. Before Tamara could gather her wits and pull herself to her feet, they'd both extended their hands to help her.

"Baby girl." The deacon's reach was longer than Delilah's and he had no problem pushing her hand aside. "What happened?" he asked as he helped a reluctant Tamara to rise.

"Sweetie, you scared us." Not one to rattle because she'd heard a scream, Delilah looked like a pop-up toy as she hopped from one foot to the other. Ignoring the deacon's slight, she rushed around him and stood by Tamara's side and asked, "Are you alright?"

"I'm fine," Tamara snapped. As much pain as she was in at that moment, she showed she was truly Delilah Dupree Jewel's granddaughter: stubborn as a mule and in no mood to forgive. She was determined not to have Delilah standing any closer than necessary. As much as she didn't really want to do it, she quickly shoved the deacon's hand aside. "I don't need no help! I can make it inside by myself."

"Baby girl." He backed off as she requested and watched her wince in pain. It took all he had, but he exhaled and said softly, "I think you hurt your foot."

Deacon Pillar found strength he didn't know he had. Even with an arthritic back and knees to match, he took the same hand she had used to swat at him, and gently pulled her to him. He then lifted Tamara off the ground. He carried her inside as though she were a feather.

Where was all that strength before? Delilah thought. But the jealous thought was fleeting because she truly was concerned about Tamara.

"Dee Dee," the deacon barked. "Woman, don't just stand there like a statue. Make yourself useful and run some warm water in the bathtub or in a pail." He swung his head toward the hallway and hissed, "It would be the room that has a toilet in it. It's a couple of doors down on the left."

Delilah was about to correct the deacon's attitude. But the sight of him showing so much tenderness with Tamara stopped her cold. She turned her head away so no one could see the pain that lately had repeatedly almost caused her to double over.

With her head drooping slightly, she sadly recalled how Deacon Pillar had once acted that same way with Jessie when Jessie was a toddler. Before a tear could fall from Jessie's eyes, the deacon would smile and say with such confidence, *Come here, little man. Let me take care of that.*

And whatever "that" was, the deacon handled it with such care, while at the same time showing the young boy how a man should react.

The memory of lost times opened the floodgate to more self-recrimination. *What mother would've done what she had? What mother would've stayed away from her child and husband without explanation, and for so many years? I don't see how I can expect Jehovah God to forgive me. I truly messed up.*

The deacon and Tamara never saw Delilah's tears. They didn't notice the way her shoulders slouched, making her appear even shorter than she was as she left to get the water for Tamara's foot.

Having dispensed Delilah to get the water, the deacon turned his attention fully upon Tamara. He laid her gently onto the couch and asked, "Baby girl, do you have any Epsom salts?"

"Yes, it's in the bathroom cabinet under the sink." The pain in her foot quickly outweighed her anger toward the deacon, although she'd certainly make sure it was temporary.

"Dee Dee, look under the sink when you find the bathroom," the deacon yelled. "There's some Epsom salts. Bring it back with you, unless you know how to pour it into the water without messing that up."

Deacon Pillar turned back to face Tamara. Gentleness replaced his annoyance with Delilah. "Tamara," the deacon said softly, "baby girl, you came upstairs for a reason. What did you want?"

Tamara tried to blink back emotional and physical tears. She couldn't. Her breathing came in spurts but she managed to answer, "I came upstairs because I heard you and Delilah arguing."

"Oh my goodness"—the deacon slapped one thigh—"I forgot how voices carry in this house."

It was only a second, but to Tamara time suddenly stood still. It was just enough time to allow her anger to return full blast.

"That's not all you forgot."

He tried to scratch a patch of loose conk, as though it would kick-start his memory. "I'm pretty sure it was—"

"You also forgot to tell me that you were Delilah's husband and you're my grandfather."

Her revelation sucked the air from the room.

And for the first time in quite some time, Deacon Pillar had no words of comfort, or wisdom, or any other snappy reply. He dropped his hands and his head. He couldn't stop the bombshell if he'd wanted to.

He needed Tamara and so he pulled her to him. The deacon didn't care if she slapped him silly or shot him dead.

Tamara didn't resist. She couldn't.

He held and rocked her as though she were a newborn. "I'm so sorry, baby girl. I'm so sorry. When Dee Dee comes back in the room, we'll try and explain things to you."

Tamara quickly withdrew from the deacon's arms. "Do we have to include her?" Her emotions ricocheted. Inwardly she was still angry, but at the same time, and in that moment, she was somewhat happy. She'd always loved the deacon anyhow.

How her father would feel was another matter. That was a bridge to cross later.

As soon as Delilah entered the room and saw Tamara nestled in the deacon's arms, she beamed. She'd recovered while out of the room; delighted she could almost feel the peace in the room despite the chaos that'd come just before it.

"You two look cozy. The water's running in a small vat I found, and I've poured the Epsom salts in it and set it in the tub." She stopped and for a moment she thought she saw the smile slide from Tamara's face, replaced with a scowl. "What did I miss?"

"Only twenty-one years of my life," Tamara said as she slid farther onto the couch. She pointed to the deacon. "And even more years of being with your husband standing here."

"Damn it, Pillar, you can't keep nothing."

"Don't blame the deacon," Tamara snapped. "I overheard it from your own lying lips."

Delilah's mind was a web of confusion; even more so than ever before. Words seemed to fly around inside her brain, each word crashing into another, and none of them making their way to her mouth. So Delilah did what she always did when confronted with the truth. She fled.

Chapter 21

It was a short time later when Delilah, now in the deacon's kitchen, heard the deacon finally return to his apartment.

"Delilah," he called out as he entered, "I'm back, and Jessie's with Tamara."

It really didn't matter. By that time she'd cried until her insides felt like a slinky toy—all turned in and out. To take her mind off the current mess, she'd also washed the few dishes in the sink. Angry, with indifference she'd already begun to mop the small kitchen floor without bothering to sweep it first.

"Delilah." Against all reason the deacon's voice almost choked with sympathy for her. She alone was catching the hell, but he'd been in the playing field, too.

But he didn't know what to do. How could he make up to Delilah for Tamara's caustic words and coldness?

He surveyed her handiwork. "You've been through a lot in the last few days. We both have, but you need to rest and you certainly didn't have to do any housework. I could've done it like I've been doing it. . . ."

"Look, Thurgood," Delilah replied as she went over and looked out from what was becoming her favorite spot—the front window. "It's getting late in the evening and too late for me to make amends to you or Jessie, and especially Tamara." She spun around and pointed toward the floor. "And I didn't spill nothing. So allow me to mop the damn floor in peace." Once again, Delilah's nasty attitude shut off the deacon's sympathy valve.

"That's fine with me! You've spilled enough for one day." He was about to say something more but didn't. Instead the deacon went over and stuck his head out the door as if he was listening for something. "I don't hear anything coming from either Jessie or Tamara. She told me before he came home that she wasn't going to say anything to Jessie before we did. But she's still pretty pissed off. When I left she was resting, and Jessie was giving her some pizza to eat. Her foot is okay and it'll be better in no time—"

"Can you just take me home?" Delilah felt twice her age. She was more confused now than before. When she got a chance to pray again, she'd ask Jehovah why He was putting her through more than she felt was necessary.

"I don't want to take you home, Dee Dee."

"Thurgood, I don't have the time or the strength. I just want to lie down and sleep until the real sleep catches up with me."

Deacon Pillar, the human Ping-Pong ball, pulled his wife to his side. "Stay here tonight, Dee Dee. I'm tired, too, and I'm putting an end to all of this real soon."

"You mean you're really not going to take me home?"

"No, I'm not taking you home."

"It's not all that late, Thurgood. It can't be no more than about nine o'clock." She pointed to his answering machine. "Oh, by the way, that she-demon in a church hat's been calling for you. You sure you don't need to get rid of me tonight so you don't have to explain our non–afternoon delight?"

"Heavenly Father"—the deacon ignored Delilah, preferring to explain his case to God instead—"Lord, I'm so tired of these women trying to run my life—" Deacon Pillar cut his prayer short. "I'm really tired, so you just stay here. Or you can go downstairs and see if your loving son and granddaughter wanna take your cute little tush back to Garden City. Which is it?"

Delilah showed she'd accepted defeat by sitting down on the sofa and crossing her legs. "Whatever, Thurgood."

"Then let's order in something to eat. We'll watch a movie on television, or I've got some real good DVDs, too."

After placing an order with his favorite Pizza Hut restaurant, the deacon turned on the television.

"Well now, what do you know about this? It's one of my favorite movies playing." The deacon turned up the sound and without asking Delilah if it was what she'd like to see, he lay back on the sofa.

"*Harlem Nights* is one of my all-time favorite movies, Dee Dee."

"It's mine, too." Delilah's eyes grew wide. She laughed at the irony of his movie choice and the scene displayed on the television.

"Oh boy," the deacon laughed, "watch how Della Reese knocks Eddie Murphy into next week."

"I don't hafta watch her," Delilah quipped. "I taught her how to do it."

The deacon was about to say something when he noticed that Delilah wasn't laughing at the absurdity of her claim. And some of the numbness returned in his lower lip.

"I never could understand why they didn't at least give me a little credit, since they based that Sunshine character on me, too." Delilah slouched back farther on the sofa. "Come to think of it, Redd Foxx left this planet owing me dinner. . . ."

The frown that grew upon her face caused him to wonder how often her mind wandered into fantasyland. It seemed to leave at will, and a lot more often these days. Just in case it was true, he also decided to remove *Harlem Nights* from his list of favorite movies.

But that was Delilah. Sometimes, with just one look, she could mind-cripple the old deacon into walking on a tightrope over a pool of gasoline holding a lit match. And she'd convince him it was safe to do so.

Chapter 22

The next morning the telephone rang, waking up the deacon and Delilah. They'd dozed off the night before on the couch, and were still there when the sound woke them.

"Can you come downstairs, Deacon?"

"Are you alright, Tamara?"

"Yes, Daddy went to have that cast removed today, and I want to talk to you before he gets back home."

"Okay, baby girl. I'll be right there. Just let me wake Delilah and let her know where I am."

"Never mind, just bring her, too."

The door to Tamara's living room was already open, so the deacon and Delilah filed through with the deacon leading.

Tamara was on the phone. She motioned for them to take a seat as she hung up.

"That was Sister Marty," Tamara said, almost too happy about it. "She's got to work overtime, but she's going to come over after. She also said don't forget you promised to escort her to the Family and Friends Day celebration next week."

"Baby girl," Deacon Pillar scolded, "was it necessary to relay that particular message at this particular moment?"

Delilah was about to say something, but Tamara's words stopped her cold.

"No, I guess it really wasn't. But I don't know how to feel, how to think. It's too much for me right now." Tamara stopped and looked straight at Delilah. "And to be honest, Sister Marty didn't say that. I'm sorry for the lie. That was the cable company."

"I'm sorry, too, Tamara," Delilah said softly. "All I've done since I've come back is to bring more worry for you and Jessie. I never meant to do that."

"I didn't think you did it on purpose," Tamara conceded, "but mama's only been gone a few months." She stopped and looked at the wedding picture of her parents. "Now suddenly I've got a grandmother who came barging into our lives, where she wasn't wanted, and loaded with all kinds of drama." Tamara stopped and pointed a finger toward the deacon. "And a grandfather who's been in my life for the last four years, pretending he's somebody else." Tamara shook her head. "How am I supposed to keep from telling Daddy his mama's married to his real daddy, who's been living upstairs all these years?"

While Tamara laid open her feelings, it was all Delilah could do not to run over and just hold her. But she couldn't worry about her own sudden maternal feelings, if indeed that's what they were. At that moment, it was all about Tamara. And she doubted if Tamara wanted her touch.

"I'm truly sorry, Tamara." Delilah was stuck on repeating *sorry*. She couldn't trust herself to say anything beyond that.

"Save it. Please let me finish." Tamara spoke in a way that dismissed any more apologies that Delilah might be about to make. "So now, just when I think I can get a break from all this insanity, I find out somebody signed me up to cook about seventy-eleven dishes to bring to the Family and Friends Day. Even with Daddy's cast removed, he still won't be able to cook. He may not be able to even play his guitar when we sing."

"I'm sorry. . . ." Delilah was still stuck on that word.

"You just oughta be sorry. Now I got to do something desperate."

"Baby girl, don't let desperation drive you to do anything. You see what happened when your grandmother was desperate."

"I married your skinny wannabe-a-thug arse! That's what happened."

Tamara limped from the couch as best she could. She swung a finger at the both of them. "Look, Bonita and G-Clyde. Hush up!"

Tamara leaned forward and raised her voice. She continued to speak as though she were the adult in charge. She pointed to an opening in the living room ceiling. "You think I can't hear you two through the living room vent? *Harlem Nights,* my foot."

Both the deacon and Delilah looked sheepish as they glanced upwards toward the vent.

Tamara turned toward Delilah and pointed. "For someone who's so short and skinny, you sure have a loud mouth and an even bigger imagination. You taught Della Reese how to knock someone out? Please. If you're good at knocking folks out, then why didn't you knock out Croc Duggan before he turned you out?"

The deacon recalled the name Croc, but couldn't remember why. And what was Tamara so mad about? *Harlem Nights* was only a movie. "You getting too excited, baby girl. Remember your hurt foot."

"My what . . . ? Give me a break, Grandpa."

"Did baby girl just sass me?"

"Shut up, Thurgood." Delilah turned back to Tamara before the deacon could react. "Well, sweetie, let me try and explain things." Delilah ignored the deacon's inability to come up with a lie or alibi. She was stalling because nothing was coming to her, either.

"Just stop it, the both of you. You two old gangsters," Tamara said. "I don't know what to do with either of you."

And that's when the deacon got diarrhea of the mouth and threw Delilah so far under the bus that all that was left was white hair, gray eyes, light skin, and tread marks.

"Baby girl, you know I've said it often, and even testified in church about it. I gave up my thuggish ways years ago. But ever since your loudmouthed grandmother returned, she's turned me into a different man."

"Not a different man," Delilah interrupted, "just into *a man*."

Tamara sat down again. She was about ready to give up trying to deal with them logically as she listened to accusations thrown back and forth between her grandparents.

"Okay, that's enough!" Tamara said finally. "I think I want a DNA test done before I believe that I'm carrying any genes from you two. Damn!"

"Hold up, young lady. Didn't I tell you before that you can't cuss? You got too much class for such language." The deacon rose from his seat to put emphasis on what he'd said. Pointing to Delilah, he continued. "Now, Dee Dee only pretends to have a lot of class. That's why she has the potty mouth."

And then Delilah and the deacon went for round two. They were scrapping like two old champions, and several times they each laid a verbal TKO. One acted like they knew more than the other when it came to God's Word.

"Stop acting like this, Dee Dee. Baby girl knows Christians don't fight like cats and dogs."

"Well, stop acting like God didn't have a mafia in the Bible," Delilah barked.

Delilah turned to her granddaughter and smiled. "Tamara, sweetheart, I know you've gone to church probably a lot more and for longer than me."

"I know I sure have," Deacon Pillar muttered.

"I don't care if I've only passed by a church or only seen a picture of it," Delilah snapped. "I still know about God. So you two can't tell me that you don't know that God gave permission to some of his folks to kill or maim other folks."

Delilah's supposed words of wisdom hung in the air like a mushroom cloud. "Y'all need to read up a bit more from your Bible. Try reading the Old Testament. There was a lot of retribution going on. I don't know how y'all call yourselves a deacon and a church girl and don't know about God's mafia. God had a hit list, too. In fact, if I recall, Moses was one of God's biggest enforcers, just like that mafioso Tony Soprano on television."

Delilah grabbed a nearby broom and threw it to the floor. "You know Moses took a broomstick and turned it into a snake, and then he sure turned that Pharaoh into a punk. He did all that after God gave him the go-ahead. And you think David would've killed Goliath if God hadn't wanted it to happen?"

Both the deacon's and Tamara's jaws dropped.

Tamara leaned over and whispered to Deacon Pillar, "She's not kidding, is she?"

"She's as serious as Obama was about becoming president."

They could've kept fighting, but Tamara again stopped them cold when she took a Bible off the table and said, "I've been reading my Bible. I'm trying to figure out why God has allowed so much to happen."

Out of respect for God's Word, Delilah and the deacon silently called a truce.

Tamara took further advantage of the welcome quiet and continued. "Daddy used to read this scripture to me whenever he and mama couldn't understand why certain things happened the way they did. They put a purple ribbon right here on the page. It's Jeremiah, the twenty-ninth chapter and the eleventh verse—"

"Well now, that's a good thing. Isn't it, Thurgood?" Delilah interrupted with a nervous chuckle. As much as she'd like to pretend she knew more than she really did about the Bible, she wasn't familiar with that particular verse and didn't know how to take the conversation further. She tossed the ball to the deacon to carry on. "Ain't there something you'd like to add, Deacon?"

"I'm glad you're reading your Bible," the deacon replied as his eyes narrowed. "A lot of time God has to knock us around like little heathen kids until we pay attention. All the while God is saying, I'll never steer you wrong. Look over here. Here's your blessing, but you're gonna have to jump through some hoops because you was hardheaded and disobedient."

"Are you sure that's what it says, Thurgood?"

"I'm pretty sure. I'll look it up later. Right now I need Tamara to explain why bringing food to the church is gonna be such a problem."

"I didn't say it was a problem. I said I needed a break from all this insanity and that Daddy wouldn't be able to cook, either."

"So what are you asking?" Delilah wasn't used to having that much patience to spare. Her newly found granddaughter was beginning to press grandma's nerves. And then she immediately cheered up, remembering the recipes she'd set aside for Tamara. "Just tell us what to do." Delilah could've pulled out an apron on demand.

"I still don't see what the problem is," Deacon Pillar chimed in. "Let your grandma cook in your place. It's not like she can't."

Tamara laughed and winked. "I was just thinking the

same thing. I guess we are related. I'll call Sister Marty right now. I'm sure she won't turn me down."

"Hold up, Tamara," Deacon Pillar said quickly. "Are you sure about that?" He let his head lean and nod in Delilah's direction to give Tamara a hint.

"You're right again. That's a lot of food for just one person to cook. I haven't seen her do a lot of things right, but Grandma Delilah can throw down for sure. I'm a witness to that." She looked at Delilah as though to dare her to back out.

All Delilah could do was smile. But she was sure the deacon had read her mind. *You've got such a big mouth, Thurgood.*

"Then it's settled. Delilah and Marty gonna get together and throw down in the kitchen."

"You about got that right," Delilah barked. "It's gonna get hot."

And then, as if Tamara weren't in the same room, Delilah and Deacon Pillar went at it again. Delilah signified that he was a pig's butt and she was gonna barbecue it. The deacon told her she needed to sue her skinny legs for nonsupport. On and on they went and when they were going to stop, nobody knew.

"Enough! I can't take it." Tamara slammed the Bible closed with a thud before she rose and limped toward the telephone.

Deacon Pillar sprang into action. "What are you doing, baby girl?"

"Whatever you need, I can get it for you," Delilah said softly as she came and stood in front of the deacon.

"Thank you both," Tamara replied. "I'm just calling the police."

"Why?" the deacon asked as he hunched his shoulders when Delilah looked his way.

Tamara picked up the phone and held it to her ear with

her fingers on the touch pad. "It's because I'm about to kill the two of you."

"You see, Thurgood," Delilah said with pride, "I told you she's just like me. Retribution is in her blood."

"Don't brag. It's an ugly habit." The deacon gently took the telephone from Tamara's hands.

She was already sorry she'd acted the way she had, so she allowed the deacon to take the phone away. Tamara limped back to the sofa and sulked, angry that she'd acted like a grown-up one moment and a spoiled brat the next. Her mother would not have approved. She could just imagine her mother fussing, *C'mon, Tamara. You now have one more person to fuss over you. Ain't God good?*

Yet she still couldn't reconcile having both Delilah and Sister Marty in their lives. She had a ton of love for Sister Marty. Even though she felt betrayed by the deacon, their love was rooted. The love she needed to have for Delilah was like looking for hens' teeth. It was hard, plus Delilah had been one of Croc Duggan's artists and probably made more on her back than she did on the stage. There was no doubt Delilah had been with the crème-de-la-crème of the music industry, but Tamara wasn't about to mattress bump to make it.

Tamara looked out the front window. She watched as Deacon Pillar and Delilah headed toward his truck.

"I almost feel sorry for you, Deacon-Grandpa Pillar."

Jessie stopped by Sister Marty's on his way home from the doctor.

"Mama Marty," Jessie called out as he entered her front door. She'd left it open to let in a breeze on that humid evening.

"Come on in, Jessie," she called out. "I'm in the kitchen."

By the time he made it to the kitchen she'd already poured cold soda into a cup he'd won when they'd gone to Disney World in Orlando for his thirteenth birthday.

As she placed his favorite cup in his good hand, she looked hard at the injured one. "Drink up." She watched him wince slightly as she gently checked out the faded area where the brace had been. "I see your hand looks like it's healing like it should."

Jessie set down the cup and tried to turn the injured hand. He had some trouble. "I'm praying for a miracle."

"Still concerned about playing your guitar next Sunday?"

"Yes, I've looked forward to playing with the deacon behind you and Tamara."

"If it's God's will, then you will." Sister Marty stopped and laughed. It wasn't her usual one. It was more of a "you ain't gonna believe this" laugh. "Did you speak to your daughter before you stopped by?"

"No, I parked and walked over here. Why? What's happened now?"

"I'll give you one word."

"Delilah?"

"She's become the word we all think of first." Sister Marty wiped her hands and sat down. "Guess what she and I are going to do?"

Jessie became a little suspicious, and with a lot of concern added, "Let me guess. The two of you are going on a Pay-Per-View WWE match."

"Something like that, but even better," she replied. "Princess Tamara has determined that her godmother and grandmother should have a cook-off for the Family and Friends Day."

"Say what!"

"You heard me. She called about thirty minutes before you came here. One of the mothers at the church checked off the Jewel family to bring food."

"That was always Cindy's job. Tamara can't cook."

When Jessie said Cindy's name the air seemed lighter inside the kitchen. He could feel the shift and he was sure Marty had, too.

"Why would Tamara want Delilah involved? It would've made more sense for Deacon Pillar to cook with you. That man is an undiscovered chef if there ever was one."

"That's something you'll have to ask your daughter about. She never mentioned Thurgood when she called me. However, she did say that Delilah had been at your house. I'm just assuming that Delilah was with the deacon."

Jessie had no doubt that Sister Marty was correct. He knew Delilah was there from the night before, but he would say nothing. "I think I'd better be leaving. I need to get home and see what else Tamara is up to. I see having a sore ankle hasn't stopped her meddling."

"Don't fuss at my godbaby. She knows I can handle things, and if she needs my help with the cooking, I'll do it."

"Even if it means you'll be cooking with Delilah?"

"Even if it meant I'd have to cook with the devil."

"We're talking about the same person, aren't we?" Jessie laughed. "So where is the throw-down going down?"

"I believe the food committee is coming together tomorrow night at New Hope's Community Center. That's when Miss Delilah and I will find out whether we'll be tossing hot or cold stuff at one another."

Jessie and Sister Marty suddenly burst out laughing. It felt good. He hadn't laughed with his foster mother since Delilah had showed up at his door.

They walked into the den and spent another few minutes catching up, like he was still a teenager and she'd asked about his day at school. They even held hands and had a quick prayer.

Jessie looked around the den, and for a brief moment he wanted to stay a while longer. But he couldn't. He knew it was anyone's guess what mischief or chaos had happened at his house. Delilah might live in Garden City, but she seemed to dwell more at his house lately.

Jessie said his good-byes and left. He quickened his pace as he walked past the brownstone houses that separated Sister Marty's home from his. *Tonight I want answers.*

Jessie burst through the door of his house, hoping to find Delilah there. He found Tamara with her iPod headphones on. She was singing. He walked over and tapped her on the shoulder, which startled her.

"Sorry it took me so long. I stopped by Sister Marty's and chatted. What's happening around here?"

"It's pretty quiet. I'm just sitting here rehearsing the song for the Family and Friends Day."

"Is the deacon upstairs?"

"Yes, he just got back from taking Delilah home. He said he was going to bed."

Jessie was agitated and he didn't try to hide it. "Who asked him to take her home?"

"She don't live here, Daddy."

"I don't need you to remind me of where my mother lives."

Jessie didn't apologize, although he knew she hadn't deserved his outburst. He had to hurry and get answers about Delilah. He couldn't continue like this. Every child deserved to know if their parent truly loved them.

Chapter 23

The deacon's sleep on his sofa was uneasy. In just a short time he'd tossed and turned so much the sofa cushions were halfway on the floor.

He'd driven Delilah back to Garden City and the truth was he was glad to do it. During the drive she kept babbling about gathering recipes for Tamara. And, of course, he was fit to be tied. For the past few days he'd done everything short of ripping out his tongue and cutting off his feet to avoid contact with or any mention of Sister Marty. Now Tamara had to put Marty and Delilah together. He felt like whipping his baby girl's butt.

He'd also heard Jessie minutes ago raising his voice downstairs. Not every word was clear, but the anger was. But Deacon Pillar was tired. Whatever they were fussing about he couldn't deal with.

The deacon finally sat up. His head throbbed as he tried to focus, but everything in his place blurred. That wasn't a good sign. He knew his blood pressure was high. "I need peace," the deacon whispered, "a peace that surpasses all understanding, Father God."

He placed his head in his hands as his mind traveled back to the days when he once had that peace of mind he now sought. He scratched around the edges of his temple where it was evident that his conk had conked out. His fingers could barely break through its nappy tangles. *I can't even find a peaceful moment to get my touch-up done.*

And then Jessie's face appeared before him. The deacon had spent as much time as possible spreading his attention between Tamara and Delilah so he could avoid the inevitable. But now Tamara knew the secret.

And what was the inevitable? Would Jessie turn on him as Jessie had done to Delilah when she first arrived on his doorstep? How could he convince Jessie that although he'd not come forward sooner, he'd still looked out for Jessie and Tamara much like any father or grandfather would? *I wouldn't buy that asinine reasoning.*

Every conflicted question that crossed the deacon's mind begged an even more contradictory follow-up question. Old Thurgood Pillar, Mr. Know Everything—and what he didn't know, God told him immediately. That's the way he'd lived his later years, since finding God. He was a hypocrite and even worse, a blatant fraud. All that time he'd hidden behind his own wall of secrets, lies, and disregard for real responsibility.

And then Deacon Pillar clasped his hands and he prayed some more. And at that moment in time, Deacon Pillar believed it was just him and God in that room; or at least he hoped it was.

"Don't let the devil win this one, Father," Deacon Pillar whispered, and then for no apparent reason the scripture Tamara had cited came before him. *For I know the plans I have for you . . .* Then, just as quick as he shook his head to gather his thoughts, Delilah's face appeared, saying what she always said. *Don't blame the devil.*

But his anger for Delilah returned. "Get back, Satan, and take Delilah with you!" he muttered as annoyance replaced the apologetic look he'd shown God just moments before.

Truly, the last thing he wanted or needed was for thoughts of Delilah to show up and break the holy connection.

While Jessie fretted and the deacon endured a restless sleep in Brooklyn, Delilah sat on her sofa with cookbooks piled in front of her. Earlier she couldn't wait to get home. If she'd known how to drive a stick shift she'd have put her foot on top of the deacon's just to get him to drive faster. Delilah didn't need him to walk her to the door. She wanted him gone so she could get started.

Delilah wasn't sure what kind of foods the church needed, but whatever it was, she was certain she could cook it, bake it, broil it, or fricassee it, if necessary. Even knowing that she wasn't Tamara's first choice couldn't break her joy. This was about more than cooking. It was about competition. Marty had already claimed her son, her granddaughter, and her husband. She'd be damned if she'd let the woman beat her in cooking, too. And she'd decided since she arrived home that on Family and Friends Day, it would be a perfect time to tell Jessie about the deacon.

Delilah had it all worked out. She was so happy, she'd forgotten to advise Jehovah of her latest plans to see if they lined up with His.

She busied herself for a while picking out an outfit to wear the next day. She was still about style just as much as substance. By the time she went to bed she was truly exhausted, but in a good way.

Jessie sat on the edge of his bed, debating whether to go back into the living room and apologize to Tamara. He was about to when she knocked on his door.

"Daddy," Tamara said softly, "are you still awake?"

"Yes, come on in."

Tamara entered. She still had the iPod in her hand. Her limp had subsided some as well. She walked slowly over to the bed and sat down next to her father. "I know you didn't mean to yell at me or be angry with the deacon."

"I'm sorry, Tamara. I just needed to see Delilah and talk."

"Is talking with her to see if she really cares and loves you as her son or if she just needs something from you really that important?"

"There's not a lot more I can talk to her about. It's not like you and me. I can't talk to her about a prom or my measles as a child. I know she doesn't know anything about my love for football or where to go on vacation. She wasn't around for that."

"But you're a grown man now."

Jessie turned to his daughter. "I need to be a whole and complete man. I need a history that's authentic. What I have with Sister Marty as my foster mother is a God-send, but with a big question mark. When it didn't seem possible I'd ever see my mother or know about my father, I wondered about it but I didn't crave it."

"And you do now?"

"Yes. I need it for you just as much as I do for me."

"I'm cool," Tamara said as she took her father's hand. "I've learned music is in our blood and I have you and Sister Marty. I'm blessed."

"You don't think Delilah's a blessing?"

Tamara laughed. "Only when she's not around me."

"She does have that effect. But I'm starting to warm up to her a bit."

"Yeah, but it's because you think she knows something you don't."

"It's a bit more than that now. I remembered something the other night. It'd bothered me for the last few weeks. I'm not sure if I should burden you, baby, but I believe Delilah was once married."

Tamara tried her best to remain calm. She suppressed her

emotions with as many face crunches as she could to keep a blank look. "What makes you believe that?"

"I remembered that the last time I'd seen her in front of Grand Central she was wearing a wedding band. I'd completely forgotten about that."

"She was?" Tamara became so nervous she wanted to throw up.

"I mean, I was a grown man by then, so I don't know when she got married or even if the ring was real."

"Is her wearing a wedding ring or being married gonna change anything?"

"Perhaps it will mean that she married before I was born and she knows where my natural father is—I'm not sure. But every time I pray about it lately, I see Delilah wearing that ring."

"What else do you see?" Tamara struggled to get him off the subject.

"Well, actually what I see is so much of you in her. You two could almost pass for twins. It took me a moment to see that clearly, until we visited her the other day." Jessie turned and looked at his reflection in the dresser mirror. "But I don't see me in her."

"Do you need to see you in someone?"

"Yes."

Tamara studied her father for a moment. She'd told so much lately and interfered when she shouldn't have. But her father was hurting and she didn't like it, especially since earlier she'd pulled out some of the old photograph albums. She'd wanted to remember the outfit she and her mother wore at the last Family and Friends Day celebration. She was going to wear it when she sang on Sunday. And that's when she saw it. The deacon and her father were standing together; the deacon with his guitar and her father with his bass. It wasn't in their complexions, or in the eyes. It was the smile.

They were grinning like Cheshire cats and it'd started her wondering if her father would see it, too. He was more sensitive and aware now that Delilah had given him more questions than answers.

"What are you thinking about, Tamara?"

"What being a father is all about," she answered, "and also marriage."

A strange look came over Jessie's face. He wondered what his daughter was trying to say. She seldom dated and if there was a young man involved, she'd have told him about it. Now she was talking about fatherhood and marriage. What had she done behind his back? "Oh Lord, Tamara, is there something you want to tell me?"

"Yes."

Jessie's heart raced. He'd always promised to be supportive of Tamara, but she was scaring him. "Just tell Daddy." He was speaking to her as though she were a young girl instead of a grown woman. "I'll love you regardless."

"Okay, here it is. . . . Delilah and Deacon Pillar got married."

"What!" He immediately thought about Sister Marty. "Oh Lord, what is Sister Marty going to do?"

"She's cool with it," Tamara said as she got off the bed and started to leave the room.

"Why would she be cool with it?"

"Because she said the deacon's gonna divorce Delilah."

"What the hell is going on with those old fools? How are they gonna get married one minute and then divorced the next, and Marty's cool with it?"

"They've been married for more than a minute, Daddy."

"I know they're old friends, but I thought they only reconnected a little over a month ago. I hardly call that a long time. And now they're talking a divorce. Did they suddenly wake up and discover they'd made a mistake?"

"According to Sister Marty, they discovered that mistake

about forty years ago. You were about two years old then. I was so mad when I found out about it that I told her and she already knew. So if it was cool with her, it was chilly with me, too."

"So what aren't you telling me, Tamara?"

"I'm telling you to start there."

"Wait a minute. How did you find out?"

Tamara had already closed the door behind her by the time Jessie got his voice back and his mind together and the question out.

Jessie heard the deacon moving about upstairs, but he didn't trust himself to confront him. But at the very least he needed to know why the deacon hadn't said anything to him. After all, Delilah was his mother. *Over forty years ago.* What did that make the deacon?

Sleep wouldn't come to Jessie. Delilah was taking his family down, one by one, without firing one shot of truth. He'd confided in the deacon that he needed to find out the truth about her and the deacon had said nothing. He'd sat at his foster mother's kitchen table sipping from a thirty-year-old cup and she'd said nothing, either. And what took Tamara so long to speak out? Delilah and the deacon obviously weren't living together, or she wouldn't be living in Garden City. Were they estranged, and that's why they were divorcing? Nobody said anything to him. He couldn't get past it. What kind of hold did Delilah have on them?

Jessie turned over. He was in so much pain. He talked to God one moment and Cindy the next.

Chapter 24

With all Sister Marty had on her plate: work, church ministry, and trying to keep Delilah's paws off her family, she still found time to fit in one more thing. Once a month she volunteered at New Hope's Community Center Multiservice office. It was a coincidence that her volunteer day fell on the same day as the food committee's meeting. But it'd been cancelled and she'd only just found that out.

Since there wasn't going to be a food committee meeting that day, she'd decided that she'd put Delilah and other trials and tribulations behind her. This day would belong entirely to God. Whoever walked through the door and needed help from the church's Multiservice ministry, she'd serve gladly.

Sister Marty straightened her dress and put on her happy-for-appearance'-sake face. She added just a bit more pep to her step and entered the Multiservice Center's main office.

She opened one of the venetian blinds. "Good afternoon and praise the Lord." She peeked at a sheet of paper pinned to a cork board. She started singing, "I'm sorry I'm late. Do we have any clients still left?"

"No, there aren't any yet. But we do have a woman who's been waiting to get in and talk to Mother Johnson, who won't be in until later on. I believe she's one of the food volunteers. She was much too early and I don't have the key to the conference room to let her wait there."

The receptionist, a young woman who looked like a mousey professor in square-frame glasses, smiled. "What's making you so happy this afternoon?"

"It's been a glorious day. I claim it as such."

"That's what I'm talking about, Sister Marty. Never let the devil steal your joy." The young woman rose and took a clipboard from the counter. "I'll recheck to see if anyone has arrived. If not, then you can do something else or I guess you can call it a day."

The receptionist left and returned in a few minutes. "No regular clients have arrived. That woman is still waiting in the intake office. It doesn't seem like she minds waiting."

"Okay, well, I'll just fill out my time sheets and do some filing. If you want you can have the lady wait over at the reading table. At least she'll have something to do."

"I'll see if she wants to do that. By the way, what's happening with you as far as Family and Friends Day?"

"Believe it or not, I'm doing more than just singing this year. I'm cooking, but I just learned the food committee meeting is cancelled. But that's okay. I need to find my way to service this evening. I can't wait to get my praise on. I'm not letting anything or anyone mess with my joy today." She stopped and put her hand over her heart. "I promise you one thing. That devil can burn an extra eternity in hell before I let that happen."

The receptionist escorted Delilah through the Multiservice Center's hallowed doors and into the office. She walked out before she could see Sister Marty's jaw drop.

At that very moment in time if at no other, Sister Marty knew for certain that salvation was hers for keeps. There were several pairs of scissors along with a cup of sharpened pencils, and even a heavy-duty stapler lying within reach. She didn't pick up any of them and go at Delilah.

Although for a brief second the thought had crossed her mind. There was no one but the two of them there. All she had to do was pretend Delilah had started something first. But miracles were Jesus's specialty. That afternoon, for a while, He'd keep Sister Marty's mind, her job, and her testimony safely at the foot of the Cross.

Instead, one of the first things Sister Marty did, in her best civil tone, was address Delilah by name and ask her to have a seat at the reading table.

"What a surprise," Sister Marty said and watched Delilah walk over to the table. She knew Delilah was probably sizing up the situation.

"You're starting to become like dog poop," Delilah hissed. "Everywhere I step, there you are."

"Well, if anyone would know about mess, it'd be you. Now take a seat."

Sister Marty waited until Delilah, walking at a deliberately slow pace, sat at the table before she walked out of the room and into a smaller one. She closed the door just enough to ensure she'd have some privacy as she dialed a number. It didn't take long for someone on the other end to answer.

". . . She's here, she's early, and she's already worked my last good nerve. They cancelled the food committee meeting. If you wanna keep her on this side of the grave, you'd better get over here."

She hadn't said it, but a prayer service may not be enough for her where Delilah was concerned.

Tamara thought since her foot felt a lot better that she would do a little shopping. She needed some accessories to wear for Sunday's event. She wanted to look as professional and star-ready as possible for the A&R rep. She also thought that with Delilah and Sister Marty at the food committee meeting, they'd be too busy going at one another to bother her. Now they'd cancelled the meeting and she doubted if Sister Marty would let Delilah know.

Instead, she raced from inside Macy's department store to the car. She struggled to take her keys from her pocket as well as hold and talk into her cell phone at the same time.

She never expected to receive a phone call from Sister Marty about Delilah. She'd almost not picked up the phone because earlier they'd already chatted about her suggested menu and how the food would get to the church. She'd also come clean and told Sister Marty what she had revealed to her father. Sister Marty was not happy. It wasn't a situation she wanted to discuss further. It might've been better if they had.

Now Tamara was in the car and taking off to see about a grandmother—one in name only. But then, if she didn't care about Delilah, why was she racing off like a fool to get her before she could cause trouble?

"I don't believe this!" Tamara blurted. Five minutes ago she was an adult with her father's credit card, about to handle her adult business.

Leave it to Delilah to mess me up. She'd better get her old butt together before Sunday. I finally get a chance where I don't have to sleep my way into a music career like she did. . . . Damn Delilah, she thought.

With one hand trying to control the steering wheel as she tore through heavy traffic on Lafayette Avenue, she yelled into the phone, "Come on, Deacon Pillar, pick up your phone." It was the third time she'd tried to call him. Each time it'd gone directly to his voice mail. "Where is he?"

Back at the apartment Thurgood sat by his living room window and looked out into the street. He'd been sitting for several hours in that same spot since he'd discovered Delilah had left early—for where, he didn't know. He opened the window and craned his neck to see up and down the block, hoping Delilah would come into view. Soon it would be time to take her over to the church so she could sit down with Marty and the other members of the food committee.

He could literally feel the heat blasting from his skull. That meant a headache was soon to follow.

He saw his reflection in a mirror. "Enough is enough." He wrung his hands and promised no one in particular since he was alone, "When she finally comes back I'm setting her straight. Enough of the drama—I'm telling Jessie the truth about everything. If she can't handle it, then it's too damn bad!"

He stopped yelling long enough to look over at the telephone. It was still blinking because it wasn't fully charged. He was convinced that Delilah left the phone off the charger on purpose. *I know she did it,* he thought.

He'd left his cell phone downstairs in Tamara's apartment. Jessie and she weren't home, so he couldn't even get his cell phone. Even Delilah's BlackBerry lying on the table wasn't useful. She'd told him there'd been no service for the past few days.

Now he couldn't make or receive calls until the house phone's battery charged. He walked over and checked the bars. Only two of the five bars were charged. Nothing he could do but return to the window and wait.

"I'm too through with women." A shudder washed over him like a burst of thunder. He remembered he'd said the same thing when he was in his sixties and caught between the amorous and vicious clutches of two, somewhat saved church mothers from Pelzer, South Carolina. By the time Bea Blister and Sasha Pray Onn finished tossing him around like he was their personal volleyball, filling him with sweet bread, collards, red velvet cake, and corn liquor, he couldn't recite his name, age, and date of birth for weeks.

But that was then and this was now. Age and stubbornness caused the old playa to forget one important rule in the two-timers' rule book.

It was the women who decided when the game was over.

Chapter 25

"Excuse me," the receptionist who'd led Delilah into the office said softly, "Mother Johnson is here. Would you still like to chat with her?"

Delilah had long ago finished reading most of the magazines on the table. She could've left, but she knew that would've made Marty happy. She didn't want Marty happy. "Oh, that would be lovely," Delilah purred.

Delilah quickly opened the briefcase she'd brought for the meeting. She took out several of her best recipes with the intention of not only making Tamara look good, but wowing Mother Johnson. She'd heard that Mother Johnson's taste buds would do the deciding once they'd test-cooked a few things. Delilah never knew cooking for a church event was so political. But she wasn't surprised, either.

"I'm Mother Johnson," the woman announced as she entered the intake office. "Sister Delilah, is it?" She didn't wait for an answer before continuing. "Well, I'm pleased to meet you. You've waited to see me for quite some time and I'm sorry about that. I understand from our receptionist you're going to be a part of our cooking team for Family and Friends." She stopped and appeared to take a closer look at

Delilah. "I thought I knew everyone. I can't recall seeing you at New Hope."

"Oh, of course I've attended New Hope before, and thank you for seeing me." Delilah edited her truth as close to the bone as she could, but she was tempted to shout *I'm Tamara's real authentic grandma,* but she didn't. It wasn't necessary to use the term *grandma.* Once she and Tamara became close they'd have to choose another term.

Mother Johnson was just a few inches taller than Delilah. Yet she looked like a snowcapped mountain as she pushed her white crocheted cap farther back onto her head. She didn't appear to have enough hair to make a bobby pin necessary. "It's almost four-thirty, and it's still a scorcher out there. My goodness, I know I must look like a wet Almond Joy."

I know you look like you eat Almond Joy bars twenty-four seven. That's what she thought, but instead Delilah came back with a Delilah reply special. "Oh, I'm sure you're not as nutty as all that." Delilah immediately burst out in laughter to hide her insincerity.

"Oh, the Lord loves the nutty ones, too." Old Mother Johnson adjusted the elastic around the waistline of her floor-length white dress. She looked well over two hundred pounds and the elastic looked pulled to its limit because it didn't give an inch. "What's that you've got laid out? Hmmm, it sure looks good."

"Thank you." Delilah quickly moved the picture out of the way before the old mother decided to eat that, too. "This is my own recipe for corn pudding."

"Do you keep pictures of all your recipes so organized?"

Now, the old church mother didn't realize it, but she was now on Delilah's fan page. Delilah couldn't stop grinning. She was beginning to like Mother Johnson and decided to make the old woman an unwitting ally.

"Please sit down." Delilah even pulled out a seat for

Mother Johnson as though the woman were in Delilah's office. Plus she knew Sister Marty wouldn't like her being so familiar, and that made her disposition sweeter. "How long have you been a church mother at New Hope?"

The old church mother seemed surprised at the question. She started counting on fingers that were bent backwards, no doubt, from arthritis; but they didn't prevent her from using eating utensils. "Well now, let me see. . . ."

"I didn't mean to get so nosy. I was just curious." Delilah didn't think the woman had to do a finger count just to answer a simple question.

"It's alright, Sister Delilah."

"Well, if it's not a bother."

"No bother. Back to answering your first question—I started evangelizing about five years after Christ convicted my heart and told me to quit my scandalous ways."

It wasn't quite the answer Delilah had expected. She became more intrigued, especially when the woman used the word *scandalous* to describe whatever she'd been doing in the past. Mother Johnson looked so frumpy, Delilah thought she'd been born saved and sanctified and filled with Almond Joy candy bars.

"Do tell," Delilah said. "You don't look like you've done a scandalous thing in your life."

"Well, that's because when Jesus takes his blood-soaked scrub brush to you, it'll change and clean you up real good."

"I suppose so. What exactly had you done when He took the scrub brush to you?"

"I guess you really wouldn't know. I used to be one of Deacon Thurgood Pillar's prostitutes."

"Huh!"

"Yes, ma'am. Me and old Deacon Pillar go way back further than pillow talk."

And that was the defining moment that Delilah knew God had indeed done something in her life. She didn't pick up anything. She didn't try to rip one of the thick magazines apart and body slam the old woman to the floor, and she didn't cuss Mother Johnson out.

Instead, Delilah smiled until her jaws felt tight enough to crack. "I've known the deacon for a long time, too. When was he ever a pimp?"

"Well now, I don't really remember when he bagged his first ho. . . ." Mother Johnson jerked her head up toward the ceiling and professed, "Oh Lord, I'm so sorry. I didn't mean to say that word. I know it ain't Your word because it ain't in the Bible."

Ain't *ain't in the Bible, either,* Delilah thought. She was pretty sure of it. "God forgives." That's all she could think to say that didn't have a cuss word in it. Delilah just kept on smiling.

Mother Johnson's eyes seemed to sparkle as she spoke about how she'd come to know the deacon. "I believe it was when he got out of prison. At least, I think that's where he told me he'd been."

For the next ten minutes or so Mother Johnson explained how Christ had saved her during the worst period of her young life. He forgave her and turned her from a wretch undone to a saleswoman for God, a president of the mothers' board and a chief taster for the food committee.

After she explained God's forgiveness to Delilah, Mother Johnson thought she'd take it a little further. After all, the food committee meeting was cancelled, but a prayer meeting was scheduled to begin in about fifteen minutes. "You know, Sister Delilah, I don't know how close you and the Heavenly Father are, but I'm certain you believe that God can reach down into a human cesspool and clean a person off." She then gave Delilah a wide grin. "I'm just handing you what thus saith the Lord."

The truth was, she'd actually handed Delilah plenty of new information to use against that old, sanctimonious Deacon Pillar. And she was going to use that info like an auger hole digger. Delilah was gonna bury that old deacon.

Whether it was her inner spirit or the remains of feminine intuition, Mother Johnson wasn't certain. She sensed a shift in the atmosphere. "You know, they conference with crazy folks in this office. I sense too many demons in this place," she announced as she pulled a bottle of blessed oil from her pocketbook. She started anointing everything in the office, including the remains of several dead cockroaches by a dry cactus plant before she finally asked, "Are you okay, Miss Delilah?"

"I'm fine." But Delilah wasn't fine. Suddenly cooking wasn't on the top of her list. Inside, her anger was volcano hot. It was a wonder she hadn't roasted every organ within her body. However, payback was a dish better served cold, so she chilled.

Tamara arrived at the New Hope Multiservice Center and found her father and Sister Marty in one of the offices near the little sanctuary.

"Hi, Daddy. Hello, Godmother. I came as fast as I could. Where is the old gal now?"

"Sorry to interrupt your shopping spree, Tamara," Sister Marty replied. "I imagine she's still in the intake office where I left her. She was waiting for Mother Johnson."

"Why did she need Mother Johnson?" Tamara remembered Delilah had questioned her about the committee members. She didn't know Delilah would seek out Mother Johnson.

Jessie's patience grew short. He wasn't usually so harsh with those he loved. "If you didn't trust yourself to be alone with Delilah, then I wish you'd called me first before you phoned Tamara." Jessie sat down in one of the vacant chairs opposite where Sister Marty stood. "She doesn't need to be bothered with Delilah. I can handle her."

"First of all, I didn't know you were in the building. Secondly, she's your child, Jessie, but she's also an adult. She is the one who asked me and Delilah to cook together."

"I know, Marty."

"You once told me that you wanted God to fix what was broken in your life, Jessie. Don't you still want that?"

"Yes, of course I do. But . . ."

"But what? What is the problem?"

"Daddy, I'm so sorry." Tamara wanted to take back every word she'd said about the deacon and Delilah's marriage; especially since there was stress growing between him and Sister Marty. *I wonder if Daddy said anything yet.*

Jessie waved away Tamara's apology and turned back to Sister Marty. "I'm just not in the place where I need to be to accept Delilah. At least until I know the whole truth."

"Truth hurts, Jessie. Remember that. I think we need another one of our son-mom chats."

"Oh Lord, I don't believe this." Tamara didn't explain, she just pointed.

When Sister Marty left Delilah, she'd never returned and seen Mother Johnson and Delilah together in the intake office. But she did see them walking arm in arm as they walked into the little sanctuary.

Delilah threw her head back and winked at Jessie, Tamara, and Sister Marty. Then she and the old church mother walked together into what Delilah thought was a food committee meeting.

Delilah was livid. She dropped Mother Johnson's arm with a thud. Instead of seeing a bunch of women with chef's hats or whatever they wore to a food committee meeting, she saw some folks kneeling and others gathered in pockets holding hands where they stood.

It took a moment or two, but it became obvious that it wasn't the meeting she'd looked forward to. There was too much prayer going on. Delilah knew that's what it was, because before she'd set up her mobile church routine, she'd attended a few prayer sessions. But that only happened when she'd gotten to church too early or too late. She'd never attended one on purpose.

Mother Johnson, out of respect for the prayers going upward, didn't say a word to Delilah. She walked to one of the altar railings and knelt down to pray. Without Mother Johnson to hold her down, Delilah turned to leave the sanctuary.

Delilah ran straight into the path of Jessie and the others.

"Delilah, where are you going?" Jessie asked the question with an authoritative tone that Delilah didn't appreciate at that moment. "With all those Bibles you have as decoration in your home, I thought you'd feel comfortable inside here."

And then it was Tamara's turn. "Grandma Delilah," Tamara said softly and as reverently as she could while inside the sanctuary, "I really didn't know the meeting was cancelled. You might as well stay for prayer. I am."

Delilah looked around the sanctuary again. *Oh Jehovah, why do you keep moving the chess pieces around? You keep dangling my family before me like a carrot.* "Okay. I don't have a choice. I took the bus over here, but I'd planned on riding back with you, Tamara."

At that same moment, Sister Marty became as confused as she'd ever been before. She looked at Delilah standing between Jessie and Tamara and it suddenly seemed right and not threatening. And at that moment in time, she also realized what she'd always confessed. *Whatever God has for me is for me.* From the very beginning she should've shown Delilah that same love and care Jesus had shown her when she was once a lost soul, too. She should've just loved the hell out of Delilah.

Jessie watched as the others prepared for the devotional service to begin. Of course, there were little cliques that always sought out one another for prayer and comfort. But then he saw Mother Johnson walk over to Tamara and Delilah.

He couldn't hear the conversation, but he could certainly imagine it. The old church mother and Tamara were going from one member to another. He saw hands extended to Delilah and wondered if Tamara had introduced her as her grandmother. That was something he certainly hadn't done, nor had he tried to. Instead, he decided he needed to stop trying to one-up God and allow the Master to play things out in His time.

"I wanna thank the Lord for His goodness and all He's done for me." That was one of the most readily used testimony starters, and it'd started with Mother Johnson. "Oh, if it were not for the Lord, where would I be?"

From around the sanctuary others called out, "Tell it, Mother Johnson."

"I made a new friend in the Lord this afternoon. Oh, we shared so much in common. We both were wretches undone, with one a little more undone than the other. . . ."

Delilah was with her newfound fan until she went there. *Who is she talking about?* Delilah looked about the sanctuary until her eyes found Sister Marty standing off to the side alone. *Oh, okay. It must be Marty. I didn't think Mother Johnson was talking about me.*

And then after several more platitudes along with legitimate praise, Mother Johnson brought Delilah to the stage. "Would you like to testify or sing a song?"

There wasn't a Martin Luther King fan waving as Delilah stood. She knew how to work her audience. She hadn't worn her signature wig, but with her snow white hair cascading about her face, she turned the prayer meeting out!

"Guide Me, O Thou Great Jehovah" was part of her first set. Her rendition was flawless and she drew the skeptics into her corner, including the pianist, who had started crying. Then she followed with a rousing rendition of Vicki Winans' "Long As I Got King Jesus." Her long white tresses took over and the way she was shaking her hair and her "pocketbook," those assets could've backed her up. But it was when she became so caught up in her own myth and screamed, "Give the drummer some . . ." that Jessie, Tamara, and Sister Marty almost passed out.

"There's no way I'm telling these folks that Delilah is my mother," Jessie whispered to Tamara. Any outing of their dirty laundry would stay in the family hamper that night.

Marty didn't know what to think. One minute she wanted to hug Delilah like Jesus would, and the next she wanted to go Jeffrey Dahmer and just go cannibal on her.

By the time the prayer meeting was over, Delilah was so happy she'd hung around. She didn't know it could be so entertaining. Delilah delivered her testimony, without prompting, diva-style. By the time she'd finished her customized account of God's goodness with a healthy dose of her celebrity status woven out of fact and fiction cloth, New Hope had a star.

But the star still needed a ride home.

Chapter 26

Delilah rode in the back of Jessie's car wondering why the others weren't feeling as good as she did. "Lord, have mercy. I truly enjoyed that prayer meeting tonight. Is this the way it always is?"

"No," Tamara hissed, "it's usually a bit more authentic, not quite so *Showtime at the Apollo.*"

Delilah was sandwiched between Sister Marty and Tamara because the trunk was full and they'd had to put some things in the passenger-side front seat. "I just love that Mother Johnson. She knows her church stuff."

Jessie stopped trying to avoid a headache and just went with it. At least the pain would keep him from killing her.

"So, Delilah," Sister Marty asked as nicely as she could, "did you ever decide what dish you and I should cook? Remember, we both were going to bring foods that complemented each other."

Delilah thought about the question. Any other time she'd say something offhanded, but not tonight. She was still feeling the spirit or something akin to it. "Well, Sister Marty, what's your best dish? We can start with that, because I can pretty much cook anything."

Tamara kept her eyes straight ahead, almost piercing the

back of her father's neck with her stare. Only now and then, when loud, piercing sounds of a fire truck or a police siren blasted as they raced to wherever they were going, did she turn her head.

As Sister Marty and Delilah went back and forth over what recipes and foods should go together, Jessie drove on, wishing both the women would just shut up.

"It's getting late. Anybody heard from the deacon?" Jessie asked the question aloud because he'd just realized that he hadn't.

"I haven't even thought about old Thurgood all day, except when Mother Johnson brought him up." A scowl appeared on her face for a second, but Delilah wasn't letting anything rain on her parade. He could wait.

"I was supposed to hear from him earlier, but I haven't," Sister Marty said.

"Has everybody checked their cell phones?" Jessie asked as he used his still aching hand to pull his from his pocket. He needed to keep his good hand on the wheel.

"There's no sense in me checking mine," Delilah replied. "My BlackBerry is in the red." She stopped and laughed at her own joke, knowing she hadn't paid the bill because she couldn't.

That left Tamara and Sister Marty to check theirs. There were no messages.

The car became quiet. Too quiet. But the deacon was a grown man, free to come and go as he pleased, Jessie thought. Either that or the old man was avoiding him. "Let's see what's happening." Without thinking, Jessie turned on the police scanner he kept connected to his dashboard. But the question still hung in the air. "Let's give the old dude his space. What trouble could he possibly get into? Aren't I riding with all the troublemakers in his life?"

That last statement broke the ice and the women laughed. One by one, each of the women raised her hand. "I know I'm a troublemaker." Delilah burst out laughing even harder than before. Marty and Tamara followed suit and claimed the same status. "I guess we're the bane of that poor man's existence," they all said together.

But no sooner had the laughter from the backseat begun to die down, than Jessie turned up the sound on the scanner. Without another word or checking to make sure the women in the back had on seat belts, he did a sharp U-turn and sped back toward New Hope.

Chapter 27

Jessie hadn't realized he was using both his good and his bad hand to drive. All he knew was he'd heard over the police scanner that unit cars had been called to New Hope Assembly. It was the code that meant serious trouble was happening at New Hope. As long as he was a cop, on duty or off, nobody would violate his church. The women hung on for dear life as Jessie weaved in and out of traffic with one hand laying on the horn.

Not one police car pulled him over, not even as he followed close behind a NYPD swat unit. His gut instinct told him something bad had happened. He was going against his police training to let on-duty police answer the call.

Arriving at New Hope, Jessie pulled up as close as the police would allow. "Y'all stay in this car," Jessie told the women as he hopped out.

The women watched Jessie rush over to one of the police officers who was apparently in charge of crowd control. They saw Jessie pull out his shield and duck under the rope.

Jessie had barely cleared the rope before Delilah, Tamara, and Sister Marty were out of the car.

The ladies sprinted over to be near the rest of the crowd.

The first church member they saw was Mother Johnson, and she was talking to a detective with his shield hanging off his belt. It shone even in the darkness. Mother Johnson appeared animated as she flailed around. By the time they reached her, she was almost out of breath.

"He's not one of our regular crazies," Mother Johnson explained to the detective. "I tried to tell him the center was closed, but he didn't want to hear it. And then one of the deacons walked in and the boy pulled out a gun. The deacon tried to fight him off. . . ." She started swinging her pocketbook. "It was a good thing, too, because I was gonna whup that young boy's arse in the name of—"

Mother Johnson stopped in midsentence. As soon as she saw Delilah and the other women she beckoned them over. As well as she knew both Tamara and Sister Marty, it was Delilah—her new best friend—whom she spoke to first. "Oh Lord, Sister Delilah, now don't you worry none. They gonna save him as soon as they can locate him. . . . I know your prayers and worship are still circling heaven 'bout now."

"Worry about whom?" Delilah asked, knowing full well that the two women had only one man in common. "You can't be serious."

Delilah was short enough not to have to duck too low to get under the rope, so she didn't. And neither did Sister Marty or Tamara. They didn't need any special discernment to figure out what Delilah knew.

Evading the police barriers was easy for Delilah. She'd had years of experience avoiding the police for one scrape or another. Her mind spun. She wasn't familiar with the area. There were too many bushes and undergrowth, and the streetlights were dim. She'd outrun Tamara and Marty. She wasn't quite sure where she was, but it didn't seem like it was that far from New Hope. She couldn't see that well in the dark, but she could hear. The sounds of the police seemed distant. *Oh Lord, did I run the wrong way?* She spun around almost like a top and still didn't hear any signs of Tamara or Marty. *Dammit, Thurgood, where did that fool take you?*

Could it be the young man was spaced out on drugs and would hurt Thurgood? "Jehovah-shammah, in your name," she prayed, "I don't want anything to happen to either Thurgood or that crazy young man. They're both your children, Father. . . ." Yet as hard as she prayed, she still didn't know where to start looking for the deacon.

Yet Jehovah, being almighty and omniscient, heard Delilah's prayer just as He had weeks ago when He'd set things in motion. But then, God never left anything to chance. And so things had happened to bring her to where she stood; knee-high in some low bushes that were clawing at her legs.

"You don't wanna do this, young man!"

The voice was low and Delilah didn't know how close she was to them, or if it was Thurgood she'd heard. So she pushed her body like a sprinter, circling the higher bushes so as not to make any noise. She made her way toward the direction of the voice.

Delilah couldn't believe her eyes when she stopped and looked behind the bushes.

Under the moonlight she could see vaguely that the young man didn't look any older than Tamara. But he was dressed up in a business suit. Who wore a business suit to a crazy interview? He had dreadlocks pulled back into a ponytail. She would've certified him crazy without paperwork. He had a maniacal smirk as he held what looked like a gun at the deacon's side. It scared Delilah speechless.

He looked completely insane as he pushed the deacon ahead of him as they walked out from behind the bushes.

Like a deer in the headlights, Delilah still hadn't moved. Not even when Jessie stumbled upon her and found the deacon in trouble.

"Stay put this time!" Jessie hissed. He was in full cop mode without his police radio and only a gun as he shoved Delilah to safety.

Jessie almost missed his chance. He'd crouched just before looking the deacon straight in the eye when the young man suddenly looked away. He could almost hear the sigh of relief as the deacon, with his hands raised in the air, nodded just slightly. Jessie knew the deacon had seen him.

". . . Like I'm trying to tell you, young man. It's not worth the headache. I've been to prison myself. I know."

"Old nigger, please. That line won't work with me. I'm a grown-ass man—I'm no baby. I can do a bid. Can you do death?"

"I ain't worth shooting, son. Hell, I'm still wearing a conk." Where that came from the deacon would never know. It just sounded like the right thing to say at that moment.

For the first time, the young man laughed. "Is that what that is around the old dome? What happened to the inside of it?"

Wasn't a damn thing funny about that. The deacon kept his arms up and his mouth shut.

The young man suddenly swung his head to the side as his eyes darted around the area. The moon was getting brighter by the minute. They couldn't remain where they were and he was tired. Hunger pangs shot off noisy rumblings from inside his stomach. He needed to find someplace where he didn't have to use his hands to control the old man. But he wasn't putting down the gun and he knew, hands up or not, the old man would continue to put up a fight.

The shed nearby was small, but the young man could tell it wasn't locked. It looked as though someone had removed all the donated clothes and whatever else folks had thrown away to clear their consciences.

It took the young man another second to realize how bad

that idea was. There was only one way in and out; so what was the point. He'd become trapped in some bushes like a wolf with an old goat.

As much and as often as the deacon testified about trading in his gangster for a Bible, he realized at that very moment that he should've reserved just enough of his gangster for such a time as this. Jessie was probably less than twenty feet or so away, and the deacon wasn't sure what to do.

He had at least forty years or better on the kid. The deacon hadn't had a physical in almost six months, but even he knew he couldn't take the young man down and live. If he moved wrong he'd either get shot by Jessie or the kid, or have a heart attack.

Another movement caught the deacon's attention. He didn't react at first, waiting to see if the young man had seen it, too. Deacon Pillar craned his neck to make it seem as though he were getting a cramp, and then he saw her. It was Delilah peeking over a bush. He'd know that white mop of hair anywhere. *Should've known my old ride-or-die gal wouldn't be too far away from our son.*

"Look, young man," the deacon conspired, "my arms are tired and I gotta take a leak. Don't you feel like pissing, too?"

The young man said nothing. It was too late. They'd been discovered. The deacon and the young man saw the prayer posse at the same time. It took several members of the prayer posse peeking out from the other side of the shed to take things to another level. The police had done a miserable job of trying to control a crowd of determined church folks.

The New Hope Assembly prayer posse quickly held hands and quietly prayed, and would've remained that way if they hadn't seen the gun. Seeing the weapon took their beloved deacon's dire situation to a new and more dangerous level. They cut and ran so fast it was as though they'd never been there.

At least they alerted the police before they left the area completely. Some of them made it to the New Hope Center and rushed inside yelling, "The deacon and the gunman are outside by the old clothes bin."

Tamara took off, with Sister Marty trying her best to keep up. Neither remembered exactly where the clothes bin was located. They'd gotten to the third barrel before they bumped into Delilah, who immediately gave them the evil eye. "Where y'all been?" she whispered and then pointed over to Jessie. He'd just raised his gun, prepared to fire.

"Look, son, I told you I need to piss. Now I'd like to do it while I still got some feeling left in my hands. Besides, you with your bad self have scared those others off. . . ."

"Piss on yourself or whatever. Just shut yo' damn mouth before I shoot it off."

Once again, the deacon shut up. He'd barely had a chance to get all the feeling back in his lip from Delilah's beat-down.

The deacon was just about to go ahead and let the pee go where it may when he saw the young man had never taken the safety off the gun.

Jessie suddenly lowered his gun. He hadn't seen Tamara and Sister Marty inching closer to Delilah. But he did see over Delilah's shoulder the outline of several men moving slowly and crouching in the distance. He estimated that they were about ten yards from where the young man held the deacon.

Tamara hunched Sister Marty before she turned slowly and followed her father's gaze as it swept over Delilah. Whatever questions she was about to ask became stuck in her mouth. "Daddy," she whispered, and pointed. "Those cops gonna get somebody hurt or worse."

She, too, recognized the outline of helmets, and for a brief moment a light from a nearby lamppost exposed their automatic rifles and dark bulletproof vests.

The deacon didn't have time to do a lot of thinking about what to do next. Anything he hadn't thought of or about before was too late now.

"Drop it! NYPD!"

The first sound Deacon Pillar heard was a strange whirring that seemed to zip past him like an angry bee. He never heard another sound. One moment the kid had a gun pointed at the deacon's side. The next moment, he felt the young man's weight as he collapsed upon him.

"Move it. Move it out!" Three members of the New York City swat team rushed from out of hiding. They had their guns drawn. They raced toward Jessie, who held his gun high with his good hand and his other hand holding his shield, making sure the swat team saw it.

As they raced forward, somehow Delilah had hiked her dress above her knees and taken off. It was an old habit for when stuff hit the fan and she needed to move freely. No sooner had she seen the young man fall than she'd made her move. She never looked to see if Tamara or Marty followed. Delilah raced toward the young man with a rock she'd picked up. If he wasn't dead or dying, she was gonna bust him upside his head with it. She never gave it a thought that the cops might've thought she had a weapon, too.

"Everybody get back!" The command was loud and clear to every onlooker.

But Delilah wasn't an onlooker. She was Thurgood Pillar's wife. They'd need more than a swat team to stop her.

Delilah ducked and dodged. By the time she got to the other side of the bushes the police already had the deacon by his arms, helping him to get up off the ground.

"Thurgood," Delilah screamed, "Thurgood!"

The deacon was never so happy to see her . . . until he saw her. "Calm down, Dee Dee. Stay back and don't move a muscle."

Just that quick Delilah reverted back to her hardheaded self. She didn't know if she was coming or going. Was it a dream or a nightmare? "Don't tell me what to do, Thurgood!" Whatever it was, Delilah wasn't having it until she heard a voice say, "Drop your weapon!"

Delilah's head jerked in the direction of the voice. She turned around just in time to see what the deacon was trying to tell her. A cop had his automatic weapon drawn.

"Last time, miss. Please drop your weapon."

Chapter 28

Delilah had the look of someone who'd just gotten caught shoplifting but didn't know who put the items in her bag.

She heard someone tell her to put down her weapon. What weapon? She didn't have a weapon, she had a rock, and it was still in her hand.

If someone had offered Sister Marty a million dollars to explain why she made the next move, she'd die a pauper. Without all the fuss and pageantry—the niceties and just plain old common sense—Sister Marty took a few steps and lunged at Delilah.

Delilah hit the ground hard enough to make sure grass would never grow in that spot again, and the rock fell from her hand.

Then it took all the restraint Sister Marty had to leave the rock where it landed and not crack Delilah upside the head.

But Delilah had only wanted to make sure Thurgood was safe, and possibly crack the young man's skull for good measure.

Sister Marty had probably saved Delilah's life when she jumped her. That had to mean something to somebody.

It certainly meant something to the cops because they arrested Sister Marty right along with Delilah.

Sister Marty faced charges of interfering with police business. The cops didn't like it when she threw herself at Delilah and kept them from shooting the woman who'd disobeyed an order. After reading them their rights off of an index card and cuffing them, they place Delilah and Marty in separate patrol cars.

From the time the cops put the cuffs on her and placed her inside the patrol car, Delilah cussed, screamed, and acted like a professional fool. She showed no evidence at all of deliverance through earlier prayers. "But that's my husband!" Delilah kept on trying to tell the cops that she was "the wife." They, of course, thought she was delusional. Every cop around knew Deacon Pillar was single.

Police procedures required Jessie to answer a few questions right there at the crime scene and turn in his weapon. He knew the drill. "I'll meet you downtown," he told the detective. "I'll piss in a cup for you when I get there, and I know I need to file a report immediately." Jessie tried to keep it professional. He had to walk a fine line, especially since he was on a medical leave of absence.

"Hey, Jessie." Another detective walked over and shook his hand. "I know you took that young thug outta here with that shot. When he comes to, he'd better send you a thank-you note from whatever nut-hotel they put him in. You ended any hope for an NBA career when you knee-capped him." The detective stamped out a cigarette he'd dropped to the ground. "Oh, by the way, Pillar's okay. He won't let the EMTs take him to the hospital." The detective stopped and rested his arm on Jessie's shoulder. "Man, I can't believe that old rooster had two women ready to go down for him. I've known Deak practically all my life and I can't pull half the women he has."

The detective treated the situation as routine because under any other circumstances, it would have been. But not that night, especially when a deranged young man had caused

Jessie to shoot to protect a man he loved, who could possibly be his father.

"Daddy!" Tamara raced toward her father. "Daddy, I don't believe all this." Tamara almost collapsed into her father's arms. "They won't let me speak with Deacon Pillar. They've arrested Sister Marty and they almost Tasered Delilah before they got her cuffed. All I could do was watch."

That was pretty much all Jessie could do, too. The patrol car carrying Delilah drove by. He hugged Tamara to him as they watched what looked like a bad B movie. There was Delilah being Delilah. She was still hopping up and down in the backseat between two detectives, like a bobble-head doll. He was tempted to leave her locked up, wherever they took her.

By the time the police finally got Delilah to central booking in downtown Brooklyn, Delilah had raised more hell than the devil allowed. On the other hand, Sister Marty, charged with police interference, kept her cool and prayed. They were like Paul and Silas, but locked up in two different cells.

Although Jessie was supposed to go downtown immediately and follow through with the rest of police procedures, he needed to take care of Tamara and the deacon first.

"Here comes Deacon Pillar." Tamara had hardly gotten the words out before she shook loose from Jessie and ran to the deacon.

"I'm fine, baby girl. You know it takes more than some punk with a gun to ruin my night." The deacon's walk was a little slow. He'd lost count of how many times in the last week he'd fallen on the same hip, but he hadn't lost his sense of humor. "I can't wait to talk to your father. He shot that fool before I could punch him in the mouth for talking about my conk."

And with that, by the time Tamara and the deacon reached where Jessie stood, the two had calmed down a bit.

"Deacon Pillar," Jessie began. "I'm sorry, Deacon."

"Sorry is what that precinct is gonna be if we don't go and check on your mamas."

"You're right," Jessie replied. "Tamara, do you want to come with us or go to Pastor George's house and wait? I'm sure they won't mind."

"I'll go. Just in case you two wind up needing bail money, too. I still got your credit card on me."

"Well, we need to get a move on," Deacon Pillar said. "Should we go to the precinct or to the courthouse? I don't know if either of them will make it to night court or not."

"We ain't that far from central booking. We might as well start there."

No sooner had they arrived, than they discovered they didn't need to make a decision. They ran into one of the detectives who the old deacon had mentored by paying unnecessary child support for years.

"Glad to see you, Deacon Pillar." Detective Gonzalez pulled the deacon aside. "Look, I've done everything I can to keep that old woman from getting her butt Tasered, or worse. But if she throws another punch, I'm afraid there'll be one coming right back at her. I don't know what her problem is."

"Damn that woman!" Deacon Pillar didn't bother to ask which one of the women Gonzalez meant. He already knew.

Both the deacon and Detective Gonzalez spun around. One look at Jessie told them he'd overheard the conversation.

"He looks familiar. Is that Officer Jewel?"

"That's Delilah's son, Jessie. You might wanna hold off on Tasering that old gal for a second."

The detective walked over a few feet and offered his hand. "Officer Jewel, I'm sorry. I didn't mean to say that about your mother."

"That's okay. To know Delilah is to want to Taser Delilah."

The deacon tried to laugh it off, but the detective didn't

know what to make of Jessie's statement about his own mother.

"She could've been released already," Detective Gonzalez continued, "but one minute she's talking about Jehovah guiding her and the next, she's talking about her lying, cheating husband who thinks he's so saved. We don't know whether to take her directly to Kings County psych ward, or wait for day court."

Jessie looked at the deacon and the deacon looked at the floor.

After listening to more of what Detective Gonzalez revealed, they knew Delilah was just being her old self. Delilah's hissy fits and determination not to cooperate had calmed down a bit. But it wasn't enough for her to be allowed to see the deacon and Jessie. They'd tried several times but couldn't.

Delilah wasn't totally alone in her holding cell. Her self-destructive imagination kept her company. At that moment she was angry with herself and disappointed with her beloved Jehovah.

"I could've been in my own home, Jehovah. But no, You just had to let me find my family and a cheating husband. You shouldn't have let me love them so much if they wasn't gonna love me back. They don't even want me around." She fought back tears as she walked about the empty cell, talking loud. "And these folks here took my good clothes, too." She tried to straighten the ugly, ill-fitting orange jumpsuit they'd insisted she wear after her arrest. But she was Delilah Dupree Jewel and hadn't gone down without a fight. She was somewhat grateful that the Spanish detective had kept one of the female cops from wrestling her to the ground. She didn't have that many clothes to rip and tear.

And then, just that quick, Delilah smiled as she remembered that she'd even fought them as she tried to read the label inside the jumpsuit. It was important that she know the designer of that ugly outfit. *Why couldn't those dumb cops see that?* she thought.

"Damn Thur-no-good Pillar!" she blurted.

"Miss Jewel?" Detective Gonzalez approached her now with more understanding. From what Deacon Pillar and her son had revealed, apparently there was a lot of family drama going on. It didn't excuse the way she acted, but it did explain a lot. He'd learned she was a sixty-three-year-old woman without family; at least without one that she believed wanted her. She'd actually risked her own life last evening and she ended up in jail. Perhaps she had a right to be angry with the world.

"What the hell do you want now?" Delilah hadn't turned around to face the man. She didn't plan on it, either.

"I'll dismiss that," the detective replied. "I just thought you'd want to know your family is here and you'll make day court, it seems."

"My son and granddaughter are here?" Delilah spoke as she turned to face the detective. She recognized him as the same one who'd kept the other cop from using the Taser on her. And she saw Jessie, who stood next to him.

"I'll let the two of you talk." Detective Gonzalez turned and walked away without looking back.

Chapter 29

Delilah's sudden outburst of tears surprised Jessie. He'd expected to find the same defiant, pint-sized woman who gave the world hell on a moment's notice, if she had to. He gave her a moment before he spoke. "I'm going to go to court with you."

Delilah wiped the corner of her eyes with the back of one hand. "Why?"

"We're all camped out upstairs. . . ."

"What do you mean, camped out? And not that I care much, but how's Thurgood and Martha . . . Marty, whatever her name is?"

Jessie chuckled. *Lord, this woman is something else.* "They're okay, but the deacon—well, he looks sadder than you. I had emergency prayer with him before that detective brought me down here to see you."

"You did? How long has he been upstairs? They don't even have a clock down here where I can tell time."

"Hmmm. Let me check. It's almost eight-thirty in the morning."

Jessie began to offer Delilah words of comfort. He walked her through the process of what would happen, or what should happen if she behaved, once she got to court. When that conversation was exhausted there were another few moments of silence between them. But it didn't last.

"Jessie," Delilah said softly, "I've made a decision."

"What decision?" Jessie asked with a great deal of caution. If Delilah did nothing else, she kept him on his toes.

She picked at something invisible on her jumpsuit. It was all she could do to keep calm. "I've decided to tell you everything. I don't want to leave anything out, but when I'm finished you might think me a coward."

"I can't even imagine you being a total coward." He still hadn't forgotten she'd abandoned her duties as a mother. But this wasn't the time or the place for that discussion. At least for him it wasn't. "Go ahead, Delilah, I'm listening."

She decided to forgo challenging him for referring to her as being not a total coward. If she didn't speak now, she didn't know when she ever would. "I'm your mama, that you can believe. But I want to start off by telling you my real name. And then I'm leaving. . . ."

He felt agitated and began to only half listen. He could've told her that he already knew she'd married the deacon, but he didn't. He wasn't sure if that was true anyway.

But if he didn't believe Delilah, he had to believe the officers who appeared to take her away.

One of the police officers called out, "Delilah Dupree Jewel-Pillar."

They were the same officers who'd arrested her. They arrived to take Delilah to court and were prepared for a possible battle. They didn't get one.

Jessie stood stunned as he watched Delilah handcuffed again and led away. She'd actually told the truth about something.

Inside the courtroom Delilah did everything she was asked. She answered only the questions put to her and she did so with deference. By the time Delilah finished her courtroom performance, the judge was ready to throw the book at the district attorney for filing a false report on the sweet old lady.

However, the judge didn't totally absolve Delilah of all the charges. After all, she did fail to obey a police order, which could've resulted in a very different outcome for her. And there was that little thing about resisting arrest, which was a big no-no.

". . . Although I've not witnessed the anger testified to by the police officers involved in the fracas, I'm not going to render any jail time besides the time—or in your case, hours—already served. You'll be given an ACD: adjournment in contemplation of dismissal. However, I'm of the mind to also have you examined to see if there is need for anger management."

The judge signed a few papers and asked for both the district attorney and Delilah's court appointed attorney to approach the bench.

After a conference that lasted about two minutes, during which the district attorney spent most of it huffing and puffing, the judge turned back and addressed Delilah.

"Miss Jewel-Pillar, it is the verdict of the court to have you attend an anger management class. The number of times you will attend will be no less than five but no more than ten, unless it is deemed necessary, in which case you will return to court and the court will revisit the charges. It also appears that your actions have led the court to wonder if you would be a danger to yourself as well. A woman of a certain age shouldn't be deliberately tossing her body around in such a manner as you have, no matter the circumstances."

Delilah looked from side to side, trying to determine who the judge was talking about. She knew for certain the old and balding Dick Cheney look-alike wasn't talking about her.

And as if he'd read Delilah's mind, the judge called her,

again, by her name. "Now, Miss Jewel-Pillar, in order for the court to release you today, instead of holding you over until you've been evaluated further, I'm releasing you to your family."

Delilah's jaw dropped.

But Jessie's opened and he mouthed, "Thank you, Your Honor."

The entire time Delilah was in court, she never saw an already-free Sister Marty seated between Tamara and Deacon Pillar. She'd probably had been rearrested if she had.

Chapter 30

Delilah learned the deacon left with Tamara and Marty before her release was completed. But she was glad they'd at least been there for her, and that Marty had an ACD release as well.

Delilah was also glad Jessie didn't try to talk during the ride home. She'd probably have said something that would've provoked him to take her back to the courthouse. But then she noticed he kept looking at her, strange-like. It was like he was trying to figure something out—as if she'd not given him enough news to handle. But he said nothing.

When they finally arrived back at the house, she noticed the deacon's Old Lemon parked across the street. "I see the welcoming committee is here."

"Let me help you out." That was Jessie's only reply.

They'd gotten no farther than Jessie's front porch when a woman Delilah had not seen before came outside. Quietly, Delilah stood off to the side on the front porch as Jessie referred to her as First Lady. She could only hear snatches of their conversation.

"Brother Jessie, I just stopped by after seeing Sister Marty. She looked exhausted, but none the worse for all she's been through. I thought I'd stop by here, too, and Deacon Pillar is snoring on the couch. It was harder getting Tamara calmed down. She's waiting for you." The First Lady stopped and looked toward Delilah. It took her a moment, but she smiled and came over.

"You must be Delilah, Tamara's grandmother."

Delilah didn't know how to react. She wasn't sure if the woman was acknowledging the fact or accusing her of something.

"I'm Sister George."

It was uncanny how the First Lady's smile put Delilah at ease, and yet Delilah wasn't certain why. "Thank you for taking care of Tamara." Delilah wanted to say more but didn't.

"We all love the Jewel family, and Deacon Pillar, too. We're grateful for all of God's miracles."

The First Lady smiled again. She looked at Jessie. "Brother Jewel, I know you and Cindy did a wonderful job raising Tamara. She's talented, centered, and she loves the Lord."

The First Lady stopped and then pointed toward Delilah. "But whenever possible, a young lady also needs her grandmother. Grandmothers can give directions without all the guesswork. They've already traveled the path and fallen off a few times. And they know when and how to get back on track. Children don't come with manuals. That's why parents make so many mistakes. Grandparents, on the other hand— and like I said, grandmothers in particular—have read the manual from the contents to the index. Grandmothers have that mother wit."

Delilah was floored; is that what she had? She'd wanted to call it that, but she had no reference. She smiled back at the First Lady. "Thank you so much."

"You're quite welcome. It was just something the Lord laid on my heart to say."

"First Lady," Jessie said as he tried to stifle a yawn, "I'm just gonna go inside. I'm so tired I'm about to pass out."

"I'm sorry. What must I be thinking? I know you two

must be exhausted. We're gonna have a six o'clock prayer call for your family, Brother Jessie."

The First Lady turned and smiled again at Delilah. "You're quite welcome to join us later on this evening if you're not too tired, or just fall on your knees wherever you are at six o'clock. I've also heard about the wonders God performed for you yesterday. The waters in the blessing pool are never calm. Just step in and take Him at His word."

"I'll think about that." Delilah smiled, too. "I guess ain't no harm in splashing around in God's pool."

As tired as Jessie was, he couldn't help but laugh at Delilah's seemingly innocent translation. It was an easy laugh in the midst of the hard trial the Jewel family faced. Jessie walked the First Lady to her car as Delilah went inside.

Although released into Jessie's custody, out of habit she headed straight up the stairs to the deacon's apartment.

When Delilah reached the top of the stairs, the door to the deacon's apartment was ajar. Peeping through it, she saw his long legs. He was sprawled across the couch.

Thank you, Jehovah God, for letting him sleep. I don't have the strength to deal with another bit of drama today. She tiptoed past him and went inside his bedroom.

Delilah showered as quietly as she could before borrowing one of the deacon's old shirts and lying down. Yet as tired as she was, she couldn't sleep. Everything that'd happened in the past twenty-four hours replayed repeatedly in her head. She hadn't bothered to close the deacon's door, so she heard faint sounds of movement from downstairs.

"What if they need me down there?" Delilah had never felt as useless in her entire life as she did at that moment. Where was all that grandmother wit the First Lady spoke about earlier? She didn't have a clue as to what her family needed, beyond their need to know the entire truth. And she'd already determined she'd give them that. Except now she'd been placed in Jessie's custody and that changed things.

Jehovah, what can I do? I can't tell Jessie that the deacon's his father until the time is right. There ain't no right time because Jessie will hate me, and the deacon, I'm sure. The deacon can move if he has to, but where can I go? I'm in Jessie's custody. I can't stay here and be hated anymore.

In her mind, Delilah's self-imposed prison sentence had just begun and without chance of parole.

Chapter 31

Delilah woke to voices coming from the deacon's kitchen. She sat up to make sure she wasn't dreaming. She slipped from under the covers and walked softly to the bedroom door. She could hear the deacon talking.

"What could I do?" Deacon Pillar was saying. "I just tiptoed back out the door and left Delilah cradling a pillow. I was shocked to find her there. I thought for sure she'd go down to the extra room in the basement to catch a nap. But, well, suh, awrighty Jesus, she's balled up like a little kitten in there."

The deacon refilled his cup as well as Jessie's and continued. "Let me ask you something. Do you want her in your life?" He'd asked the question knowing full well it was on Jessie's mind. It had to be. It would certainly be on his.

"I'm not sure if I want her beyond what the court says is mandatory."

Delilah's heart sank. She'd been right. Yet, instead of returning to the bed, she kept on eavesdropping. She might as well hear everything.

"What are you talking about, Jessie?" the deacon asked. He wasn't sure if he really wanted to know.

"I didn't have time to tell you after I came back from answering questions and leaving a cup of piss downtown. Delilah's been released into my custody."

And that's when the deacon relaxed and started laughing. He laughed until he was holding his sides and almost threw up his tea and liquor, which he'd said was for medicinal purposes.

Jessie couldn't help it. He started laughing, too. The absurdity of the whole situation was laughable, and if they didn't laugh, then both men would start bawling.

Behind the laughter each man wondered what the other knew and when he knew it.

Delilah quietly closed the deacon's bedroom door. *Damn, I thought I was deceitful. Those two could teach me a thing or two,* she thought.

While a few doors down Jessie and Deacon Pillar chatted in the deacon's kitchen, Marty jumped up in her bed from a sound sleep. Her doorbell rang and she thought it was part of a dream. One look at her clock told her she'd not slept that long, three hours or so at the most. The bell rang again and she heard her front door open.

Tamara was almost too exhausted to use her spare key to enter her godmother's house. "Sister Marty," she called out as she sat down in the nearest chair. Everything in the living room looked nice and neat as always, so why was the situation all a mess?

Tamara called out once more, "Sister Marty."

Marty rushed through the house toward Tamara's voice, wearing a nightgown. She hadn't bothered to put on a robe. "What's wrong, Tamara?" She knew it was a stupid question. Her goddaughter looked more of a wreck than she did, and she'd been locked up in jail.

Sister Marty snatched a tissue from a box and sat down next to Tamara. "If you're worried about me, I'm just fine."

"I'm worried about everybody." Tamara took the tissue

from Marty's hand. "I've never seen Daddy shoot someone before. I've never been so scared for the deacon. And I don't know what I'd have done if you'd been hurt, too."

"That's okay. We weren't hurt. We're doing just fine. Even Delilah made out okay. You know that. You were in the court-room, too."

"I know she did. But I'm too ashamed to face her right now."

Marty's face couldn't hide her confusion. "Ashamed of what, Tamara? What did you do?"

"It's nothing that you don't already know about. . . ."

"Then what is it?"

There was a reddish halo around Tamara's gray eyes as she looked up. She'd cried so much she appeared much older than her twenty-one years. "I thought I was gonna die when the cops told Delilah to drop that rock and she didn't." Tamara stopped and tears began to drop. "They could've shot my grandmother. I would've lost her. How could I feel that way about her, when I have you?"

Marty looked at Tamara's sudden admission of her love for Delilah as a sign. She didn't feel threatened, nor did she make any subtle jabs or put-downs about Delilah. She'd al-ready promised God, as she sat in that cell with people who probably had less than she, and even those who more than likely deserved to be there, that she'd back off. She'd done and felt too many things that went against her nature. She wasn't some teenager who had to fight over a boyfriend. She'd never done that anyway. God had given her Jessie for a reason, and perhaps her season with him was finished. God's will was His, and she'd be okay no matter how things turned out. Even if Jessie got angry because she'd not spoken up about Delilah and Thurgood sooner, she'd still be okay.

"Where's your father?"

"I heard him go upstairs to the deacon's before I left the house."

"And where's Delilah?"

"I don't know. I checked before I left and there wasn't any sign of her downstairs in the basement room. I know Daddy brought her back, and now I don't know where she is. She doesn't have anyone." Tamara started rocking and crumbling the tissue she held.

Marty's heart was breaking piece by piece watching Tamara in so much pain. "Come on, Tamara."

Marty helped Tamara to her feet and then led her into one of the spare bedrooms. "Rest here, baby."

Tamara didn't fight it. She lay down fully clothed on her godmother's bed and before Marty had crept out of the room, Tamara was sleep.

Marty went into her kitchen. As tired as she should've been, she was now wide awake. She wondered where Delilah could possibly be. And she also wondered if she should get involved. She'd just promised God she'd stay out of it. Yet she'd already started dialing her phone. As much as she hated doing it, she called the deacon's house.

"Hello." The deacon answered his phone almost on the first ring. He didn't want Delilah to waken. ". . . Jessie's right here. How are you? . . . Okay, we'll chat later. . . . Let me put Jessie on. . . ."

The deacon took the cordless phone back to the table. He used the palm of his free hand to cover it instead of putting it on mute. "It's Marty," he told Jessie as he handed him the phone. "If I didn't know any better I'd think she was upset with me. What could've changed since this morning?"

The only thing the deacon knew for sure that could change things was sound asleep in his bedroom. He was certain he'd detected a hint of aggravation in Marty's voice.

". . . She's upstairs. . . . Why? . . . Can't you tell me?"

Jessie placed the phone into the deacon's hands. "Wake up Delilah and give her the phone."

Chapter 32

No one was more surprised than Delilah when the deacon knocked on his bedroom door with a phone in his hand. She'd barely tiptoed back to the bed and gotten under the covers. She wasn't in the mood to talk.

"Delilah," the deacon called to her as he approached the bed. "Wake up, Dee Dee." He waited to see if she'd respond, but she didn't. He spoke into the phone. "Marty, I'm sorry, but she won't wake up."

Delilah sat up and snatched the phone from the deacon's hands almost at the same time. She didn't want to talk to him, and not Marty, either, at that moment. But she was curious.

The deacon started to say something but he didn't, especially when Delilah waved him away. It was obvious she wanted privacy. He wasn't sure when he stopped being the king of his castle, but it had to be about the same time she had arrived back into his life.

Jessie and the deacon continued chatting at the deacon's kitchen table while Delilah was on the phone. They talked about nonsense, wondering what was going on between the two women. Jessie was certain that their not being in the same room wouldn't stop drama from happening. He and the deacon looked up as Delilah raced from the bedroom. She flew past them, tossing the phone as she went. The phone nicked the deacon across his forehead and before he could holler "ouch" Delilah was out the door.

Marty met Delilah at the door and led her to the spare bedroom where she'd left Tamara.

Delilah stood in the doorway and watched her granddaughter, praying she'd know how to handle things. Moments later, urged on by Sister Marty, Delilah quietly came around and sat on the edge of the bed. "Hush, baby, just let Grandma Delilah hold you."

Marty looked on, marveling at how easy the word *grandma* finally rolled off Delilah's tongue. Had she realized what she'd said?

"C'mon, Jehovah," Delilah prayed, "my grandbaby needs peace." With that Delilah started to make up a refrain, which she sang softly. "Jehovah-shalom . . . He's peace in a storm. Jehovah-shammah . . . for He is here with us . . ."

Tamara fell into her grandmother's arms and immediately went back to sleep.

Jessie had left the deacon's apartment as soon as Delilah raced away. He didn't try to follow her out the front door, knowing she'd probably gone over to Marty's house. There was nowhere else she could've gone. He'd already decided that he'd go over to Marty's right after he'd checked on Tamara.

As soon as he discovered Tamara was missing, he put two and two together and came up with Delilah and Marty. When he ran over to Marty's, she met him at the door but didn't let him in.

"Tamara and Delilah are both here. They are both fine. Delilah wanted her real grandmother. I'm fine with that. I'll call you later." She closed the door, hard, and left him standing flat-footed on her porch.

There was nothing for him to do but return home. *She wouldn't have lied about that,* he thought.

For the second or third time that day, Jessie rapped lightly on the deacon's apartment door. He could hear the old man shuffle across the vestibule floor.

The deacon opened the door slightly and then all the way when he saw it was Jessie.

"Come on in, Brother Jessie. Are those women alright? I figured that's who you'd taken off to see about."

Deacon Pillar pointed to the other love seat. "I've got more tea and Jack. Which do you prefer this time?"

"At this moment I'll take Jack heavy and tea light."

The deacon poured the concoction into a large cup and handed it to Jessie. He watched Jessie take a sip and then waited for the shoe to fall.

"You'll never guess what happened at Marty's."

"Does it involve your mother?"

"Yep."

"That's funny, I didn't hear any more police cars or ambulances."

The men laughed softly and that broke the tension again.

"Would you believe that Tamara chose Delilah over Marty?"

"What are you talking about?" The deacon quickly poured some of the Jack into his chamomile tea and leaned back to listen. All his tiredness suddenly fled.

"I was already shocked to hear that it was Marty on the phone for Delilah," Jessie confessed.

"Tell me about it—" The deacon quickly put the cup to his lips to keep from saying anything more.

Jessie took the opportunity to probe once again. "How did you feel when you heard the judge refer to Delilah as Mrs. Jewel-Pillar in court?"

The deacon almost choked, but it wasn't like he'd expected Jessie not to figure things out. But he still wasn't ready for full disclosure. "I was going to speak to you about that when things calmed down a bit around here."

"We're alone now." Jessie took another sip from his glass while his eyes stayed glued to the deacon's. He'd learned to read body language years ago and he probably should've watched the deacon closer.

"Back when I met your mama, we used to hang tough. I mean, we were in some of the same bands, hung out at some of the same clubs. We were thick as thieves. But your mama wasn't old enough to do a lot of things that we did, so I made an honest woman out of her."

"You gave her your name?"

The deacon hadn't thought of explaining it so simply without flat-out lying, but since Jessie had provided the explanation, he went with it. "Yes, I gave her my name."

"And what did she do with it after you did that?" Jessie still sensed the deacon wasn't as forthcoming as he should've been, but he could wait. This was a start.

"Well, let me see," the deacon said slowly as he took another sip. "We traveled a bit."

"Traveled?"

"Yep. It was mostly around the five boroughs, but now and then we managed to make it out to the Hamptons for gigs and such."

Jessie was about to say more, but he saw the deacon fidgeting a bit. He decided to cut the old man some slack. It had been a hell of a ride in the last twenty-four hours.

"I don't know about you, but I don't think I'm gonna make it for prayer service this evening. I still have to pick up some things for this Sunday. What are you going to do?"

"I gotta mix and match an outfit and make a couple of phone calls." The deacon saw the look on Jessie's face and smiled. "I promise to keep it at no more than three colors or patterns—how's that?"

"That's a deal."

"Jessie, I want to ask you something before you go."

"What is it?"

"Do you think about that young man you shot?"

"Why do you think I haven't slept yet? It's all I can think about, when I'm not thinking about my family. But I did what I had to do. If I hadn't, we might not be having this conversation."

The deacon didn't respond. He rose and walked over to Jessie. He patted him on his back. "Thank you. You saved my life by shooting that young man. And you don't take it lightly. I'm proud of you."

"As proud of me as if I were your son?"

"Yes."

The deacon walked Jessie to the door. They shook hands, and again neither said what needed to be said.

Chapter 33

Saturday Night

No one could tell that any of the women had been through something as traumatic as time in jail and witnessing a shooting by the way they were laughing and spending time together. Yet, the past two days had worked wonders.

"Delilah, you put your foot in these collards," Marty said as she stood in the kitchen, cramming forkfuls into her mouth.

Delilah nodded as she wiped dripping cheese from the corner of her mouth. "Well, if I put my foot in the greens, you sure enough dropped your drawers in this macaroni and cheese."

"I don't know who hooked up the yams with all these gooey marshmallows, but somebody added the funk to them."

"Now that's just nasty," Delilah said as she sucked her teeth.

"That's why we don't allow you to cook," Marty chimed in.

"I see." Tamara laughed. "But feet and drawers are allowed in the pots."

"Grandmama"—Tamara's eyes sparkled when she called Delilah by the dreaded name and Delilah smiled instead of shuddered—"I know I keep asking and I guess I'll continue. . . ."

"You already know the answer, sweetie."

"Humor her, Delilah." Marty winked. She truly liked the Pillar-free zone she and Delilah had agreed upon. Amazing how much alike they were when jealousy wasn't an issue.

"But I want you to do it." Tamara tried her best to pout, and all it did was make both Marty and Delilah burst out laughing.

"Okay, you two go ahead and laugh. I'm telling you it will work. All we have to do is choose some outfits with a bit of swagger to them and grab microphones. We can turn out the Family and Friends Day. Ain't that right, Daddy?" Tamara called out. "We know you're standing around listening to us."

Jessie stuck his head into the kitchen. "I am not." He walked inside and stood by the dishwasher. "I'm not getting caught up in whatever craziness y'all creating."

"Tamara wants us to add swagger to our outfits. I've never heard of that designer. Have you?" Marty looked at Jessie and smiled. She was blessed to see him still smiling, knowing what he did and not being able to share it.

"Well, first of all," Jessie said as he cracked one of the dozen crab legs lying on the counter by the dishwasher, "I don't do swagger. I don't even know what swagger is, but it sounds sinful to me."

"Lord, please have mercy, Jessie. You're my son. You can't help but have some of that swagger," Delilah bragged.

Delilah turned to Tamara. "Swagger is a good thing, right?"

It was Tamara's turn to laugh. "Yes, it's a good thing. And as handsome and well dressed as my daddy is . . . he's got swagger to spare."

"Sounds like some type of disease to me," Marty added.

Crab and lobster shells went flying around the kitchen like missiles as Jessie roared with laughter.

It was a first for them, and truth be told, they truly liked it.

By that Sunday morning everything was in place for the Family and Friends Day celebration at New Hope Assembly, and the Family Jewels, Deacon Pillar, and Sister Marty were so nervous they couldn't stand it.

The deacon had gotten up earlier and dressed not to impress. He'd kept his word and limited his outfit to three colors. He wore a neon red, peach, and navy blue polka-dot custom-made bow tie, to make sure he was seen. He hadn't bothered to make it laugh-proof, too. He finished his fiasco designer outfit with peach-colored suspenders, a navy blue dagger-collar shirt, and bright neon red pants. Of course, his shoes were black. He'd already gone to the airport the night before and picked up Zipporah Lamb; she was the A&R representative who'd flown all the way from Pelzer, South Carolina, to hear Tamara sing. He'd convinced her to stay with Sister Marty, since she had the room, and he'd pick them both up this morning before service.

Deacon Pillar's cousin, affectionately called Sister Betty by most of the folks in Pelzer, couldn't make the trip with Zipporah, which was too bad. It was she who set it up for the deacon and Tamara. But for Delilah's sake, it was also good that Sister Betty couldn't come. Years ago, when the deacon and Delilah stayed a few days with his cousin, Delilah did some nasty little Delilah tricks and his cousin wasn't happy. He knew they both had long memories—or, they'd probably forgotten everything except that.

"Will y'all ever stop yapping and come on?" Deacon Pillar called downstairs as he stuffed his purple Royal Priesthood cap in his back pocket. "It's getting late."

A short time later, Tamara and Delilah stood by Jessie's car while he piled the food into the trunk. "Are the two of you sure we have everything? I'm not trying to come back here for nothing."

"You won't have time to come back here. I guess you forgot you need to take me to Garden City later on so I can check up on my house and get my bills. . . . I mean my mail."

Tamara laughed and hugged Delilah's shoulders. "Am I going to be like you when I get older?"

"No, sweetie. You'll be much wiser than me."

Jessie smiled. It was becoming a habit lately, despite all they'd been through and all they still needed to know. And he liked it.

"Okay, we're ready." Sister Marty walked with her dress bag flung over her arm. This morning she'd wear her nurse's uniform for the grand march. She didn't think she'd have much time to change so she brought a "swagger" outfit with her. Tamara had chosen a bright yellow and a coffee brown knee-length outfit for them. The suits looked fabulous. The A&R rep, Zipporah Lamb, walked a few steps behind.

Everything was fine. Delilah waved at Sister Marty and smiled. As soon as she took one look at Zipporah all bets were off.

"Is that the gal that Jessie said he spoke to last night about you singing for the record company?" She hunched Tamara so she wouldn't have to talk so loud.

"Yes, that's her. She and Daddy spoke for a long time last night. He said she has a very high opinion of the deacon and that she was the goddaughter-in-law of Deacon Pillar's cousin Betty."

Delilah turned back to look at Zipporah once more, and then she stared at Jessie as he looked at Zipporah, too. He was looking a little too hard for Delilah's taste.

Zipporah Lamb was a married woman with a small child, yet she looked like she'd just stepped off a runway. Her svelte figure and five-inch heels made her olive-skinned legs look long and lean. She had long, shoulder-length, curly auburn hair. Her hazel eyes with specks of green glimmered in the sunlight. She'd worn a designer two-piece tangerine dress with matching pillbox hat, complete with netting that rested upon a perfectly shaped nose. The sight of her caused some on the block to stare as sun rays shimmered against white-on-white teeth. Everything about her screamed *I'm just visiting Brooklyn and I'll be leaving shortly.*

She's as out of place as Monica Lewinsky at the Clinton dinner table, thought Delilah.

By the time Sister Marty and Zipporah reached Jessie's car, Delilah had already decided who she would ride with.

Deacon Pillar drove his Old Lemon as though it were the first time. He'd almost hit several squirrels and there wasn't a pigeon along the way that didn't have its wings tested for flight.

Delilah hadn't stopped verbally beating on him since they'd pulled away from his apartment. By the time she finished with him, she'd cussed him out and threatened to be the bane of his existence for as long as he lived; as though she weren't already.

"Thurgood, you can't tell me that music woman from Pelzer, South Carolina, being your cousin Betty's godson's wife is just a coincidence. You can't tell me that with a straight face and expect me to believe it."

"Dee Dee, the problem is that you won't let me tell anything."

"What the hell are you talking about, Thurgood?"

"Stop your cussing, Dee Dee. We're on our way to the Lord's house."

"So how far are we from the church?"

"About another fifteen minutes after I make a stop."

"What the hell do you mean, after you make a stop?"

"I need to pick up two more people."

"And put them where, Thurgood? Put them where?"

"I guess you've been running your trap so much you haven't noticed that I've had the truck done over."

Delilah's head spun around as she followed the deacon's gaze. Sure enough, he'd had another seat installed as well as two long bars that ran along the sides of the interior.

"Well, it's a good thing that you at least had the sense to make enough room for all of them you promised rides to."

"Please be quiet, Dee Dee. They're waiting over there." The deacon pulled up to the curb and parked. He got out of the truck and went around and opened a side panel.

Delilah's first thoughts were to get out and take a tire iron to the deacon's head. But there were too many witnesses and she wasn't sure how she'd explain going to anger management classes while still displaying violent tendencies.

A middle-aged woman with her head leaning to the side, her hands pulled almost into an arc shape, managed a smile when she saw the deacon walk toward her. She was in a wheelchair. Mother Johnson from New Hope Assembly was with her.

Mother Johnson started to push the wheelchair toward the truck. "I can't thank you enough, Deacon Pillar."

"Than ya." The woman's speech was slurred, but she was trying to thank the deacon, too.

"It's no bother," the deacon replied.

"Sister Green, honey," Mother Johnson said slowly, "this is Deacon Thurgood Pillar. He's the man that's gonna testify on your son's behalf. He ain't harboring no grudge from the other night."

"Than ya." The woman strained to say more but couldn't.

"I'm so grateful." Mother Johnson spoke as though for the woman. "I hadn't seen Sister Green in so long I didn't recognize her son when he came to the center for help. Lord,

I feel just as responsible as you must feel. I've asked the prayer team to come visit Sister Green here at the nursing home."

"I'm sure they'll do that." The deacon would be surprised if they didn't. He'd seen the prayer posse pray for the blind, crippled, and crazy. The woman's son fitted in one of those categories.

"Who's in your truck?" Mother Johnson had gotten the wheelchair close enough to see that there was someone with the deacon.

"It's Delilah."

"Delilah," Mother Johnson said once they had Sister Green secured inside the truck. "It's good to see you again. This here is Sister Green. It was her son who caused all that fuss with the deacon, if you get my drift."

"It's good to see you again, too. And you, too, Sister Green." Delilah couldn't look the other woman in the face. It wasn't that Delilah pitied the woman, because she really didn't. But she'd wanted to take a rock to the woman's son's skull and she felt convicted.

For the rest of the ride to the church, the deacon traded old Family and Friends Day stories with Mother Johnson. To Delilah, he said not another word. She'd gotten jealous for no reason and started off his day with a nasty attitude. He'd placed her in a supporting role because at that moment she was no longer the star of his Lifetime movie.

By the time the deacon arrived with Delilah, Mother Johnson, and Sister Green, New Hope Assembly's Family and Friends Day celebration was in full swing.

The celebration had started earlier with the sunrise morning service and it would end, as Pastor George always said, "When God said so."

They found Jessie and Zipporah seated in one of the pews in the center aisle. They followed Jessie's finger as he pointed to the seats he'd saved by placing bags on them.

"Tamara's gone to join up with the choir," Jessie told

Delilah, who sat down next to him. "I haven't checked the program yet, so I don't know when we go up."

"I'm feeling the spirit already," Zipporah said to the deacon. "I'm so happy I came."

Delilah continued to ignore Zipporah. Instead she watched with a bit of unexpected sadness as the church nurse rolled Sister Green over to a nearby aisle where the other attendees in wheelchairs sat. She thought about telling Jessie who the woman was, but decided it could wait. She obviously wasn't going anywhere. Yet Delilah found herself looking over at the woman again, knowing how the woman must've felt losing her son once to a mental problem, and then again to the system. Delilah patted Jessie's knee and smiled, but inside she'd begun to feel sadness because she'd hadn't lost her son, she'd given him away.

But sadness had to vacate the premises of New Hope because when the musicians started playing, it was time for fire to rain down. In no time two overweight sisters wearing hats that should've come with a warning label hit their tambourines and that lit the match.

And then the real churchy-hallelujah good time started when the choirs marched in.

The combined choirs' colorful robes looked as though Crayola had hooked them up. Then it was time for the vocal Olympics. Singers of all sizes and lifestyles tried to one-up each other. One singer would send a note up through the church rafters and another would bury it in the church basement. There wasn't a note left that wouldn't have made Patti LaBelle green with envy.

And if that wasn't enough of a show, the combined choirs lost their minds and turned into steppers with their versions of the grand march. And it was Sister Marty and the nurses unit that led the madness. It didn't matter if a marcher had one leg or two, crutches or arm slings, they high-stepped,

Cabbage Patched, butterflied, Laffy Taffied, and even Tootsie Rolled when they could get away with it.

Everyone sat on the edge of their seats while Pastor George and the First Lady sat like proud parents as the event took off. Everyone knew the NHA auxiliaries delivered when they marched around the walls of the church like Joshua around Jericho.

And of course, the choirs and the nurses units weren't the only shows. Any true spirit-filled Family and Friends Day march had to have a knockout finale. It happened when someone in the musicians' pit hollered, "Give them mothers some." So of course they knew they could always count on the mothers board to be ready and available to pass out the hallelujahs at a moment's notice. And when Mother Johnson got up and led those old gals they didn't disappoint.

At the end of the march and other spectacles, the ushers always received a nice collection to divide among themselves. The church affectionately called it the usher board combat pay. Those gatekeepers earned every dollar.

Zipporah was no stranger to a boisterous church. She immediately felt at home and acted like she was about to lose all her professional cool. From the first note Tamara sang until the last, Zipporah was secretly overjoyed. Of course, she couldn't let the others know because business was still business and she knew she'd have to negotiate for Tamara's awesome talent. Yet there were still other parts of the service to shout about. So Zipporah went about getting her praise on and loving it.

Jessie wasn't too far behind Zipporah. Just like any proud papa would, he, too, leapt for joy with every solo Tamara led. The only time he kept quiet was when he thought of how proud Cindy would've been had she seen their daughter on that day.

And as for Deacon Pillar—well, he sat peacock proud on

another pew with the rest of the deacons., No one would've known he had a jacked-up conk hidden beneath his purple Royal Priesthood cap. But then he got caught up in the spirit and then caught out there, in embarrassment. Without thinking he jumped up and threw out one too many hallelujahs, so his cap jumped off, too.

And when that happened, that's when Delilah almost fell out.

She started whooping and doubling over from trying not to laugh harder than she already was, until she caught the attention of some of the ushers. They thought she wanted to shout, but was confined by space. So a few of the ushers raced to her pew and snatched her into the aisle to let her get loose for the Lord.

At first Delilah was doing what she always did. She was giving her audience all she had. She bucked, jerked, and nearly danced the electric slide before something got a hold of her.

And if Delilah had to describe what that something was, she couldn't. At first she felt a warm feeling spread throughout her body. In her mind she heard the words *Thank you, Jesus* repeatedly, but couldn't figure out who was saying it.

With her eyes shut tight and her body shaking, Delilah suddenly remembered sitting in her car outside of New Hope those many years ago, and she cried out, "Thank you, Jesus."

And then she remembered that less than a few months ago, she'd thought it next to impossible to get close to her granddaughter and her son. Even the thought of Thurgood not mentioning a divorce, and that he was safe from the young man who wanted to kill him caused her to cry out again, "Thank you, Lord."

The floodgates opened in her mind and she recalled everything—from the time her mother, Claudia, left her without even looking back, until the day Thurgood found her in the church's parking lot. And she remembered God had allowed her to see her son again, and she wept, "Oh, Jesus, I thank you, Jehovah-shammah."

"Call on him," one of the ushers coached Delilah. "Let Jesus in."

"He's waiting on you, my sister." It was Mother Johnson, who raced over and tried to encourage Delilah to continue praising God.

But then the prayer posse members got into the act and the First Lady came down from the pulpit. She ripped off her giant, white, three-layer church hat and went to work. She grabbed hold of Delilah and whispered into her ear, "Wade in the blessing pool, Delilah." The First Lady placed her wide palm against Delilah's small forehead and pushed her backwards. "There's deliverance in that water."

Delilah sprang forward.

"There's precious healing in that water." The First Lady cradled Delilah's head and rocked her back and forth, fast.

Delilah passed out completely . . . and it was for real this time.

And when it was all over Jessie and the deacon, along with Sister Marty and especially Tamara, didn't care at all that they'd not sung a song together. For on that night they rejoiced because Delilah's Jehovah had brought his prodigal daughter home.

Outside in New Hope Assembly's parking lot, it'd taken Jessie, the deacon, and two other female ushers to get Delilah, who hadn't stopped praising God, into Jessie's car. Although the pastor had volunteered to bring Delilah to Jessie's after he and his wife prayed further with her, Jessie had said, "That's okay. She's my mother."

He wanted to drive his mother and was glad when Zipporah said she'd ride back with the deacon instead.

All the way home Delilah kept repeating, "Thank you,

Jesus. Thank you, Jehovah God." Jessie wasn't sure what to make of it all, but every time she said it, he and Tamara would join in and say, "Thank you, Jesus," too.

Once inside the house, Delilah still hadn't stopped praising God. Not even by the time Tamara had helped her to take off her clothes for bed. So for the first time in her life, Delilah wasn't the star. She was well on her way to becoming a servant of the Most High and she'd never be able to tell anyone why or how.

Chapter 34

A month had gone by since the Family and Friends Day at New Hope Assembly, yet the joy had continued inside Jessie's home.

This morning Delilah, Tamara, and Marty had decided to have a brunch. So they were in the kitchen chattering, cooking, tasting, signifying, and just having a grand time.

They were making too much noise for Jessie, so he decided he'd give them room to work. He was glad Cindy had insisted on having a large kitchen. He looked up and laughed. "She'd have loved to see this."

Though his hand had healed and he'd returned to limited duty on the night shift, with not much else to do he decided to give the deacon another chance. He enjoyed the peace that was present since the Family and Friends Day, but he was still finding it hard to let his need for the total truth go, even though he'd promised himself that he would after Marty had finally told all she knew. He'd made her promise, against her better judgment, to keep their conversation private. He believed she had.

★   ★   ★

"C'mon in, Brother Jessie." The deacon came to the door with a jar of goop in his hand. He still hadn't found time to touch up his conk since the Family and Friends Day.

Jessie stepped inside and it was almost like he'd never been there before. The deacon's apartment looked a lot less masculine than it'd been a few weeks ago.

"What's happened to your apartment? What's with all the frills and lace scattered about?"

"Your mama happened to it."

Jessie laughed. "Enough said."

After Jessie sat down, he and the deacon discussed everything from church politics after the past Family and Friends Day to Delilah finally coming to the Lord.

"I'm telling you, Brother Jessie, when your mama was not downstairs shouting and praising God while she's quoting Bible scriptures, and then off collaborating with Marty, no doubt, about some mysterious women's stuff, she was up here ordering stuff off that QVC channel to redecorate my home. And then, just that quick, as soon as she'd marked the place so no other female could mistake me for a single fella, she stopped coming up here so much."

"Better you than me," Jessie said as he continued to laugh. "You mean to tell me she's not upped your blood pressure with her newfound religion and 'just-gotta-do-good' attitude?"

"Not as much as she's trying to turn Tamara into a singing diva who'll make Whitney Houston and Mariah Carey beg to sing backup for her. And when I left, I overheard them say something about getting their hair done."

The deacon's laughter took on a hint of pain when he said, "Ain't zeal without knowledge a dangerous thing?"

The two men continued to evaluate Delilah's state of grace and the growth they'd witnessed over the past month or so.

From out of nowhere Jessie suddenly changed the subject. "You know, Cindy's been gone almost a year."

"I know," the deacon replied. "I think about her a lot these days."

"I often wonder what she'd think about Delilah's sudden appearance. How she'd take knowing that I had to shoot Sister Green's son; not that I wouldn't do it again to save a life. . . ."

"I believe Sister Cindy would've told you to stop wondering about things. Lord knows, I ain't mad at you for keeping me above ground. But look how everything turned out since Delilah's returned into your life. I believe Cindy would've loved it."

"I'd still like to know why I couldn't have them both, Delilah and Cindy."

"Maybe Cindy's season was over." The deacon hadn't planned on putting it out there like that, but it was too late. He knew by the pained look on Jessie's face that his son was still mourning.

The deacon didn't give it much thought as he instinctively reached over and lifted his guitar. He began to strum a melody.

We'll understand it better by and by . . .

While the deacon and Jessie had their man-to-man chat upstairs, Delilah and Tamara arrived home. They'd taken Sister Marty to the hairdresser. It was Delilah's idea. She always believed that a new hairstyle or a wig was one way to keep a woman's feminine side ignited.

"Grandmama Delilah, why in the world would you have that lady give Sister Marty a flip?"

"Tamara, I've so much to teach you. Now listen. When a lady wears her hair flipped it means she's ready to take things up or tear things down."

Tamara started laughing and that started Delilah's laughter, too.

"You're only twenty-one," Delilah teased, "so you ain't flipping nothing until you're my age."

"And why is that?"

" 'Cause I'm gonna pray on you that you stay innocent or at least don't get any guiltier."

"What makes you think that'll work on me? I have had a boyfriend or two. I'm just not ready to get involved until things calm down for Daddy and me."

"Sweetie, listen. I know what you're trying to say. Right now, me and Jehovah are real thick. Lately, it seems that just about anything I ask Him to show me or fix, God does it. I know you don't want to date and bring up memories for your father. I get that. But Jessie is never going to forget your mother. You need to live your own life. But while I'm still on Jehovah's good side, I'm gonna have Him keep a close eye on you until you're about seventy."

"I don't know how well you did in math, but if God keeps me chaste until I'm about your age, He's gonna stop blocking about ten years earlier than you'd like. You must've forgotten you're only sixty-three."

God had brought both grandmother and granddaughter to a place where they could continue their teasing as though they'd been at it for years.

Chapter 35

Delilah sang and pranced about Jessie's kitchen as she prepared the food. She'd finally come to a place where she and Jessie were a little more comfortable together. He'd broken her down and had her move out of her Garden City rental— "What sense does it make for you to use your entire social security on a place you visit every other week or so?" he'd asked. He'd made a good point. And though neither of them easily hugged or kissed yet, the laughter was never forced. It just seemed to happen naturally.

"Has the deacon returned yet?" Jessie had just returned home from working his night shift. "It looks like the record label is going to sign Tamara."

"No," Delilah quickly replied.

"Well, I need to talk to him since he was the one that set it up with Mrs. Lamb."

Jessie went on to explain that Zipporah Lamb had called two days ago and said she needed to chat with him and Tamara. She'd convinced her label to sign Tamara, but wanted to go over some details in person. Again, she would stay with Sister Marty, and that still didn't sit as well with Delilah as it should've. Delilah did claim that God had entered her heart, bringing with Him love, compassion, and forgiveness.

"I wouldn't know," Delilah said slowly. "Haven't heard from him since he said he was picking her up at the airport."

"Why don't you like this woman? She is the goddaughter-in-law of one of the deacon's cousins." Jessie decided he might as well find out what was on his mother's mind, whether it was jealousy of a younger woman or something more.

"I do like her better now than before," Delilah admitted, "but I get a strange feeling when I hear her name or see her. I cannot tell you why."

"Are you jealous?"

"Should I be?"

"I know you and Sister Marty have become joined at the hips and I thought you might've felt a little left out since those two got along so quickly."

Delilah stopped and laid down the string beans she was preparing for supper later on. "Jessie, I honestly don't know. I spoke to Mother Johnson about how I feel and she says I'm experiencing some kind of 'cernment."

"You mean discernment?"

"Yes, discernment. She also said that God sends warnings, but not every warning is a bad one. She said we hafta watch and pray." Delilah picked up the bowl of string beans and went back to preparing for supper.

"We definitely need to do that." Jessie turned and left the room, wondering why he didn't get that same strange feeling when he spoke to Mrs. Lamb. But he was too tired to deal with it. He needed to rest up for Tamara's back-to-college spending spree later.

Meanwhile, the deacon was unusually quiet as he drove Zipporah back to Brooklyn from the JFK airport.

"So, Deacon, you're very quiet. What are you thinking? I hope you're not gonna let the devil steal your joy because your cap came off in service the last time I was here." Zipporah thought that incident might've embarrassed him, but she wanted to hear whatever the problem was from him.

"I've been naked and worn a hospital robe backwards by mistake, and that didn't embarrass me. I did last month, but I don't care about my conk right now."

"I'm glad to hear that. So what's bothering you?"

"If I wasn't confused before, I am now. Can you explain to me what happened at the church? Delilah's got me twisted since she's found Jesus. One minute she's redecorating my place and the next thing she's moved downstairs, with Jessie. It's like she's trying to keep an eye on me or put the bad eye on me. I don't know which."

"For someone who's so deep into God's Word, I don't understand how you can ask that question about your wife with a straight face."

"Well, I'd laugh about it, but right now a straight face is about all I got."

"God happened, that's what happened." Zipporah laughed and added her own hallelujah.

"I know God happened," the deacon conceded. "Lord knows I've known Delilah long enough to know when she's acting, and she wasn't acting that night."

"Of course she wasn't acting. Do you really believe that there wasn't a time during all these years that Delilah hasn't wanted what she's seen others have with God?"

"How do you know so much about that woman and you haven't known her long enough to spell her name correctly?"

"I don't have to know her. God knows her, and He gives knowledge to those He chooses." She let out another laugh. "Have you ever heard the saying that a prophet is never honored in his own home?"

"I sure have. I read my Bible."

"That's good, so now you know why God didn't use you or even Jessie to get to Delilah. Delilah knew the two of you too well. She probably felt judged every time she was in your presence. Since you've confided your true relationship I guess I'd have to call you and your *son* a couple of Delilah's spiritual blockers."

"How did you get to be so smart in the ways of the Lord?"

Zipporah smiled and it set the deacon at ease. She kept smiling even as she said, "I was lost just like Delilah, and even more so like Jessie. I'm a little bit of both of them."

She'd opened the conversation to discuss Jessie. They were almost off the Belt Parkway, so if they were gonna discuss him they needed to get to it.

Zipporah explained to the deacon the conversation she'd had with Jessie the day of the Family and Friends event as they drove to the church. She told the deacon that she felt she'd touched a nerve with Jessie when she talked about God's season and reason for taking folks in and out of His people's lives. "He'd opened the door when he spoke about his wife and how awful it was to have her snatched away. Then he mentioned Delilah and how she only represented one part of him. So I told him about my mother, Areal, placing me for adoption without laying eyes on me, and then me, many years later, finding my father, Jasper, after I'd been living in a homeless shelter. I told him to give his hurt over to the Lord and when it was right, it'd be alright. I truly believe I got through to him. You just let God show you when to deliver the news. And when God does it, don't you rebel."

Deacon Pillar dropped Zipporah off at Sister Marty's house. He and Marty had come to an understanding of sorts. They'd never really broken anything off because after all she'd given him a deadline and he didn't meet it, so what was there to say? He didn't fight the quasi breakup because she'd begun to push his buttons. He already had an estranged and strange wife who did that. So from the night of the Family and Friends Day they'd been, more or less, friends.

Back home, he came through the door and immediately heard Delilah and Tamara inside. He didn't bother to knock or see what was happening, deciding he'd rather just go upstairs and relax.

The deacon went over in his mind the conversation he'd had with Zipporah. There was a lot of wisdom in the young woman. Her father was like that to some degree. *Who'd have thought old Jasper and I would be in the same fix?* the deacon thought. He was glad Jasper had found Zipporah and managed to make things as right as he could before he died.

Thinking of Jasper and the old times they had playing with different groups up and down and in and out of the Bible Belt, caused the deacon to smile. He reached over and picked up his guitar. Perhaps if he strummed softly he could get his thoughts together.

"Deacon Pillar, can I come up?" Jessie called out just as the deacon picked the first note.

The deacon wanted to say no, but he was sure Jessie had already heard him come in. He hadn't shut the door behind him. *Jessie probably wants to chat about what went on with Zipporah when I picked her up.* "Come on, Jessie."

Jessie came through the door, winded like he was an eighty-year-old man who'd just learned to climb stairs. "How are you? I'm sorry to bother you, but I worked the night shift and I still cannot relax." He stopped and pointed his finger to the floor. "Do you hear Delilah and Tamara downstairs? They seem to be having a good time. They're probably on pins and needles waiting for Zipporah to stop by and talk more business. I hope it's soon. Tamara still has Juilliard in a few weeks." Jessie winked at the deacon. "Ha! Listen. Who would've thought it?"

The deacon laid his guitar to the side. He rose and went over to the floor vent to hear clearer.

"I knew their voices were coming in from somewhere," Jessie said as he rose to join him. "I'd almost forgotten about the floor vent."

"Don't worry," Deacon Pillar replied, "I never listened in until your mama came around. And even then, whoever's talking has to stand almost directly under it."

"It sounds like they're starting to chat about something fiercely funny or serious. I guess we really shouldn't listen in. It ain't the Christian thing to do."

Jessie said all the right words, but he didn't move from his spot.

"Well, I'm going to let those chatterboxes chat on. Can I get you something to drink from the kitchen? I'm parched."

That seemed like as good a time to discuss with the deacon what he'd wanted to say all along. His talk with Zipporah really stirred him, and in a good way. "I'll have whatever you've got that is cold. I don't drink anything with ice, so even if it's room temperature, that's okay."

"Anything else you need?" The deacon asked the question because Jessie still hadn't said anything about what Zipporah had mentioned.

"Yes, I do need something. But it can wait until you come back from the kitchen."

Jessie watched the deacon leave the room. He was about to move away from the vent when he heard Delilah and Tamara again. But they weren't laughing. He could've sworn that they were arguing instead. He wondered, *What could've gone wrong in just a few minutes?*

Chapter 36

Moments before, while they were in the basement spare room, Delilah and Tamara's conversation had turned sour as soon as the deacon's name flowed from Tamara's mouth. Even as she followed Delilah up the steps and into the living room, she wouldn't stop pushing.

"Don't you care about the deacon?"

"Of course, I do. I'm a Christian now. I gotta care about everybody."

It wasn't so much that Delilah didn't still care about the deacon. It was that she cared a little too much and hadn't figured out how to do so without shortchanging God. So she'd just stopped visiting him any more than she had to. They'd been married in name only for a long time, and she didn't know if there was an expiration date on that sort of arrangement.

"Grandmama," Tamara pleaded as she fidgeted with one of the doilies on a shelf, "okay, if you won't do it for the deacon's sake, what about Daddy? We can't keep telling Daddy how much we respect and love him but not tell him the truth. It's not right."

"Do you like the peace and quiet that Jehovah has provided for this family? Do you think Jehovah would've saved me and cleaned me up for my son, just so I could break his heart?"

"His heart's been broken for years. And he has his suspicions." Tamara's voice rose as she continued to challenge Delilah. "Saved by God or not, I think you're being selfish."

"Watch your tone, sweetie."

"I'm sorry, Grandmama. But you and the deacon have put me in the middle of something that could even ruin my relationship with Daddy if everything's not out in the open. That's not right."

Tamara's words pierced Delilah's heart. How could she put such a burden on someone she loved now more than her own life? It wasn't that she hadn't thought about it before. She just hadn't thought about it a lot since Jehovah took her into His inner circle.

"I'm sorry, sweetie. I truly don't know what to do. And unless Jehovah has someone to open their big mouth and reveal that Thurgood is really your grandfather, I just don't see it happening no time soon."

Tamara walked over and put her arms about Delilah. "You and I can always tell him together. We're Jewel women. We're not afraid of anything."

"Well actually, sweetie, since Thurgood and I never divorced, don't forget I'm really a Jewel Pillar. . . ."

Deacon Pillar returned to his living room carrying two tall glasses of raspberry tea, one without the ice and not too cold. His hands shook just a little. All the time he was out of the room he'd prayed again, and asked God to give him the right words to say.

So it was up to him, and unless God had an ass to speak like the one in the Bible, there'd be no going back.

It took the deacon a moment to realize that Jessie's complexion had reddened and it looked like his eyes were red, too. He wondered what could've happened while he was in the kitchen. He almost dropped the glasses.

"Brother Jessie"—the deacon rushed to his side with the glasses still in his hands—"what's wrong?"

"Hypocrites," Jessie shot back. "I can't stand them."

"Well, I'm not partial to them, either, but don't let them upset you."

"All this time it's been secrets and more secrets and half truths." He stopped and pointed down to the floor vent. "She knew what it meant to me and my mother never said a word about it."

"Well, don't be too mad at Delilah. She's just gotten reborn. She hasn't been at it as long as me and you. She's bound to have a secret or two."

"What about your secrets?"

The deacon thought it was a strange question, but he'd answer it anyway. He placed the glasses down and spread his arms wide open to prove a point. "I don't have anything much to hide. Everyone knows I'm an open book."

"Oh really, Deacon," Jessie said slowly as he left the floor vent and sat back onto the sofa. "Then why don't you come on over here and read *your son* a bedtime story."

Chapter 37

Jessie never gave the deacon a chance to respond or to give a follow-up lie. He jumped off the couch and left quickly before he punched the old man.

He fled down the stairs two at a time, and then raced inside his apartment. No sooner had he gone into the living room than he saw Delilah and Tamara.

"Daddy, what's wrong?" Tamara's voice shook. Her father looked about as bad as he had during the weeks after her mother passed away.

"Jessie." Delilah was a bit more seasoned than Tamara. The first thing she did was to look up at the ceiling. It took her only a moment to realize she and Tamara had stood there and revealed everything she'd wanted to keep a secret.

"Jessie, let's pray about this." Delilah couldn't believe her own words. Her son looked as though he'd had his heart ripped out and all she could do was think about praying.

"Daddy." Tamara started toward her father. "Please. What's wrong?"

Jessie's anger spared no one in the room. "Shut the hell up, Tamara. How many times you gonna say the word *daddy?* You've already called it out twice."

"I don't understand. You're my father. Why are you upset with me?"

"I'm upset with you because you don't have the right to call me daddy."

"Jessie, don't do this." Delilah was beside herself. She didn't know what else to say. If she wasn't saved, she could've slapped him or knocked him out with something until he came to and made sense.

"Don't you ever try and tell me what to do," Jessie shouted at Delilah, "you selfish witch."

And then, as if he'd seen Tamara for the first time, he lit into his daughter. "You have a daddy. Why wouldn't you want me to have one, too?"

"I don't know what you're talking about." Tamara thought her father was having breakdown. But what would've brought it on? And then she remembered the hints she'd given him weeks ago. She'd taken him to the edge of a lie and waited for the truth to save him. But it didn't. The truth pushed him over the edge.

"All of you made a fool of me."

Upstairs the deacon's back was against the wall. He could hear Jessie screaming and accusing Delilah and Tamara through that hellish floor vent.

Without a plan of his own, but relying completely upon God, the deacon raced down the stairs to Jessie's house. The anger inside Jessie's apartment seemed to darken the hallway, but it didn't stop the deacon from barreling through Jessie's door.

Jessie spun around when he heard the door crash open. "Well, ladies, it looks like your cavalry has arrived." Jessie snatched Tamara by her shoulder and almost flung her in the deacon's path. "Here, take my daughter. She needs a daddy. I've never had one, so I won't miss it."

"If you put your hands on baby girl again, I'll whup you like the daddy you need and not the one you want."

"Thurgood, please stop. We all just need to calm down and talk this out." Delilah was the only voice of reason in the room. That was enough to cause a break in the commotion for all of two seconds.

"Oh, I know damn well you've returned to crazy now." Jessie started toward Delilah as if he were stalking prey. "I could kick my own ass for allowing you into my home and my life. You just couldn't be satisfied ruining my childhood. You just had to come back and finish the job."

That was enough for Delilah to place a temporary hold on her salvation.

"Jessie, I wish you would step over here and think I'm just gonna let some nigger throwing a hissy fit whup my ass."

"So who's gonna stop me—you?"

"Leave him to me, Dee Dee." The deacon rushed toward Jessie. "You don't have to like me or even love me," Deacon Pillar exclaimed, "but dammit, you will respect me and your mama!"

Tamara pushed the deacon to the side. "Don't threaten my father, Deacon Pillar."

"I don't need your help." Jessie tried to wave Tamara away.

"But I need yours." Tamara stood with her feet planted and her hands on her sides. "Now I could cry like I want to, or I can be the adult and try to get some clarity about this."

"Didn't I just tell you to leave me alone, Tamara?" Jessie stepped back. He really didn't want to confront her but he would.

"I don't give a damn what you want, Daddy. This isn't all about you."

"Did you just cuss at your father?" Delilah's voice suddenly rose several levels and she didn't care if the whole neighborhood heard her. "You don't cuss at your father. That stubborn ass I gave birth to is still your father."

Either Delilah was backsliding into crazy or she'd found a way to make crazy work.

Deacon Pillar stood tall in the middle of the floor. He seemed to tower over them all. He looked like Mount Kilimanjaro with his salt-and-pepper conk sprinkled around the top of his head. "Both of y'all need to step back. This is between me and my son."

That word *son* coming from the deacon shocked Jessie and sent him to a place inside his head where confusion reigned. It felt like the word handcuffed him and made him unable to move an inch. So he didn't.

"I went to prison for my son. Neither of you did." Deacon Pillar pointed to Tamara and Delilah. "I stopped pimping for my son. Neither of you had anything to do with that, either. I searched for God and found him, and God brought my son to New Hope. I became his friend because I thought that's what he needed more than a long lost daddy!"

"Thurgood, what are you doing? What are you talking about?"

"Stop butting in, Delilah. This is between me and my son. I ain't telling you again."

The deacon turned to Jessie once more. Jessie hadn't moved or spoken since the deacon called him son and handcuffed him with that word.

"Now you are a father, so you know Tamara didn't come preprogrammed, and you sure didn't come with a book of instructions when your mama gave birth, either. Me and that woman standing over there were in some kind of fix back then in Harlem."

The deacon stopped and pointed to the other sofa where he wanted Delilah and Tamara to sit. "I'm coming back for you two."

And then the deacon removed his belt and held it in his hands. Jessie was in his forties, a cop with a licensed gun, and the deacon was letting him know that it didn't matter.

"Now I'm sorry for all the hurt you've been through. But you can't sit here and tell a lie that whether I called myself your daddy or Deacon Pillar that I wasn't here for you when you needed me."

Jessie's jaw tightened as he struggled to fight against the truth. He wanted to hold on to his anger to where he need not compromise or be kind.

"Now I could continue to go through our trials and joys, year by year, but I'm not. You ain't having a meltdown or anything convenient like that tonight. You're gonna be a man and take what I'm about to give you."

The deacon took the strap and struck it a couple of times against his thigh as he walked toward Jessie.

"Thurgood, don't you dare hit my baby!" Delilah jumped up.

"Didn't I tell you to sit your arse down?"

There was something about the deacon's tone and his stride that made a believer of another kind out of Delilah. She sat down on the sofa and took Tamara's hand.

Jessie didn't budge. "Gimme your best shot! I can take it like a man. I just hope you can take it like one, too."

The deacon struck his thigh with the strap again. Just as he got to the edge of Jessie's seat he threw down the strap and leaned over Jessie.

The deacon pulled Jessie to his feet and quickly wrapped his arms around him. "Take this like a man, son."

Jessie was larger in girth and height than the deacon, but he felt like a feather in his father's arms as Deacon Pillar gave him what felt like a bear hug of love.

Epilogue

One Year Later

The sun rose long before Delilah did. She stretched and looked over at the deacon. He'd finally fallen asleep clutching a month-old early morning edition of the *Amsterdam News.* There was a full-blown color photo of Tamara in the entertainment section. She was accepting her Stellar Award for the 2009 Best Gospel Jazz Album and Artist.

That Sunday night she, the deacon, and Jessie almost lost their minds when Zipporah called and told them Tamara had won. They'd been too nervous to watch the awards show on television.

Delilah laughed softly as she gave thanks to God for His favor upon her precious grandbaby. Tamara had gone further than Delilah had in the music business, and Delilah was not only okay with it, she was bursting with pride.

Hmmmm . . . Delilah touched a stiff strand of the deacon's now part Afro, part conked hair and smiled again. With little effort she sat up and wrapped her arms around her knees. If there was stiffness in her limbs, she didn't feel it.

She turned and looked at him. Covering her mouth, she struggled to keep from laughing aloud. He'd fussed a little yesterday when she'd finally returned from taking Mother

Johnson and Sister Green to see Sister Green's son. Although the deacon had testified on the young man's behalf, he was still sent to Rikers Island. The deacon wasn't too thrilled about the women paying so much attention to the crippled thug, as the deacon still called him, even if one of the women was the boy's mama. But Delilah had learned the hard way about the ferociousness of a mother's love, and if Sister Green needed her, she was going.

She continued to watch the deacon as he lay sprawled out across the other side of the bed. He'd suddenly started grinning while he slept.

"You'd better be dreaming about me, you old rascal," Delilah whispered.

For the next few moments Delilah reminisced about the powerful love they'd shared so many years ago. And it was still powerful after they'd renewed their wedding vows barely a week ago. It was a beautiful ceremony at New Hope Assembly and, of course, she was a beautiful bride. Folks said she looked more like Lena Horne that day than Lena ever could.

She was certain there was also a lot of talk about why she and the deacon had to have such a large wedding party at their age. *Because we can* is what the deacon told those who'd dared ask openly.

"Thurgood, you certainly looked handsome that day," Delilah murmured.

He'd had Jessie as his best man. He even had the word *son* typed on the wedding program right next to *best man*. And the deacon had had the pleasure of having Reverend Cordell DeWitt and his lovely wife, Janelle, along with her sister Chyna, the former First Lady of New Hope Assembly, fly in from California. Without hesitation the Reverend DeWitt had cleared his busy television schedule to fly in and be one of the deacon's groomsmen. After all, the deacon had stood up for him at his wedding, too. To hear the reverend tell it, the deacon had saved his marriage even before he said the words *I do.*

And, of course, Delilah had had Tamara as her maid of honor. Sister Marty threw hint after hint to be one of Delilah's bridesmaids. *I'd have beat that heffa to the ground if she hadn't been there,* Delilah thought. She actually would've understood if Marty hadn't been at the ceremony. But she'd never admit it. Yet the highlight of the wedding came when she and the deacon joined Tamara and Jessie in song. They turned the wedding out. It made Zipporah, who'd come with Sister Betty, start thinking about offering Delilah and the deacon a chance to record a track on Tamara's next album. It'd worked for Mom and Pop Winans, so why not?

The alarm clock on the side of the bed chimed that it was eight o'clock. She didn't need reminding of the time.

If she didn't know better, the way the deacon made her feel last night, she'd have thought that time had stood still. It certainly wasn't all one-sided, either.

Last night, several hours after she and the deacon had watched their favorite *Harlem Nights* movie, she started feeling like sunshine; a lot better than she had in weeks, perhaps even months. She'd sexually jacked that deacon up. He had to limp into third base.

But she couldn't spend the entire day in bed. She was somebody's wife and she had to keep her man happy.

Less than thirty minutes later, still smiling in the afterglow, Delilah buzzed about the kitchen that used to be for the deacon only. For years, she'd claimed she couldn't or wouldn't cook in a kitchen that wasn't painted bright sunshine yellow, with plenty of counter space. Yet there she was, dressed in nothing but that smile and another one of the deacon's old shirts.

Everything is mellow, she thought. One thing was for certain—if they came together as intensely as they had the night before, she'd have to cripple him before he'd ever let her go again.

"Good morning, Dee Dee."

Delilah jumped. She was so engrossed in her thoughts she'd not heard him wake up or move about. And yet there he was.

The deacon stood in the doorway to the kitchen. He looked almost two shades lighter than normal and was dressed. He'd changed his usually tacky outfit into one that was even worse. He'd donned a purple and brown robe that barely covered the green striped trousers and red shirt. "I feel so good, I could eat a pig with his oink dipped in barbecue sauce."

The sound of his satisfied voice earned him a pass on his crazy getup, and it put her back into a good mood. "Good morning, Thur-*so*-good Pillar."

The deacon smiled so wide his jaws ached. Her praise had put to rest any doubts he had, and he'd done it without any help from a blue pill for a headache.

Delilah suddenly broke out in song. She sang over and over.

"Something and you certainly smell good this morning, my lovely wife."

She loved the sound of "my wife." It was enough to make her break out in song again.

"Something about my man, some don't understand; it's not that he's so much bigger, it's because he ain't fast on the trigger. . . . If I put him in my kitchen, he can bake a mean ham. If I put him in my garden, he don't stop until I drop . . . oh, oh, oh . . ."

"Sing that song, Dee Dee. My goodness, woman! You still got it, gal."

"Well, you know I always could cook," Delilah purred, "and I make a mean pot of grits and cheese, too."

He tried to look serious to keep from agreeing with her. "Just make sure you put water in that pot right away, gal. You know grits stick like glue. I don't have a dishwasher—except for the one you're about to become." He laughed at his own joke.

Delilah started to say something that the old Delilah would've said. It'd be about how the deacon didn't have any Teflon-coated pots and pans and she'd be damned if she was gonna be anyone's dishwasher. But she didn't want to break the mood; just in case he was up for a doubleheader.

"Take a seat, Thurgood. Let me show you how a sixty-four-year-old woman who moves like she's thirty-five can serve her man."

"Oh, you served me until I was full last night. I haven't felt this good from my rooter to my tooter in quite some time. For a moment, you were serving me so good I didn't think I was going to live to see seventy-something; and wouldn't have cared if I didn't."

They laughed even more when the deacon boasted, "Dee Dee, I still can't believe you remarried me." He winked. "I realize when I asked, you made the promise during a moment when you were hollering yes to everything I did."

"Tone it down, Tarzan." Delilah started spreading butter on his toast. "It wasn't hard for me to say it and mean it. After all, I can chew gum and walk at the same time."

"Really," the deacon said as his chest expanded, "I know about the chewing gum and walking ability, but why wasn't it hard to say?"

It was the third time he'd asked her that same male-ego-feeding question. She decided it was going to be the last time.

"Oh, Thurgood," Delilah purred, "stop acting like we were ever divorced. Remarry is all we could do."

"You mean it wasn't my . . ." The deacon stopped and put on his most sad-looking face. "I'm hurt."

"You oughta be hurt. I tried to break your back!"

The two seniors laughed as Delilah reached over his shoulders and wrapped her arms around his chest. She kissed the nape of his neck and moved the plate closer to him. "Quit playing around and eat this food. I don't cook this good for any old deacon husband."

"You'd better not." He laughed again before he chided, "Just how many old deacons did you know, anyhow?"

"Do you mean in or out of the church?" Delilah could hardly keep a straight face.

The deacon stood and turned to face her. And despite the fact that less than a year ago he'd questioned God's wisdom and blamed Satan for her return, he cupped her chin and whispered, "Thank you for coming back into my life, Dee Dee."

He didn't want to chance Delilah destroying the moment with some truth he didn't want to hear, so he playfully patted Delilah on her hips. "Woman, put it in gear so we can go shopping for your new car. Meanwhile your husband's ready to eat whatever your perfect little hands have prepared."

"I'm going to get dressed. I just can't decide between a Porsche or an Audi. What do you think the Lord would want me to drive?"

"Well, let me see what the spirit is telling me, Dee Dee." The deacon pushed his chair aside and threw his head back. "I see a HONDAAAAAAAAA."

Delilah's and Deacon Pillar's laughter turned almost into giggles. Delilah in particular couldn't believe how much at home she felt.

After eating a big breakfast, they washed the dishes together. It wasn't quite noon yet, so the deacon grabbed his old guitar. His fingers strummed a few chords until he found the right ones. Within minutes, and as though they'd never stopped singing duets, he and Delilah sang a couple of soft melodies. They kept their voices low so as not to awaken Jessie.

When it was all over, the deacon put away his guitar and sat back on the sofa. "Bring your sweet self over here." The deacon chuckled and patted a space beside him on the sofa. "I'd place you on my lap, but neither one of us would stand a chance—if you know what I mean?"

"You mean, you wouldn't stand a chance." Delilah winked. "You know I've learned a lot in the last six decades."

"Well, I've got almost another decade on you. You'd better watch out now."

Delilah and Pillar chided one another, their laughter getting louder and louder, until they fell across one another like two teenagers. The only thing missing was the tickling.

"Delilah DuPree Jewel-Pillar." The deacon repeated her name over and over. And with each time he spoke the words, his voice took on another tone; a more reverent one. It was almost as though he were about to open a church service. "It's still hard for me to understand what's going on at this stage of my life. I don't know why God is handing me a second chance with you—the love of my life. . . ."

"Thurgood," Delilah said while she, too, struggled to understand.

"Don't interrupt me, Dee Dee. I need to get this out."

"Okay, Thurgood."

"I've decided that if the Master thinks enough of me to give me a second chance at having a family, then I'm going to treat this opportunity like the golden treasure it is."

"What do you mean?"

"I'm the Chairman of the deacon board. . . ."

"I know that."

"Of course you do. Nothing much gets past you." The

deacon started to laugh. "I'm just teasing, Dee Dee. But you need to let me finish."

"Well, you'd better hurry up. I don't think you want me taking this much time getting undressed when you want me to hurry."

"I get your point." The deacon kissed Delilah. "Okay, here's what I'm thinking. I think since I'm a deacon that you should consider becoming a deaconess."

"Thurgood, are you serious? I haven't been in Christ long enough to take on such an important title."

"My goodness, woman, this title is for man, not God. He doesn't care what you call yourself as long as it's not 'Satan's spawn' or something like that."

"But I'm still struggling every day to do the right thing. I don't want to disappoint the Lord; or you, either. I'm not quite like you."

"What do you mean, Dee Dee?"

"You don't sin anymore."

"Woman, please. Everyday I sin." The deacon reached across Delilah and took a small Bible off the table. "In between the pages of this book lie all the reasons why we go through hell to get to heaven."

"I've never thought of it like that. . . ."

"Now, what we did last night and what we're gonna do later on—now that's about as close to sinning as I can think of."

"Then why do it?"

"Because, my lovely Dee Dee, just like us humans, God loves it when we make up with him."

"So how often are we gonna make up?"

"We're gonna do it like the Word says, seventy times seventy times seventy times seventy. . . ."

"My goodness, you two! Talk about something else. I've

worked all night. Can't y'all take up knitting or go cruising or whatever it is old people do? Damn!"

Jessie's voice sailed up through the floor vent.

Later the next day, it wasn't their lovemaking or any cooing that kept Jessie from getting sleep. It was the sound of hammering. Delilah and Thurgood nailed a covering over the floor vent. That freed up the oldsters to do whatever they wanted, as loud as they wanted, and as often as they wanted. And they thanked God every time.

DON'T BLAME THE DEVIL

Pat G'Orge-Walker

ABOUT THIS GUIDE

The questions and discussion topics that follow
are intended to enhance your group's
reading of this book.

DISCUSSION QUESTIONS

1. Have you ever had a lost relationship that you felt was impossible to restore? Did it matter whether it was with a parent, other relative, or friend?

2. What were the obstacles and the triumphs?

3. For a sixty-year-old woman and a seventy-year-old man, estranged wife and husband Delilah and Thurgood have a very healthy sexual appetite. With the advent of Viagra and other medicines, what impact do you feel sexually transmitted diseases have had on the senior community, if any?

4. Do you believe in generational curses? Delilah's mother and grandmother abandoned their parental responsibilities. And yet, at a young age and still feeling the sting of her mother's disappearance, Delilah did the same. Discuss whether or not there are times when parents are needed for a season, and then ultimately removed by God-ordained circumstances to further His plan.

5. As a Christian, was Jessie a hypocrite for not accepting his mother back into his life as the prodigal father did in the Bible? Was he cautious, or had his anger and abandonment issues consumed him? Would the outcome have been different if he'd not been a recent widower?

6. In the Bible, Abraham lied about Sarah being his wife, because he feared for his own life. Yet Deacon Thur-

good Pillar, known as a man with all the answers and God's go-to guy, was not in harm's way, sorta. Why did he fold when it came time to tell the truth to Jessie? Why did he give in to Delilah without a fight? Why was he not completely honest with Marty?

7. Should the deacon be forgiven easier than Delilah because he acted as a substitute granddaddy for Tamara?

8. Do you approve of people engaging in sex after a certain age, whether they're married or not?

9. Sister Marty was also a woman of God and yet she became combative almost immediately after meeting Delilah. Did she have a good reason? Should she have fought for the deacon? Did she have a right to claim Jessie because she'd been his foster mother during Delilah's absence from his life?

10. Was Tamara's involvement in her father's predicament appropriate?

Don't miss Pat G'Orge-Walker's wickedly funny,
uplifting novel of love and betrayal,
good karma and bad karma, sin and redemption in . . .

Somebody's Sinning in My Bed

On sale now from Dafina Books

Here's an excerpt from *Somebody's Sinning in My Bed.* . . .

Chapter 1

Violent March winds swirled viciously along Brooklyn, New York's Linden Boulevard, showing little respect for a supposedly holy and consecrated Sunday night. From the second earth took its form, God set that seventh day aside for everything He'd created to praise His work. However, as if mocking God, the very winds He'd created angrily kicked around empty wine and liquor bottles along a small section of Linden Boulevard that struggled to hide its poverty. Small yet powerful wind funnels seemed to mock heaven as they propelled scraps of paper toward the night sky. In a blink of an eye, it then turned its anger on small, colorful plastic crack vials, tossing them against the street curbs like dice.

And then, without a warning, evil shifted its shape and intention as it prepared to release its minions.

That night, chaos of another sort was about to visit Linden Boulevard and fierce gusts of winds and signs of poverty along that stretch were the least of its problems. That night, some folks would learn that what goes around certainly does come back around, bringing with it the proverbial flip-top can of vicious comeuppance.

Further down Linden Boulevard the distant purring of an automobile somehow reached through the howling wind to make its presence known. As if on cue, a nearby broken street-light suddenly flickered, revealing a slow-moving powder-blue 2006 Mercedes.

The car's driver found a spot, parked, and slowly stepped out. The embers of a lit cigarette flickered as a figure of a man was outlined. He puffed once more before tossing it to the ground.

As if accepting the challenge to step up its evil, the wind suddenly changed its direction toward the Mercedes, abandoning its game of tossing about litter. Loud wooshing sounds accompanied its assault. It homed in on the rear flap of the man's expensive chocolate-brown trench coat, causing the material to fan rapidly.

The man suddenly stood still. With eyes narrowed and determined, he suddenly looked back toward his car. It was as though he were daring the wind to do its worst. He muttered, "Go to hell!"

He had dark, penetrating brown eyes that were set deep into an extremely tawny-complexioned, handsome face that hinted of a possible mixed heritage. Then he sucked in a deep breath of night air as though it were his last.

He'd only taken a few steps when one hand suddenly flew up and grabbed at the tan fedora about to fall off his head. He was too slow. The wind would not be denied and blew the expensive fedora over into the middle of the filthy street.

Through it all, he kept his eyes focused and determined. Without a word, he walked a few feet and retrieved the hat, placing it snug onto his head, and turned back to the side-walk. He'd ignored the filth not so much from fear but almost as a reflex because of what he was about to do. With his hat now secured, he used the same hand to hold the front of his coat, not wanting anyone to see what he had hidden.

There was no turning back now.

Across the street there was a working streetlight. It burned bright on the man as he crossed the street as though to make up for those lights that didn't.

The man moved toward a two-story building nestled between a totally abandoned building and a closed Neighborhood Multi-Service Center. He came within a few feet of his destination and stopped. Despite the darkness, he could see clearly through a small square glass pane. He scowled briefly at a sleeping, obese man.

The portly man was supposed to be alert, but it was nighttime and sleep had claimed the bouncer for the Sweet Bush. Despite nodding off in a deep coma-like sleep and snoring like a bull with asthma, he somehow managed to keep from falling off a stool that was much too small for his wide girth.

The man was tempted to snatch off his unclean fedora, slap the bouncer, and stuff one of those disgusting snores back down his throat, but he needed to stick to the plan.

The man hugged his coat, again, against a body that had been well worked out and buffed. Being a bit of a health fanatic, he hadn't even started smoking until recently when it seemed as though his life was falling apart and brought him to where he now stood.

With one hand, he angrily pushed hard against the oak wood door. The door swung open and closed quickly. It almost nipped the hip of the man as he poured into the front room of the Sweet Bush Lounge.

Noise affected the bouncer much like a sleeping pill; with his barrel chest heaving slightly, he shifted his weight on the stool and continued sleeping soundly.

In a deep sleep, the bouncer would not be a problem.

Fool. The man suppressed a rising growl in his throat as he dismissed the bouncer as a threat. He chose, instead, to adjust his eyes to the dim lounge lights. While he slowed his heart to a manageable beat, he stood transfixed between the panels of a red velvet curtain and peered through a wall of love beads.

His handsome face was stoic. With little effort he inhaled the streams of thick, cloudy, cigarette and reefer smoke for what seemed like an eternity.

But it wasn't.

It'd only taken a moment before he fully understood that none of the other few patrons inside the dark smoky din of lust had paid particular attention to his entrance. Why should they? He wouldn't be the first, or hardly the last, to stumble through that door looking peaceful or angry, on the hunt for whatever was forbidden and getting it.